ADULT FICTION
W

c.1

Erdman, Loula Grace
Years of the locust

8000014608

ADULT DEPARTMENT

1. Fine Schedule
    - 1- 5 days overdue . . . . grace period, no fine
    - 6-10 days overdue . . . . 25¢ per item
    - 11-19 days overdue . . . . 75¢ per item
    - 20th day overdue . . . . $2.00 per item
2. Injury to books beyond reasonable wear and all losses shall be paid for.
3. Each borrower is held responsible for all books drawn on his card and for all fines accruing on the same.

FOND DU LAC PUBLIC LIBRARY
FOND DU LAC, WISCONSIN

The Years of the Locust

The Gregg Press Western Fiction Series
Priscilla Oaks, Editor

The Years of the Locust
Loula Grace Erdman

with a new introduction by
Jane Nelson

Gregg Press
A division of G. K. Hall & Co., Boston, 1979

With the exception of the Introduction, this is a complete photographic reprint of a work first published in New York by Dodd, Mead & Company in 1947. The trim size of the original hardcover edition was 5¾ by 8⅛ inches.

Text copyright, 1947, by Loula Grace Erdman
Reprinted by arrangement with Dodd, Mead & Company
Introduction copyright © 1979 by Jane Nelson

Frontmatter designed by Designworks, Inc. of Cambridge, Massachusetts.

Printed on permanent/durable acid-free paper and bound in the United States of America.

Republished in 1979 by Gregg Press, A Division of G.K. Hall & Co., 70 Lincoln St., Boston, Massachusetts 02111

First Printing, September 1979

Library of Congress Cataloging in Publication Data
Erdman, Loula Grace.
   The years of the locust.

  (The Gregg Press western fiction series)
  Reprint of the ed. published by Dodd, Mead, New York.
   I. Title. II. Series: Gregg Press western fiction series.
PZ3.E67Ye 1979 [PS3509.R28] 813'.5'2 79-16721
ISBN 0-8398-2595-1

FOND DU LAC PUBLIC LIBRARY

Introduction

IN 1946, Loula Grace Erdman won the $10,000 Dodd, Mead-*Redbook* prize for *The Years of the Locust,* an achievement which signalled the end of her apprenticeship as a writer and the beginning of a productive relationship with Dodd, Mead.

Prior to 1946, while teaching school in Amarillo, Texas, Erdman had published a few sketches and stories as well as two books about the teaching profession: *Separate Star* (1944) and *Fair is the Morning* (1945). The latter received some national acclaim, and was reviewed by Eleanor Roosevelt in her newspaper column, "This is My Day."

She was further encouraged to write by Ida Jewett and Dorothy Brewster while studying with them for an M.A. degree at Columbia University, and won second prize in a writing contest sponsored by a New York literary agency.

When a staff member of the agency reported that her manuscript for *The Years of the Locust* had "absolutely no promise," Erdman was piqued enough to enter the $10,000 contest on her own behalf. As she later learned, her novel did not easily win. The Dodd, Mead staff reader, Mrs. Shepherd Butler, liked it but could not convince Mr. Dodd that a story written in flashbacks would work. Finally consenting to read it, Dodd decided the book was prize quality only when the flashbacks "tricked" him into the past three times in succession.

Erdman acknowledged that winning this prize was the turning point in her writing career. Within three years after publication of *The Years of the Locust* (1947), Dodd, Mead published two more novels of equal quality: *Lonely Passage* (1948), a book similar in setting and theme but much bolder in characteriza-

v

tion; and *The Edge of Time* (1950), an historical novel of homesteading in Texas which established her reputation as a Southwestern writer and which won the admiration of her panhandle neighbors. At the time of her death in 1976, she had published 21 books, won several awards, had her books chosen by numerous book clubs, transcribed into Braille, and translated into several languages. She achieved this success while teaching creative writing at West Texas State, participating in professional organizations, and generally dealing with the problems encountered by women writers who must, she pointed out in her autobiography, *A Time to Write* (1969) "merely add writing to all their other duties."

Erdman's impulse for writing *The Years of the Locust* came from her father's death in 1944. This marked for her the end of a lifestyle that she had known in her Missouri childhood, described by her in *Life Was Simpler Then* (1963)—country life dominated by extended family relationships which resulted in a comfortable security. Her father, as a child, had helped his mother plant the walnut trees that eventually shaded the house he built on the land that had been his grandfather's homestead. He had worked in the nearby town of Blackburn, where more kinfolk and friends lived:

> It is not a bad thing, this clan business. The strength it offers, the solidarity, the pride. The feeling of being a part of something bigger and stronger than oneself. The need for loyalty. Even, perhaps, the chance to work off steam in your own private fights.

This theme, and the characterizations presented in *The Years of the Locust*, continued to inspire her for 30 years of writing.

When her mother moved to Amarillo, and she began a new career at West Texas State, Erdman felt that she could never again "go home." In *A Time To Write*, she identified this juncture as particularly significant: "With this evaluation of the past, this contemplation of the future, came a certain detachment, a feeling of objectivity. It was under these conditions that I started another book." Her father's death had an even more specific effect on the novel she decided to write—it provided the central occasion for the plot:

Introduction

I had long held the conviction, strengthened by my father's death and burial, that if one wanted to know the true folkways of a community you went to one of its funerals. More nearly then than at times of birth or marriage you saw people as they really were.... It was almost as if time stood still, or even moved backward.

True to this plan, *The Years of the Locust* opens with the death of Dade Kenzle, a patriarch of family and community in a small Missouri town. For the three days of funeral preparations, the community obeys "some deep tribal instinct within them struggling through all the layers of civilization, through the deep, soft folds of the dullness of their ordinary lives" (p. 9). Each person is "an actor in a play as old as life itself, and as meaningful" (p. 10). Underneath the ritualized behavior, however, each person must also face the personal consequences of this death.

In a series of flashbacks, Erdman develops the responses of six characters. The least affected and the most objective of these is the gravedigger, whose memories provide a necessary realism and humor to temper the patriarchal presence of Dade. The other five are women profoundly influenced by Dade in their individual relationships with him and by the values he represents. For these women, Dade's death signals a significant threshold: each in her own way evaluates the past and contemplates the future.

The primary value represented by Dade is stability, the source of which is the land that he so fiercely loves and possesses. Dade and his land come to symbolize "the merging power of God and man—patience and wisdom fused together into a great partnership" (p.49). To perfect this love of land, Dade marries Ellie, an independent woman who matches his own strength of character and who becomes an equally powerful presence in family and community. The two of them live in the old Kensie place, and together they create a compelling variation on traditional Missouri life.

Land and family combine into a style of living that encompasses all kin, however distant, and the entire community, including the very poor. Their pattern of life is maintained primarily because the life itself is valuable and comfortable; there can be good things to eat only if the corn is harvested at the right time, the beans canned properly, the hens watched so the chickens will hatch in the spring. This pattern also symbolizes, however, an order on which others can rely for emotional strength. People seem to feel better knowing that the Kenzie cellar and linen closet are well-stocked, that the spring housecleaning is done with precision and care, that the family dinners every Sunday are prepared with plenty of cream and lard. Even those who reject the particular life-style, like Dade's son Barry and his granddaughter Allison, depend on knowing that the pattern endures as they once lived it.

Such a life does not necessarily insure its own perpetuation, however. When Ellie and then Dade die, the stability they created threatens to collapse. Dade's sons are too weak or too uninterested to assume the responsibility; the daughter-in-law Julia is ungenerous to a fault; the grandson Mark is spoiled by his mother; the granddaughter Allison follows her own interests by travelling to the East and West coasts. Fortunately, Mark marries Beulah, an outsider from Illinois who wins Dade's approval because she so clearly and candidly understands her destiny. Not as dynamic as Ellie but with a quiet assurance of her own, Beulah models her life with Mark on the Kenzie pattern, realizing that the concessions she makes do not compromise her if the pattern itself is valuable. The one sin she admits—marrying Mark with the knowledge that she cannot bear children—is finally resolved when she assumes the responsibility of maintaining the Kenzie tradition in the Kenzie house after Dade's death.

It is not important that there are no children to bear the name but rather that there is someone to shoulder the burden of tradition, someone who believes an "exulting sense of freedom" can be felt within stability and order. For Beulah to win this freedom, she must also convert Mark from his spoiled ways, since a patriarch must gain the respect of the community as well as of his family. Dade can die knowing that Beulah has succeeded in her plan. At the Sunday dinner following the funeral, Mark will assume Dade's role; the tradition will be maintained with a confident pair at the head of the family.

The theme of tradition and stability permeates most of Erdman's fiction. Land, family, kin, and community are the sources of rural values that her characters learn to accept. The

Introduction

patterns of home and the communal activities of the village that Erdman herself knew become the matter for fiction: family dinners and parties, revivals and chautauquas, fruit picking and canning, births and deaths. Ruling over all of these is the sense of place—Missouri, the meeting point of south and west. The commitment to southern tradition, based on a Virginia model, provides the pride of family that sustains many of Erdman's characters through severe trials. A western energy that recognizes no tradition is equally important, however. Missouri land is fertile western land, not yet exhausted by too many generations' use. Western values of independence and self-reliance, a pioneer spirit that impelled grandparents and great-grandparents to move in the first place, are as crucial to survival as the memories of a southern aristocracy. Thus, in Erdman's Civil War novel *Another Spring* (1966), the characters who survive the rigors of Order Number Eleven are those who accept with grace the destruction of a genteel society based on a Virginia ideal and who begin to build a new communal order based on a more democratic spirit.

In her novels about homesteading in the Texas panhandle, Erdman develops the same theme. The major lesson to be learned by Bethany in *The Edge of Time* is that the Texas plains cannot be made into Missouri farmlands, and, more importantly, they contain a beauty and enduring fertility of their own. Nevertheless, the rosebush that she plants in front of her dugout insures that she will not deny her Missouri heritage. The rosebush had been brought from Virginia to Missouri by her great-grandmother; Bethany's bush, started from a slip she cut from the Missouri plant, reminds her of tradition, family, and community. Other symbols and activities also help to establish stability: a kitchen calendar to mark daily events, the mail-order catalog, the celebration of Christmas, a dance, a church service.

The conclusion to another homesteading novel, *Far Journey* (1955), completes this transformation of Texas. Near the end of her overland trek during which she has learned self-reliance, Catherine Montgomery loses all of her belongings in a flash flood. In the meantime, her husband Edward has lost their homestead in Texas through a surveying error. Before they meet again, both destitute, Catherine spends her last dollars on a fashionable new dress so that Edward will first see her as a member of society, not a defeated pioneer. Edward then decides to study law, since the panhandle will need lawyers to maintain the more complex social order implied by homesteads and towns. In Erdman's sense of history, homesteading in Texas marks the end of individualism as the cowboys practiced it and the beginning of a rural society dominated equally by men and women.

Though the theme of tradition, family, and community pervades her fiction, Erdman herself disclaimed it as the central idea in her novels. Instead, as she told her biographer Ernestine Sewell in "An Interview with Loula Grace Erdman," "I like to think that in my books I have upheld individualism mainly. What counts is what a person really is." Certainly Dade Kenzie affirms the value of individuality as well as the value of family. He does not admire Elaine Courtney, for instance, because she shows no spunk, though he is unfailingly kind to her because she is kin who depends on his support. His granddaughter Allison, on the other hand, earns his respect because she alone understands his devotion to the land and she alone searches for an ideal to which she can be equally committed. Dade supports her in all her radical schemes, from her refusal to recites poetry at the traditional talent show to her acting studies in New York City.

Though the family and community disapprove of these rebellions, they agree that of all the children and grandchildren, Allison is most like Dade. His death, consequently, could be a tragic loss to her. Significantly, she turns to Beulah for guidance, and she finds in Beulah's life an acceptable model for her own future. The concession of her individuality to a larger idea implies, however, that she, like Beulah, will always be a little lonely. In Erdman's fictional world, the tension between individual and community seems to strengthen both. The individual depends on family and community for stability; the community depends on the individual for the creation of new values which it can then embrace as its own.

By far the majority of characters who successfully portray this tension in Erdman's novels are women. To critics who complain about women's fiction, Erdman responded, in *A Time to Write*,

Introduction

It seems to me that, all things being equal, it is better for a woman writer to use a woman's point of view. Occasionally a critic or reviewer will say, 'She writes like a woman,' about a woman author of a current book. Why not? She is a woman and when did good writing come as a result of denying your own identity? . . .Writing like a woman is not an automatic indictment any more than writing like a man is a badge of quality.

One of the most outstanding features of Erdman's fiction is, in fact, her depiction of a complex female community. Once again, the pattern she developed in *The Years of the Locust* served her well for future novels.

A central figure in most of her books is a young woman, in her teens or early 20s, who must learn how to cope with her love for a man. It cannot be denied that these romantic love stories constitute a major weakness in Erdman's fiction. Perhaps the weakness derives from her decision not to characterize fully the male point of view in the romances. The men are dreamers who actively pursue their ideals whether or not their lovers approve of and participate in them. Apart from their dreams, we know very little about these men; they appear as forces only, not as people who question the patterns of their lives.

As the prototype of the female characters, Allison, in *The Years of the Locust*, is also the most independent. She, at least, had defined a life of her own far before she met Harlan. But very few of Erdman's young women in her later novels discover lives for themselves apart from the men they love; in fact, they must learn how to conform their lives to the dreams of those men. However, despite the weakness of the romantic plot, we are sympathetic to these women because of their complex doubts and their quiet assertions. As initiates into the adult world, they must learn that if they cannot actively follow their dreams, they can at least define the values they will bring to another's dreams.

Such a discovery must be made in the social world of small communities and family clans. Many of Erdman's adult female characters have the faults associated with closed societies. They gossip, they snoop in each other's closets, they are quick to judge on the basis of externals, they snub outsiders, they do not understand their children. These characters are not stereotyped, however. The old maids seem eccentric because society paradoxically rejects and values them at the same time. The poorer members of the family clans learn to rebel quietly against the tyranny of kin. Dominating mothers, who spoil their sons and daughters, sometimes learn to cope with their mistakes, sometimes acknowledge too late the tragedy of their dominance. Together and perhaps intuitively, these women maintain the patterns of community life that have value beyond themselves. The task of the young initiates is to differentiate between the universal values and the more provincial expressions of private fears and hatreds.

The heroines do not lack guidance in this process of distinguishing truth from error. If one of the weaknesses of Erdman's fiction is the romantic plot, one of its strengths is her portrayal of the wise, independent female by whom the entire community judges itself. A source for this character type was Erdman's grandmother—a respected matriarch of the family clan and an important influence in Erdman's life—of whom Ellie Kenzie is the fictional counterpart. Miss Bea, the matriarch in *The Short Summer* (1958), is a similar character. She is more clear-headed than the family she has raised, and judges the community from the vantage point of age, experience, and a realistic assessment of values.

Erdman's women are not always old, however. Beulah is young when she inherits Ellie's wisdom, a wisdom which consequently makes her seem ageless. Erdman develops the most successful character of this type in her second novel about a Missouri family, *Lonely Passage*. Sarah Pemberton, one of three sisters in the novel, never marries. Instead, she finds complete satisfaction in the nursing profession. The insights she gains from her position of independence and self-assurance allow her to help other people in the community, especially women, in more than medical ways. When her integrity is threatened, however, she chooses to leave her family and community rather than lose her work. This kind of characterization is Erdman at her best.

Though Erdman portrays female characters more successfully than male, she does not restrict herself to the woman's point of view. About her male characters she said, "You will

Introduction

notice that I picture successfully the moody, poetic, sensitive young man, but I never attempt to describe the rugged, outdoorsy type. I succeed with old men, too, for they are after all, asexual." When Erdman chooses to speak through a man, his character is integrated well with the other voices. In *The Short Summer*, for instance, Tony Gregory must decide between the city life that seems to offer independence and the farm life that he loves. His doubts and yearnings are much more interesting than the passive romance of his sister. The Civil War, seen through the eyes of Matthew Weatherly in *Another Spring*, is a tragic affair of misguided and misunderstood loyalties. In these occasional uses of the male point of view, Erdman shows the man to be as lonely and reluctant to compromise, as committed to family and community, as the female.

Historians and literary critics often claim that the frontier myth in America is a male myth. Erdman's fiction reveals the limitations of this view. Her depiction of Missouri and Texas farm life depends on a sense of tradition, a love of place, and a commitment to community. The individuals who assert independence in her novels do not thereby reject community values; instead, they affirm tradition by making what is valuable in it completely and uniquely theirs. Both the individual and the community are strengthened by this assertion; both men and women participate in its dynamic exchange. This perception of American life is shared by major novelists of the American Frontier—Willa Cather, Paul Horgan, Harvey Fergusson, and Wallace Stegner, to name a few. Erdman deserves to be remembered as a writer in this tradition. *The Years of the Locust*, the first of her novels to explore a more comprehensive frontier, is a fitting introduction to her fiction.

Jane Nelson
College Station, Texas

SUGGESTED SOURCES
Ernestine P. Sewell,"An Interview With Loula Grace Erdman," *Southwestern American Literature*, 2 (1972), pp. 33–41.
Ernestine P. Sewell, *Loula Grace Erdman*, Southwest Writer Series No. 33 (Austin, Texas: Steck-Vaughn Company, 1970).

To my family—
For reasons they know well

DRAMATIS PERSONAE

They each took a portion of their past, examining it, remembering Old Dade and the part he had played in their own lives, recalling things they had not thought of for years, stretching out all the bright tapestry of memory before them . . . for three days, time and memory were something they held in their hands.

These were the people who had most to remember:

BEULAH FULTON KENZIE—the outsider from Illinois in whom the Kenzies could find no flaw, yet who married Mark with a sense of guilt.

ALLISON KENZIE RANYAK—Dade's granddaughter and "only child," who defied small things and small souls with a stubborn, bright courage which carried her far from the farm.

BARRY KENZIE—Dade's youngest son, to whom books, not the farm, were home.

MARK KENZIE—Dade's grandson, weakened and spoiled by Julia, loved by Beulah, and changed by her into the man who could almost fill Dade's place.

JULIA CALLAWAY KENZIE—faithful wife to Dade's oldest son, Tom, a conscientious mother and dutiful daughter-in-law, whose feeling of inadequacy made her take refuge in sharp, veiled insults.

ELAINE COURTNEY WARING—a sort of cousin of Dade, who married Henry Waring rather than die an old maid and wandered through the routine of her days as though asleep.

MISS LAURA MEEKS—who did her Christian duty for sixty years and always wondered what would have happened if Dade had kissed *her*.

VIRGIE AND JIM MEADORS—to whom Dade meant luck and courage and escape from the Bottoms.

CONTENTS

THURSDAY 1

FRIDAY 95

SATURDAY 161

SATURDAY EVENING 217

Thursday

~ I ~

OLD Dade Kenzie died at three o'clock on the morning of May 26.

It was a most inconvenient time. To begin with, the season had been late, and monstrous wet besides. Corn was not yet all planted, and now that a warm, dry spell had come, everyone needed to be in the fields. The women wanted to get the young chickens out into the sun and clean the coops. And because there had been so little sunshine, house cleaning was far behind schedule.

If, at the last, Old Dade was aware of these things, he gave no inkling of it, and was in no way apologetic over the trouble he was causing. After all, these people had given him trouble enough in times past. Nor was he frightened at the prospect of dying. He lay in the bed that had been his for more than fifty years, watching the proceedings as if they were a thing which was happening to someone else. Certainly he did not want to die, for he enjoyed life as much as the next one: good food, and his children and grandchildren, his friends, and the farm stretching out—black, lush acres—in three directions from the house. His had been a good life, and eighty was a goodish long time to live it. There are things that one can enjoy at eighty, he had discovered, just as one found things to enjoy at twenty, and yet others at fifty. Although he was a good and upright man and a steward in the church, he felt none of that sentimental twaddle about only sitting around waiting to be taken to his heavenly home. He could have lived on another year, or ten, or maybe longer, had things come out that way, finding something to enjoy in all those added years. Only, life had lost most of its flavor with Ellie gone.

There had been a great fuss when he and Ellie had lived together fifty years. Everyone had come in to celebrate, and the house was full of friends and kin. There had been gifts, and their pictures in the paper. He and Ellie had lived together still another year and nothing was made about that anniversary, although fifty-one years married is a greater thing than fifty years. It was almost fifty-two when she had insisted on running out in the rain to look after her chickens, had caught pneumonia, and died of it.

There had been a great to-do after that, trying to work out what he should do now that Ellie was gone. Tom, his oldest son, said why didn't he rent the home place and come to live with him and Julia. Dade had no notion of renting the farm. Almost all his consciousness of living was centered in this place. Here he had been brought by his father and mother when he was only a child. Here he had grown up, so that he knew every foot of ground on the place, every indentation of land, every tree and shrub. Here he had brought Ellie as a bride and here they had lived and brought children into the world. He was rooted here, like one of the great trees on the lawn, and he had no notion of leaving, any more than they had of picking up and traveling to another location.

Besides, he did not want to live in the same house with Julia, Tom's wife. She was a good enough woman—a faithful wife to Tom, a conscientious mother to her children, a dutiful daughter-in-law. But she irritated him. When her opinions were questioned she had a way of retreating like an outraged, squawking hen, clucking to herself scandalous things no one could quite catch. Like a hen, too, was the wrinkled and loose skin on her neck. Dade had always liked firm-fleshed women, like Ellie. She had never got scrawny, but had kept her flesh as she grew older and had a full bosom and a firm neck to the end of her days. She had nice legs and ankles, too. A man could look at her and feel he had something wholesome and strong and substantial for his own. He never could understand why men picked out for themselves women who they knew would be nothing but a rack of bones by the time they were sixty. It turned him sick to see them—stockings bagging down around their skinny ankles and wrinkles webbed across their faces like gullies washed in a plowed field after a heavy rain. More often than not they also wore rouge and crimped their hair and simpered. He had no use for them. He wanted natural prettiness, like Ellie's.

He told them all he had no notion of renting out the place and moving in with any of them, that he would manage as he always had to take care of things. And while they were all stewing around, he went over to see his grandson, Tom's boy Mark, and his wife Beulah. He asked them straight out to come live with him, making no promises of what he would do for them if they came, putting it up to them entirely as a business proposition. So Mark and Beulah had moved in with him, and life had gone on with very few actual changes in the ritual the place had always known. Only, of course, the light of it went with Ellie.

It seemed only yesterday, the first time he had seen Ellie. The Fullers were giving a party for her and had asked him. At first he hadn't much wanted to go, but they had begged him into it, and he had said all right. He even took a girl with him. Who was it? Oh, yes—it was Laura Meeks. He had a new buggy, the very first one that had come into the community. He was so taken with it, and with Pete, his high-stepping horse, that he had little time for Laura. He remembered what a time he had getting her into that high buggy, with her so prim and prissy that she got all flustered every time he tried to boost her.

The Fullers had invited a lot of people, and by the time Dade and Laura got there, the house was good and crowded. When Dade came in, they took him at once to meet the visiting cousin. And when he saw her, something came over him. That was the best way he could ever describe it—"Something just came over me," he would say.

She was a tall girl who held herself straight and firm. She wore a blue dress much like the dresses all the other girls were wearing—straight up the front and built out in the back so that the wearers looked all on an angle, like a barn that needed to be propped back into shape. Only, Ellie gave the impression of standing straight, with no lean to her. Her hair was different, too. Not frizzed in front, like wisps of dried hay. Just a nice smooth look to it like maybe it would be fun to touch it. Later he found it was. All he could say now was,

"Who is that girl?"

The Fullers said it was the cousin, and took him over to meet her.

"Ellen," they said, "this is David Kenzie. Dade, this is Ellen Sparks, our cousin."

David Kenzie hadn't thought so much about himself until this moment. Here he was, twenty-three years old, helping his father on a farm. It was a good farm, for the Kenzies had more than most around these parts. He was no saint, but he wasn't as bad as the grannies made him out. Seeing this girl, he suddenly became aware of himself. Now it seemed important that he was the tallest man in the room, that his hair glowed warmly auburn and his teeth flashed white and even when he smiled. He knew he was stronger than most, both in body and in spirit. He knew life was a good thing and he wasn't afraid of it.

He knew he wanted this girl.

Just like that, things cleared up for him. His own power, and his own desire, and the things he wanted from life. He had never really known until that moment. Every hope and dream he could ever have centered around that tall girl in the blue dress with her soft brown hair and gray eyes.

Of course, they didn't dance that night—goodness knows what the preacher and the church members would have said about dancing. But there was no preacher living, and no dead, long-faced saints, who could find a way to cheat youth out of life. Forbidden dancing, they still found ways in which they could touch hands and maybe even do a little hugging and kissing as well. They played "singing games" and Dade, with Ellie's hand in his, found it strong and firm and wonderful to touch. And then they played forfeits, and Ellie lost to him, so it was his power to collect. He said she would have to kiss the doorknob.

When he told her to, she went into the back living room, closing the door behind her. There was no squealing, no fuss. She just laughed and went, although she hadn't the faintest notion of what the trick was. He left her kneeling on the floor, ready to kiss the doorknob, once he gave her the signal.

"Get your mouth all ready," he told her. "I'll tell you when the time comes."

He went back into the other room, just on the other side of the closed door. Everyone was laughing. Most of them knew the forfeit. But Ellie didn't. He could swear to that.

Dade called to her, "Now," and opened the door at the same time. Ellie, her lips all puckered up, leaned forward at the command.

Dade kissed her, square on the lips.

The people in both rooms roared with laughter. Ellie reached up to rub her lips with her handkerchief.

"Well," she said, "I must say it's the first red-headed doorknob I ever saw."

Just like that. No pretense at being offended. No coy assumption that it was more than a party joke. No brazen easiness betraying the fact that it was all an old story to her. Just simple, natural, casual acceptance.

He laughed, too, but he could not forget how her lips had felt under his. Cool, and firm, and sweet. Because she was ready to kiss something, she had had no time to draw back. There was life pulsing through those lips. While he knew, as well as if she had told him, that she was not sorry her lips had met a substitute for the china knob, he still knew she would not be easy to kiss.

Nor was she. It had been hard enough work getting her, goodness knows, although he set his heart on doing it and went after her with complete singleness of purpose. There was really no reason that they should not be married quickly. He was an only child, now that his two sisters had died of diphtheria, and his parents were both eager for him to marry a nice girl and settle down and start a family. Certainly the house was big enough for two families, and the farm could well support them all. Everyone in the community thought it was a good match, too, and agreed that it was fitting and proper for a Sparks and a Kenzie to marry.

But Ellie held things up for a while—not coquettishly, but just until she could make up her mind for sure. She was not the one to be hurried into anything. But when she did make it up, it stayed made without wavering for more than fifty years.

Funny thing—suddenly he wasn't just remembering that long ago party where he first met Ellie and knew he wanted her. He was *there*. Ellie was there, too. The light shone on her blue dress, and on her brown hair. She was coming toward him, swift and graceful, like she always moved—no nonsense about her, and no dilly-dallying. She was holding out her hands to him and leaning forward a little, as if her heart and eager mind were pushing her forward faster than she could follow.

"Dade!" she cried, and her voice was a girl's voice, warm and lovely.

"Ellie—" he answered, very firm and strong.
And rose to meet her.

~ II ~

Under Ezra Dowlin's urgent fingers the crank at the side of the telephone box was a small whirring disk in the dimness of the room.

Up and down the length of the country line men and women, in their night clothes, hurried with sleep-dazed eyes to find out who was using the telephone at this hour of the morning, and why. And as the news came to them, there was great activity in the farmhouses, dotted across rolling Missouri hills. Cars were wheeled out of garages, their lights dim in the half-light of dawn. Men and women talked in quick, hushed tones and children, disturbed more by the urgency in the voices than by the noise itself, stirred in their sleep. Dogs barked and horses, ever sensitive to nervous tensions of their masters, moved restlessly in their stalls.

Soon telegraph keys began their staccato clicking, hurtling their message across miles of singing wires—southward to Texas, to Kentucky, to Tennessee. Eastward it went its singing way also—to Indiana, and on to Ohio. In Illinois, receivers came off hooks to catch the import of the news. It reached Chicago; it came to California, still sleeping in a gray dawn.

For David Allison Kenzie, a good man and full of years, had passed to his eternal reward and all those who knew him —relatives and friends and acquaintances—swung into the solemn age-old pageant that is the community ritual for the burial of the dead. As a single man, they rose to meet the exigencies of the occasion, some deep tribal instinct within them struggling through all the layers of civilization, through the deep, soft folds of the dullness of their ordinary lives. Each person knew well the role he was to play and took over his part, superimposing it over his normal one so that he was no longer himself alone but an actor in a play as old as life itself, and as meaningful.

And as they went about the business that was peculiarly theirs in this matter, they each took out a portion of their past, examining it, remembering Old Dade and the part he had played in their own lives, recalling things they had not thought of for years, stretching out all the bright tapestry of memory before them. Past, present, and future were all held in solution in the days that were present now, no one thinking beyond them, no one living an individual life or an independent one. Time and space and all separate entities had been sucked into the whirlpool that began with the small circle the telephone crank had made in the early dawn.

For three days, time and memory were something they held in their hands.

~ III ~

ELAINE COURTNEY WARING had not slept well that night. Indeed, she had been so long going to sleep that it seemed she had only just closed her eyes when the telephone began its nagging, persistent jangling. One long—three shorts; one long—three shorts. Over and over again it rang.

"Henry," she said, trying to waken him, "the telephone—go answer it—"

Henry was sleeping heavily, his mouth wide open, his crooked front tooth showing. Ever since their marriage she had begged him to have it pulled and a straight false one put in, but he always said heck, no, he wasn't going to have a good tooth pulled and then pay money to have a dummy put in its place.

THURSDAY

"Henry!" she said, once more trying to pierce through to his consciousness.

"Huh—" he mumbled, but did not move.

There was no use trying to rouse him when he was like this. In the chilly half-light she got up, not taking time to reach for either robe or slippers, threading her way past pieces of furniture until she came to the dining room where the phone was still ringing.

"Hello," she said.

"Hello, Elaine? This is Ez—Ez Dowlin—"

"Yes—?" she said, knowing what it was he wanted, and yet asking. "What's wrong?"

"Uncle Dade—" Ez said.

"He's—?" her voice came thickly and she shivered as she stood there in her thin gown.

"Yes, 'bout an hour ago. He didn't suffer any at all. Just went to sleep."

"Do you want us to come right away?" she asked.

"No—not unless you want. I'm staying to see to things—" his voice trailed off in unctuous importance.

"Henry will come as soon as he's finished the chores. I'll come, too, if Beulah needs me."

"You needn't. Nell and Cousin Julia are here. The others will be coming, too. Maybe later on we'll need you worse—"

By the time she got back to the bedroom Henry was awake, sitting on the side of the bed.

"Uncle Dade?" he asked.

"Yes. Ez called. I said you'd be over as soon as the chores were finished."

Already he was pulling on his clothes—the heavy overalls, the blue shirt, the work socks and shoes.

"Gosh," he said, "looks like we are never ready for a thing like this. He was an old man, and had lived his life, and all. But we're just never ready."

"That's right," Elaine agreed vaguely. "I said I'd come, too, but Ez didn't think they'd need me. I'll fix breakfast while you milk, so you can hurry right on over."

"Want me to cut some ham for breakfast?" he asked.

"No," she said. "I have some bacon already cut. You go on with the milking."

The screen door slammed and he was off to the barn, two milk buckets clanking against each other as he walked. Elaine pulled a robe over her nightgown, wadded her hair in a knot at the back of her neck, and went into the kitchen. The coal oil stove, when she lighted it, gave off an acrid odor and, although she was still shivering, she opened the window to let in the morning air. And as she set about the preparation of breakfast, her mind went racing back across the years.

She could not remember a moment of her life that had not been dominated by an awed fear of Uncle David Kenzie, who was not really her uncle at all, but was related to her mother by some sort of remote, intricate degree of cousinship dear to the hearts of Missourians and especially cherished by Adelaide Courtney, Elaine's mother. Adelaide had married Horace Courtney who had taken her away from home and kinfolks to live, so that all she had to hold to was bright memories of them. They were her shield in time of trouble, her vindication, her anchor in storms. When things went bad for the Courtneys, which happened more often than not—Horace being a small, ineffectual man given to failures and minor disasters—Adelaide would say briskly,

"I'm going to write to Uncle Dade. He'll see that we get a job—or a horse—or a new plow—" or whatever the nature of the mishap might be.

Always Adelaide was prevented from carrying out her intentions by Horace Courtney himself who must have both hated and feared this important member of his wife's family, and with good reason. For Old Dade was Adelaide's genteel way of reminding her husband that she had married beneath herself. It was only when Horace Courtney died, the summer Elaine was twelve years old, that his widow made good her ancient threats and let Old Dade know, at last, the plight into which she had fallen.

Elaine had only to shut her eyes, even now, to see once more all the details of the trip they made (on tickets sent by Uncle Dade) to come to him—the musty green plush of the seats on the day coach, the smell of bananas and peanut butter in the lunch boxes, the dizzy rush of scenery past the train window. She remembered her mother's face—thin and tense and triumphant above her shabby black dress.

They came to Dade Kenzie's place one fall day when the trees in the orchard were dark with blackbirds resting briefly in their flight south. Their raucous cries filled the air as their black bodies filled the branches of the trees. Forever after, the whir of their wings and their tuneless songs were tied up inseparably with the memory of her coming to the place. A great flock of them had settled in the trees that bordered the lane up to the house, and as the car came in, it frightened them into noisy flight. So, it was through a crowd of blackbirds that she first saw the Kenzie house.

It was a large, squarish house, painted white, and set back in a yard filled with great trees—box elders, elms, ash, walnut, and honey locust. A wide porch ran completely across the front of it, turned the corner, and extended to a side door which opened into the back living room. It was at this door that Elaine and Adelaide entered, as was the custom of the family and more intimate friends. Ellie met them at the door, the great warmth of her greeting reaching down even into the frozen spot in Elaine's heart—the spot that had been there ever since Papa left—putting the child quickly at her ease, so that she could look about her and feel a certain comfort in the room, a sense of home-coming. There was nothing pretentious about it—the furniture was sturdy mission type. A library table sat squarely in the middle of the room, on it were piled farm magazines, copies of the *Kansas City Star* and other newspapers, a few books. A divan with worn leather upholstery and several fat pillows was pushed back against the wall; a big Morris chair with a footstool beside it and a lamp near by were Uncle Dade's special property, as Elaine later discovered. Ellie's little rocker was in the room, too, and her sewing machine, and various other pieces of furniture which were too good to discard, but still not quite the thing for the "front room." A door opened into the wide hall, from which also opened the doors of the dining room and the parlor, or front room.

This room held the piano, the new chairs, the best rug, a new divan and a table. Elaine had never seen things like this —she reached out to touch them shyly, as if her very touch were a profanation. Nor had she seen anything to compare with the bigness of the dining room furniture—the table that could be extended to almost unbelievable lengths, the massive buffet, the china closet behind whose glass doors cut glass, hand-painted china, and snowy Haviland showed like brilliant jewels. And even she, who was braced against the Kenzies and all their ways, could see nothing overdone here, but knew instinctively that the things she saw were only sturdy and substantial, fitting well to the family and their way of life.

Later, she was to know the house better, to see that the whole plan of it was one that had been adapted to family needs. Forty years ago it had started out according to a definite idea of architecture, but as time went on, had been expanded in order to meet the needs of a growing family. Two bedrooms had been added, and a bathroom. A screened-in back porch (running the full length of the house and having on it a closet large enough for the storing of winter overshoes, gum boots, raincoats, and such things) had been tacked on almost as an afterthought. These additions had been made with little thought to what they might do to the original plan, and yet they presented an effect neither cluttered nor unharmonious, but gave to the house an air of individuality and charm. Just now, however, Elaine had no chance to explore the house, for Aunt Ellie said to come on—dinner was just ready.

The very lushness of Uncle Dade's table was, in itself, overwhelming. There was a plate of baked ham at one end of the table and one of fried chicken at the other, while in between, as thick as they could sit on the cloth, were bowls of potatoes, both sweet and Irish, late butter beans, green beans (Aunt Ellie called them pole beans), slaw, and innumerable dishes of fruit, condiments, sweet pickles, relishes, and preserves and jellies. Elaine recalled the meagerness of her own mother's table—how thin the bread had always been cut and how chicken was never fried because "stewed chicken took less grease and went farther, besides." Adelaide's cooking always had a queer blue look that came of too much water and too little cream and butter.

Elaine thought, that first day, that Uncle Dade was the biggest man she had ever seen. It was not so much a matter of size as of spirit and force. When he spoke, everyone listened, and when he came into a room he became, at once, the center of it. When he left, it was as if a light had been turned out. He overwhelmed her and she was afraid of him, even as she suspected her father had always feared and resented him. The most she could hope for was that he would not notice her, and, even as she hoped, he turned toward her.

"Here, child," he rumbled. "Eat another piece of chicken. You look like you'd been living on skim milk. No color to you at all. Make her eat, Adelaide."

"She's never been a hearty eater," Adelaide said as she herself took more chicken. "I think she'll do better here. Things are so delicious, Aunt Ellie. That comes of having plenty of cream and butter to cook with."

"Here," Dade Kenzie said, putting a piece of chicken on Elaine's plate, "eat it, child. A body's got to eat."

That was where she made her first mistake with him. If she had thrown a tantrum and refused to eat, he would have thought better of her. She was not hungry. She had a queer, sick feeling in her stomach, as if the very act of eating was disloyal to Papa. She felt that way, and still, she tried obediently to choke down the food he put on her plate. He knew she did not want it, yet she went on trying to eat. That was why he did not have much respect for her, even from the start. He had no use for people without spirit.

Barry Kenzie sat next to Elaine. The boy was fourteen, much younger than the other Kenzie children who were, by this time, married and away from home. Tom, the oldest, had married Julia Callaway, and they lived on an adjoining farm. He and Julia and their two children, Allison and Mark, often came by, dropping in sometimes for meals, sometimes just for a casual visit. Ben Kenzie, who had married Opal Gregory, lived on another farm close by. The Ben Kenzies had three girls, and now, since Opal had had such a hard time with the last baby, there was no hope of a son for them. Years ago there had been another Kenzie girl—Mary Ellen, Dade and Ellie's only daughter, who died when she was ten. It was almost a year later that Barry was born, and the old wives said it was often so—the Lord sent another to take the place of the one He took. So Barry grew up, as it were, almost as an only child, not much older than Allison and Mark, his nephew and niece.

The boy was tall, but very slender, with gently sloping shoulders. All his features were delicate and fine with the clear-cut lines of a cameo. His skin was fair, and his hair a golden blond. Behind his heavy gold-rimmed glasses, his eyes were the clear soft gray of a pigeon's breast.

"Nose in a book all the time," Dade said. "Won't do the things other boys like. Guess we had him too late, eh, Ellie?" Aunt Ellie said nonsense, and to pass the ham again. Adelaide didn't have a thing on her plate.

There was nothing fearsome about Aunt Ellie. She gave out confidence and courage as a stove gives out warmth. Her bones were well padded with good, firm flesh, and about her there was always a faint, tantalizingly delicious odor. Afterwards Elaine was to know the source of it—dozens of little bags of dried rose leaves tucked away in everything the woman used. Her underwear, her clothes, even her household linens, were redolent of the scent. This first day the child knew only that it was a part of the personality of Aunt Ellie, distinct as the shape of her nose and the curve of her chin.

"Do you like to read?" Barry asked Elaine, under cover of the grown-up conversation.

"Oh, yes—" Elaine told him.

"Hurry and finish your pie," he said. "I got a new *American Boy* today. We'll go read it."

"I don't want any pie," she said, emboldened by his presence. "Let's go now."

They got themselves excused and went into the sitting room. Barry stretched out on his stomach on the rug and she sat cross-legged beside him, her soft brown plaits falling across her thin chest as she bent forward to catch the words he read to her. Presently one of her feet went to sleep but she did not move, fearing that any motion of hers would stop the even flow of the boy's voice. She had never known playmates; she had no faith in her own ability to hold one. She and Barry sat there in a small circle of their own on which no one else offered to intrude. In the dining room across the hall the voices of the adults went on, brisk and efficient, making plans for Adelaide's future, and for Elaine's, a concern about which the girl neither knew nor cared. All that mattered was the sound of

Barry's voice, and his complete acceptance of her as a friend and equal. It was small matter that in the next room the loom of her life was being set up.

Before Adelaide and Ellie and Dade had ever left the table, they had settled things among themselves. Adelaide and Elaine were to move into the Kenzie house. There was plenty of room —too much, now that all the children but Barry were gone. Adelaide could help Ellie, who was not too well this fall. Elaine would be good for Barry—he was too much alone with all the others gone. Later, if the Courtneys wanted to move away it would be all right, but just now the only sensible thing for them to do was to stay here.

So Adelaide unpacked their meager belongings and got them into place in the room over the kitchen. Ellie said Elaine could have a room to herself—there were plenty. But Adelaide, setting the deprecating pattern for all her relations with the Kenzies, said no—it was bad enough for them to take one room. Two would be unthinkable. Just outside of their bedroom was a great elm tree, its arms reaching out so close to the window of the room that Elaine could climb out and sit on the branches, munching apples and reading—always reading. Often Barry would join her and they would sit together, each buried in his own book, through an entire summer's afternoon. Sometimes it would be almost sunset before they would raise dazed eyes to see that the magic world in which they had spent the afternoon existed only in the pages of the books they read.

She and Barry started to school together, that first fall she came to them, walking the two miles, carrying books and dinner pails. Each morning as they went through the orchard they would stop to cram their book sacks full of apples—Jonathans and Winesaps and York Imperials. Later, after frost, the Genitans were ripe and, although the children had just finished enormous breakfasts, they would gather these small pinky-green apples and eat them on their way to school. The juice, so cold it hurt their teeth, would stream down their chins, chapping their tender skins until their mouths were red and raw. Ellie would rub camphor ice on them and say they were exactly alike— skin like babies, and why did they insist on eating while they were out in the wind and cold.

(Elaine could not bear the sight of a Genitan apple now. She kept at Henry, that first winter after they were married, until he cut down the one tree on the place. She said the apples were good for neither eating nor cooking, and besides, the tree shaded the strawberry bed. Henry demurred, saying that he knew the things weren't worth giving orchard room, but he kind of liked them, anyway. Made him think of when he was a kid, and carried them to school in his book sack. But Elaine insisted, so he cut down the tree and they burned the wood in the kitchen stove.)

Barry was forever quoting poetry, in a full rich voice, surprising in one of his slender frame. On Friday afternoons he would stand on the platform at the front of the schoolroom, his eyes half closed as if he did not see anyone—as more than likely he did not—and recite poem after poem. He was not good at games. He could not throw a ball straight nor hit one. But he was fleet of foot, which won the respect of the other boys, so that they accepted him as one of them, even though he was poles removed. They respected, too, his ability in books. They were awed, as Elaine was awed, at the way in which he could recite poetry. Something in this power of his seemed to fill a deep, if unconfessed, need for beauty in their lives, so that they did not tease him or call him "sissy" as they might have done less gifted boys. They did not even make capital of the fact that he chose to walk home with Elaine rather than with them, even though they were at an age when girls were things to be ignored or even actively despised.

In the morning, the walk to school was always a race against time. They took short cuts, scarcely looking to either side, so great was their hurry. But in the afternoon, they came around the road and, since there were no specific chores for them at home, they took their own good time. They passed through a lane bordered with trees which everyone in Missouri called "hedge" but which Barry said were really bois d'arc. Sumac bushes grew on both sides of the road, masses of ruby flame after the first frost. There was goldenrod, too, which Barry complained made him sneeze and feel "all choky inside." Old Dade said nonsense—that was before anyone had heard much about allergies—goldenrod was a good Missouri flower and Barry was imagining things. If he'd get out into the sunshine instead of mooning over books all the time, he wouldn't have so many colds in the fall.

Sometimes on warm afternoons Elaine and Barry would sit in the shade of the hedge while he read poetry—"Horatius" and "Eve of Waterloo" and "Thanatopsis." Even when she did not quite know what he was saying, the music of his words and their rhythm stole into her soul so that she was all shaken with the beauty of it and wanted to cry. To cover up this emotion, she gathered the "hedge apples," those round green balls that were the fruit of the bois d'arc tree, and built them into neat pyramids. While she was busy with this, she did not have to look at his face, with that strange rapt look upon it. She could not bear to see it. She was never able to understand how poetry was the thing that drew them closest together and, at the same time, took him out of the world and away from her. Perhaps he was always away, and it was only through poetry that she was able to follow him, even a little way.

After supper, the two of them would sit at the dining room table, doing their home work together. In the sitting room Aunt Ellie and Adelaide busied themselves with knitting or sewing and Uncle Dade read the *Kansas City Star* or the *Daily Drover's Telegram*. Adelaide Courtney, as Dade had foreseen, made herself useful in many ways. Always expert with the needle, her hands seemed now to find an almost sensual pleasure in mending Ellie's fine damask or Dade's good shirts, or in setting patches on household linens.

"Look at this material," she would say with awed delight. "I haven't seen anything like it since I was a girl at home. This tablecloth is like satin. And these shirts! That comes of buying good stuff, a thing I was never able to do in all my married life."

Apparently she felt no shame in confessing it. Or, if she did, it was a shame that was swallowed up in gloating satisfaction that now, at long last, she was back to the kind of life she had known as a girl and from which her marriage had temporarily separated her. It was Elaine who felt the shame for her, and then knew added shame that she should feel it in the first place. She would remind herself quietly that she must not, even in her mind, criticize Mama. Things had been hard for her, always. Now that she had at last come into a measure of security for herself and her child, she could not be blamed for clutching it gloatingly to her heart.

Adelaide was not privileged to enjoy this new-found security of hers for long. Before she had been two years at Uncle Dade's she slipped quietly away, going quickly and painlessly as she would have wanted to go, and without giving Old Dade any great trouble or expense for her sake. Kinfolk—most of whom Elaine had never seen—came from far and near to pay respects to the dead woman. Ellie shed tears of real grief, as if Adelaide had been a beloved and respected sister. Uncle Dade was as gentle and thoughtful of Elaine as if she had been his own daughter. Elaine looked at her mother's still face, feeling the last bit of shame and bitterness leaving her own heart. Now she understood how Adelaide must have felt at coming here where there was so much of everything flowing without stint or grudging. It was a generosity of the spirit, as well as of material things. The funeral of Adelaide was not that of a dependent relative. It was that of a well-loved member of the family. The spirit of Dade

Kenzie was something that Adelaide had known well, on which she had depended with unerring faith, when she decided to write him about her widowhood and in which she had rested securely when she brought herself and her child under his care. She must have known she was not well, and how much it meant to her to realize that Elaine would be forever safe and cared for.

It was this same unstudied generosity and largeness of spirit that went with Dade and Ellie's matter-of-fact statement that, of course, Elaine was staying on with them. Ellie said she was a real comfort and help around the place, and company for Barry besides, who was lonesome with all the others gone. Dade said to be sure she was staying, not expanding his statement beyond that. Elaine had the feeling, quickly stifled, that he had her stay on exactly as he would have suffered the children to bring in another kitten or stray pup, or as he himself would have asked a casual acquaintance to stay for dinner if one happened to pass by at mealtime. His was a broad and embracing generosity that took in everyone he knew. He could not stand unpleasantness or skimping or sordidness. Old Dade was a product of an era and of a region in which indigent female relatives, no matter how distant the relationship, attached themselves to the households of their more fortunate kin. He would never think of that relationship as anything but natural and right. Nor would he ever be able to understand any hesitation Elaine might feel at accepting such an arrangement; neither would it occur to him that, in accepting, she should feel any special gratitude to him. For her to stay on was a natural and normal thing, and he liked arrangements of that kind. It had nothing to do with whether or not he liked the child. It was in no way colored by the fact that she suspected he found her lacking in spirit and had no great interest in her as an individual.

So Elaine stayed on with the Kenzies and there was really no change at all in her way of living. She had her room to herself now, and began to contrive things for it—feminine things, like blue ribbon ties on the curtains and fancy pincushions. Later on, when she took painting lessons, she added pale water color pictures in light gray frames. But this was much later, after Barry went away, and Ellie thought she needed something to take her mind off her loneliness. The summer after Adelaide's death, Ellie thought it would do the child good to have the room prettied up a bit, so she bought new furniture for it—white enamel with little pink wreaths of roses painted on the dresser and the bed. Ellie was too busy to sew, and Elaine had no knack for it, so they bought a spread and curtains—pale pink organdy with ruffles. It was all so beautiful that Elaine sat in the middle of the floor, looking at it and wanting to cry.

The days and the months slipped by, each blending into the next one so smoothly that there seemed to be no change at all, until one morning she would look out and see that the trees, which only yesterday had been thick with their curtains of leaves, were now bare. And then, magically, the leaves were back again, and it was hard to remember that they had ever been gone. And so the years passed, and she had been with Uncle Dade and Aunt Ellie four years, and she herself was sixteen.

She was small, with flat breasts and a body that seemed soft and boneless, like a kitten's. Her brown hair lay close to her small head. Like the girl herself, it had no body to it, but was soft and straight and thin. Her hands and feet were slender. Because she had little strength or endurance, Ellie never put her to difficult tasks. Always her eyes were her best feature—large and gentian-blue, with thick dark lashes and strongly marked brows. In contrast to them, her face looked even paler than it really was. People looked at her eyes first and then at her, thinking she was a right sweet-looking little thing, but wasn't it a pity she was so frail. Few ever got past the eyes to notice her mouth—eager, sensitive, tender.

Barry was eighteen. At that age, Old Dade had been, as he

was fond of saying, a ripsnorter. It was not strange, then, that he should regard the boy, still thin and slight and bookish, as a mere child. Again it was midsummer, merging into early fall. The blackbirds were flying south, as they had been that day when Adelaide and Elaine had first come to the Kenzie place. It was Saturday, and in the kitchen Ellie and the little Negro girl who was helping her that summer were busy making preparations for the Sunday dinner. The Kenzie boys and their families were all coming home—Tom and Julia and their children, Allison and Mark; Ben and Opal with their girls, Ellen and Kay and Frances, so close together in age that they were all three almost the same height. Others had been asked as well—perhaps a dozen friends and neighbors, so that there would be more than twenty people there for dinner. The kitchen smelled divinely of baking ham, of spice cake, of warm bread, and of dozens of other delightful things.

Dade sent Elaine and Barry to the melon patch, perhaps a quarter of a mile away, for watermelons. These would be buried this afternoon in the icehouse, down beneath the straw, close to the great chunks of ice that had been placed there last January. Tomorrow they would be brought out, freezing cold, to be eaten during the long afternoon when everyone sat around talking. So cold they would be that they would send shivery little pains through Elaine's teeth, just to nibble them, but their icy sweetness had a sort of beauty, too.

Barry hitched old Kate to the two-wheeled cart so there would be something to haul the melons back in, once they were picked. He and Elaine both got into the cart to ride to the melon patch. The day was warm, and the girl's thin blue dress clung to her body. She pushed the sunbonnet back off her head, letting it fall to her shoulders. Barry said she looked like a pioneer woman, crossing the plains, and she thought it would sort of be fun, she and Barry riding off into a West of purple sunsets and blue mountain peaks.

The melon patch was just at the edge of a cornfield. This had been a good year, with plenty of rain, so the cornstalks were tall and thick, shedding their long shadows on the patch. Barry went out to pick the melons, thumping them, selecting the ones whose sound he liked best. Elaine sat at the edge of the patch in the shade of the corn, watching him, until presently the cart was full and he came to sit by her. The exercise had made him warm, and he took off his glasses to wipe the perspiration from his face. Without them, his eyes had a vague and unseeing look. She was glad when he replaced them, bringing him back into the world with her. Then he settled himself and took a book from his pocket and began to read aloud. It was with a start that she realized that he was calling her name:

"Elaine the fair, Elaine the lovable," he began,
"Elaine, the lily maid of Astolat—"

A flock of blackbirds had settled in a tree across the field, far enough away so that their cries were not unpleasant but rather a soothing undercurrent for the sound of Barry's voice:

"High in her tower to the East," he went on,
"Guarded the sacred shield of Lancelot."

His voice rose and fell, and the beauty of it and the beauty of the poem were one. Its sadness swept over Elaine so that she was filled with a great aching sweetness, and suddenly she was sobbing, why she could not have told.

Barry dropped his book and turned to her.

"Elaine," he said. "Elaine—"

He put his arm across her shoulders, patting her as he did when she hurt her foot in the haymow or found her home work too difficult. She dropped her head back on his shoulder, the tears wet upon her long lashes, her mouth sweetly trembling. And suddenly Barry's arm tensed around her.

"Elaine—" he whispered.

Her lips, under his, were cold and frightened; it was really only the merest peck he gave her. After it he drew back, and looked at her. She could not raise her eyes to meet his, could not lift her head off his shoulder. Her lashes lay heavy on her cheeks, and she slumped, a dead weight, against him. Apart from him, she had no power to hold herself erect.

He bent to kiss her again. This time she was conscious of a great clarity of senses, drawn out against his lips. Kissing a man was different from kissing a woman. Frail and delicate as Barry might be, there was still a leathery feeling to his skin, different from the skin of a woman. This time his lips were warmer against hers—not so timid and frightened.

"Elaine—" he said, and she answered so low it was only a thread of a whisper, "Barry—"

It was then that they were dragged back to unwilling consciousness at the sound of a horse approaching down the lane. They drew apart dazedly, just as Dade rode into sight. How much he had seen they were never to know. Too much and too little, actually—too much to have any doubts as to what the situation was, and too little to be able to judge it in all its innocence. Whatever his thoughts were, however, he kept them to himself. He only said they'd better be getting the melons back and into the icehouse if they were to be cool enough by tomorrow.

It was at the dinner table the next day that Dade made his announcement. The meal was finished and everyone was sitting, relaxed and content, in that magic period that comes after a good meal, shared by happy people. Dade looked down the long table, flanked on both sides by friends and relatives, and said,

"Guess we'll have to call this a sort of farewell dinner for Barry. He's going off to school next week. Nose stuck in a book all the time, so there's no use trying to make a farmer out of him."

THURSDAY

Everyone thought it was a fine thing, and said so.
"Where's he going?" Tom asked. "State?"
"No," Dade said, "Chicago. Got a notion Columbia's too little for him. Wants to see a city."
Elaine sat very still, her hands linked tightly in her lap, every drop of blood seeming to drain away from her body. Chicago. That was the edge of the world. He would not be home until Thanksgiving, if then. Columbia was close. He could come home nearly every week-end from there. She raised stricken blue eyes to see how Ellie was taking it. And Barry.
Ellie's face was as smooth and bland as cream. And Barry's eyes were shining. They both knew; the announcement was no surprise to either of them. They had talked it over, and without her. She was only Elaine Courtney, a sort of cousin, who didn't really belong to the family. Why *should* they tell her. She lowered her eyes to the plate, and in her heart something died.
In the week that followed, they were all so busy that any thought was crowded out by action. Elaine moved about, in a sort of drugged silence, helping Ellie with Barry's things—the shirts and the underwear and socks and ties. They had to make a trip to Rockwell to buy new things—a trunk and a new suit and luggage and the other things the catalog said he'd need. Barry spent the time in a dazed delight, reading all the information in the catalog, scarcely realizing the trouble everyone was taking for him. Ellie shed a few tears when she was out of sight of the others. If anyone noticed that Elaine went around looking like a wan and stricken ghost, nothing was said about it.
And then the day came for him to leave, and he told them all good-by, kissing his mother and then turning to Elaine, as he would have kissed a smaller, and beloved, sister. He turned back to his mother once more, held her tight and kissed her several times and then, without looking back, got into the car with his father. Just as they were driving away, he turned once more to Elaine.

"Write," he said. "I'll be lonesome. Be sure to write—"

"I will," she promised thickly.

She watched them as they drove off, until even the dust which the car had raised had settled back into the road. Then she went upstairs to her room and, without even bothering to remove the organdy spread, threw herself across the bed and cried, until finally, exhausted, she fell asleep.

That had been sixteen years ago. And now Dade was dead, and Barry would be coming home for his funeral. And she, Elaine Waring, was standing with shaking fingers, measuring out the coffee for Henry Waring's breakfast.

~ IV ~

DR. BURGESS had sent Beulah Kenzie upstairs to rest, so she was not in the room when the end came. Mark came up to tell her and found her lying across the bed, still wearing her print house dress and shoes. Scarcely had he set foot in the room when she was awake, sitting up on the side of the bed.

"Grandfather—?" she asked.

"Yes—"

"Oh, Mark—"

She began to cry, the tears spilling out of her big brown eyes and falling down on the front of her dress. She cried with singular ease, so that there was no distortion of her face. Mark came to sit by her, and put his arm around her.

"Don't cry, honey," he said. "He was an old man and had lived his life. He didn't suffer at all. It came just as easy. Like going to sleep."

She got up and went to the dressing table, reached for a piece of tissue, wiped her eyes, and blew her nose.

"I know it," she said. "But I'll miss him so. He was good to me, and I loved him as dearly as if he had been my own."

THURSDAY

Beulah Fulton Kenzie had, indeed, loved her husband's grandfather dearly. And he had loved her. The first time he ever saw her there was warm approval of her in his eyes, and afterwards he came to love her as much as he did any of his own grandchildren.

Beulah was the only Kenzie bride who had come from "away from here," as the community expressed it. Always the Kenzies had married local people, so that the young couples settled down with double blessings and with the comfortable assurance of knowing each other's way of life and family background almost as well as they knew their own. Mark Kenzie did things differently.

He went to Illinois one summer for a visit to some of the innumerable and untraceable cousinships, and there met Beulah Fulton. Beulah was twenty that summer. Since her mother's death, more than two years before, she had been keeping house for Papa. Goodness knows he needed someone to look after him so that he could get his sermons prepared without being bothered by the members of the Ladies' Aid or the factions in the church choir. Beulah herself sang in the choir—a cool, clear soprano. She could play the organ, too, but long ago Mama and Papa had decided it was best for the minister's family to take as few conspicuous jobs as possible, so it was only in cases of emergency that she offered to play.

She could still remember every detail of that day when Mark Kenzie first came to the church where Papa was preaching. She was wearing a sprigged muslin dress and a new hat. The skirt of the dress was made in three tiers, with lace edging each one. The hat was a leghorn, with a black velvet band and a big pink rose on it. All the time she was singing she was conscious of a strange young man, sitting out there in the audience, never taking his eyes off her. He was good-looking—tall, with dark eyes and brown hair that, when the light struck it, showed warm bronze tints. After church, his cousins brought him around to meet her, and she found his name was Mark Kenzie, and he was from Missouri. That evening he came back to services. And the next day he came to the parsonage, with a cousin along for manners' sake, and asked her if she would go with him to the ice cream supper the Masons were giving that evening.

The ice cream supper was exactly like all the others she had ever been to. The same long boards were stretched across the same sawhorses; the same heavy church plates held the same kind of rich, melting ice cream; the same women had brought the same kinds of homemade cakes. Yet everything was different. Every word she said was important, trembling with meaning, filled with some delicate and beautiful import whose real significance she could not even guess. Her blood flowed light and quick in her veins, and she felt she was more beautiful than she had ever been in all her life and yet, filled with a great aching desire to be even more beautiful.

For two weeks it was like that, with Mark Kenzie coming to see her every time she would let him. And then he had gone home with something on his mind which she did not know at the time, but which he was to tell her later. He was determined to marry her as soon as he could talk his family into consenting.

Tom Kenzie was not at all sure about the marriage. Mark was young and flighty. People said it was a pity Allison wasn't the boy in the family—she had more push and drive in a minute than Mark had in a month. Tom must have been thinking of these things when he said he wasn't sure. After all, the boy was not yet twenty-one.

Mark had no notion of waiting. He had never waited for anything in all his impetuous young life. His mother (she had been a Callaway, a family never noted for its backbone) spoiled him ridiculously, so that he always got, either by wheedling or tantrums, whatever he wanted. This, however, was one thing his mother could not win for him. Tom was firm. Mark must wait the four months until he attained his majority and then, if he was still of the same mind, they'd consider the matter.

Mark had not the faintest idea of giving up. He went to his grandfather, choosing with a perfect eye to strategy a time when the old man was richly steeped in content. It had been a good year—the corn was hanging heavy on the stalks, past all danger of the vagaries of weather. The haying was going well, the smell of it filling the air as the hard, rectangular bales filled the barns. Late fryers were coming into their prime and watermelons were beginning to ripen. It was August, a time when Dade Kenzie's soul expanded to meet nature's lavish fulfillment.

Mark came, with a spoiled child's directness, to the point.

"I met a girl in Illinois," he said. "I want to marry her, but Dad says no."

Dade smoothed the ear of the hound-dog that sat with his head on the old man's knee.

"What's she like?" he asked.

"A little like Gran'ma," the boy told him.

Dade looked at him sharply.

"What makes you say that?" he asked.

"I don't know. She just is, that's all," Mark told him with candor in which there was no guile. Old Dade recognized the ring of truth in his voice.

"Bring her out for a visit," he said. "Maybe your dad will feel different when he sees her."

Julia Kenzie, thus encouraged, wrote the correct letter of invitation, and in due time back came Beulah's letter of acceptance, saying she would be pleased to come, and they were nice to ask her, and she was looking forward to the visit.

Torn between her fierce desire to see that Mark had what he wanted and her fear of the consequence of the visit, Julia began to make preparations. It was a pity, she thought rebelliously, that Allison was not here to help her. But then, her daughter never had been much comfort or help to her. The girl had no notion, no notion at all, of the value of things—cut glass, and pretty china, and satinlike damask cloths. She could not see why it was important to have an angel food cake just so, or chicken fried exactly right. Allison would just as soon open a can of beans and eat them, cold, from the can, as to have a dinner well cooked and served in style. Here she was now, off in Kansas City, learning to sing. Not just the sort that she would do in a church choir, or at parties, but the kind people did on the stage. A Callaway, all smeared up with grease paint, singing on a stage! Only loose women did that. Julia'd never feel any different about it, even if it was what her own daughter chose to do.

She was all the more firm in her disapproval because she was so utterly unable to tell Allison how she felt about it. Everything she said seemed to amuse the girl, who would meet her objections with a mixture of gentle ridicule and a cool insolence. Julia could feel her face turning the brick-red of embarrassed humiliation, her head jerking back and forth with quick, frustrated motions, when the matter came up for discussion. The fact that she made herself ridiculous every time she tried to say the things she knew were right and true about the matter only served to set her more firmly against her daughter's actions.

Allison should be here now, helping to clean the house, prepare the food, and plan the social events that would have to be given for this girl from Illinois. If Beulah Fulton was the nobody that Julia suspected she was—the daughter of a smalltown Methodist minister was pretty sure to be a colorless creature—all the Kenzies were going to have to rally around in order to make her seem important to the neighborhood. Allison wouldn't be any help there—she had spent most of her life antagonizing and outraging the home people—but she could find out what the girl was up to where Mark was concerned. Although she would not have admitted the fact to her daughter, Julia did know that Allison possessed a keen insight that enabled her to see at once to the bottom of people and their motives. The woman sighed when she thought of how unfair life had been to her. With a daughter like Allison, she should have got a daughter-in-law of her own choosing—a good, biddable, correct little thing, one that everybody would approve of and admire and say wasn't Mark Kenzie lucky to get her. One like Jane Markham, over at Midland.

Beulah Fulton, quietly unaware of any of these things, came for her visit with Mark's family. She was a tall girl who moved with a placid ease and unconsciousness of self. Her smooth olive skin was warm with rich undertones of color, so that no matter how tired she became, she never looked dragged out. Her hair was dark, and inclined toward coarseness. She could arrange it the first thing in the morning, and it would stay in place all day. Her eyes, dark and beautifully expressive, were her greatest asset. She had a way of looking directly at the person who was talking with a look that brought confidence to the speaker. Whoever happened to be talking with Beulah Fulton felt, at that time, that he was a most important person, and Miss Fulton recognized the fact.

Especially were the men drawn to her, although there was not about her the faintest trace of coquetry. Even Ezra Dowlin, pompously critical of most women, found no fault with her. A natural and spontaneous warmth pervaded all her relations with others. She laughed often, with such genuine and unfeigned mirth that her very laughter made everything seem right and happy.

Old Dade was no more able to explain it than Mark had been when they discussed the matter, yet he knew the boy was right in saying that the girl was like Ellie. He was drawn to her at once. At first, he deliberately sought her out, feeling sure that she must be putting up some sort of front, trying to reassure and impress these people who were, quite openly, looking her over to see if she were the proper wife for Mark Kenzie. Her mother was dead. Her father was a minister; just now, he wasn't very well. She had a brother and a sister, both married and living on "little farms." Each had two children, and sometimes they had "rather hard times, for you know how farming goes." She had lived in a great many places, all of them small. "You know how it is with preacher's families—"

The old man recognized the complete honesty back of every word she said. If any of the Kenzies ever went to Illinois to check up on the details—or, if they checked with the Kenzie kin already there—they would find things just as the girl had pictured them. Too many people went into a great deal of dramatizing about their families so that later, when the real facts showed up, there was embarrassment for all concerned. Not so with Beulah.

All these things were commendable in the girl, but they were not the reason for her resemblance to Ellie. Dade, trying hard to put his finger on it, felt that at last he came to the truth of the matter. It was her complete femininity, in the very best sense of the word. Men felt for her a complete, but entirely male, respect and admiration. Between her and them there was no rivalry for power, no vague antagonism. They saw in her the qualities they idealized in womanhood, and all too seldom found. They preened before her, feeling somehow that she brought out all their best points. That was where she was like Ellie. All women should be like that. They should be warmth and strength and sweetness and beauty instead of simpering foolishness, or struggle for power, or temperamental nonsense. Surprising thing was that a spoiled young whelp like Mark would have sense enough to recognize these qualities when he saw them and go after the girl. He would be a darned lucky boy to get her.

Dade was not the only member of the family who approved of Beulah. Allison came down from Kansas City and liked the girl on sight. Ben and Opal and their three girls came over for supper the first night of her visit. Ben found a great deal to say to her and Opal was not jealous, although, as a usual thing, she became nervous when he noticed other women, laughing too much and talking with strained animation. The little girls were charmed with her, and begged her to go home to spend the night with them. Even Elaine was more animated in her presence, and Henry Waring forgot his hands and feet sufficiently so that his conversation became easy and almost fluent in her presence. Beulah must have sensed all this, but she moved quietly and naturally among them, giving no hint of her awareness.

Beulah Fulton had always been poor, but she could never remember that it mattered much to the family. That was a part of the way they lived—that, and going from parsonage to parsonage, sometimes every year, sometimes at longer intervals. The family took these parsonages as they came, making the best of them. This quiet acceptance was largely the influence of their mother, a gentle, placid woman who set to work, as soon as she had removed her hat, cleaning the new home into which fate and the Presiding Elder had sent them. Usually there was a double duty attached to moving—not only must she leave immaculate the place vacated, but she must clean the new one as well. Once Joe, the oldest, burst out,

"I don't see why we have to clean this one so good. Why don't you leave it the way you found it? Like that lazy Mrs. Egbert left it!"

"Don't criticize," his mother said calmly. "Mrs. Egbert is not strong. She is a good woman, and does the best she can."

That was Mrs. Fulton's creed. One never criticized, and never apologized, or made things out different from the way they really were. Others might brag of rich relations and former grandeurs, but the parsonage family never could. They took things as they came, and made no fuss. In dress and behavior they must be quiet and dignified, so that no one could find grounds for criticism. With their mother's help, her children did this with no outward rebellion, but with great certainty and quietness of spirit. Whatever happened, they knew her way was the good way, and the true.

It was while they were cleaning the house after Mrs. Egbert that Beulah fell. It was a nasty fall; she was unconscious so long afterwards that they called the doctor. He told her to stay quietly in bed for a week, and then to drop by his office for an examination. At the last minute, on the day she was to go, a delegation of Ladies' Aid members appeared to check the parsonage needs, so, since her father was away preaching a funeral, there was no one to go with the girl to keep the appointment. Dr. Finley was an older man, a member of the Methodist Church, with daughters of his own, and altogether highly respectable, so her mother took the sensible view that it was quite all right for the girl to go alone. Which she did.

Beulah had never forgotten that office. It faced west, so that it was warm in mid-afternoon. Potted plants were in the window, and on the walls were hanging a steel engraving of Lincoln and a calendar bearing a copy of "The Doctor" in brash, bright colors. The office smelled faintly of medicine and dust and heat. The doctor sat in his swivel chair, slumping a little, for he was very tired. His hair, gray and quite thin on top, was rumpled.

He was very gentle and impersonally kind with her. After he had finished with the examination he talked with her as she sat on the old black leather couch, worn down into hollows until the springs showed through the shabby black covering. He took off his gold-rimmed glasses, looking at them as he talked, polishing them, blowing his breath on them and wiping them with a dingy handkerchief.

She was all right, he told her, but, at times, she might have considerable pain. She must take care of herself and not lift heavy things nor allow herself to get overtired. Outside of that, she was all right.

"Except," he hesitated, putting his glasses on, and then taking them off again to lift them to the light, to find another speck and begin anew his polishing, "except, it is extremely unlikely that you will ever have children. With a delicate and dangerous operation, perhaps. But even then, it is not sure. Bring your mother down some day and we'll talk it over. In the meanwhile, do not worry. You are quite all right in every other way."

She did not tell her mother about the conversation. At first, it was because she did not want to worry her. The complicated and delicate business of getting settled in a new parsonage and becoming adjusted to a strange congregation was, in itself, a big drain on Mrs. Fulton's courage and poise. To burden her with a problem touching upon the welfare of her children was the last thing Beulah wanted to do. Besides, the girl did not quite know how to go about the telling. With Mother, one did not glibly discuss having babies. So she pushed the matter back into her mind until a more appropriate time for discussion should come. And before that time ever presented itself, her mother died, unobtrusively, as she did everything.

Joe and sister Myra were already married, leaving Beulah the only one at home, so the girl took up the job of managing the house for her father. So busy was she, so stricken at the loss of her mother, that she seldom thought now of what Dr. Finley had said to her. There were times when, as he had promised, the pains came and then she crept off to bed with the memory of his words in her ears. As the months went on, these pains became less severe, and she began to think of him less often, especially after they moved to another town.

And then, Mark Kenzie came visiting. Brief as his stay was, it was long enough so that she felt she knew what he wanted. Although he had never, in so many words, told her what his intentions were, he had gone about his wooing with the guileless energy of a child after a lollipop. She had thought he would forget her once he got back to Missouri and to that family he talked so much about. The thought came like a chill wind over the bright glow of her thoughts in the days after he left. She put it resolutely away from her, telling herself sensibly that he was only a visiting boy, and that, quite likely, she would never hear from him again, and she must not hope, nor must she feel bad if she did hear no more.

And then Julia Kenzie's letter came, asking her to visit the family.

She hesitated over the answer to that letter, even going so far as to talk it over with her father. He sat in his shabby study with books piled high about him and a small pad covered with notes for his Sunday sermon on his knee. These he put down when she indicated she wanted to talk to him, pushing aside papers on the table to make room for the notes, securing them with a paper weight, getting things in order, so that, once he began talking with her, there would be nothing that would make either one of them feel that he could not give her his attention. Thus prepared, he listened quietly as she spoke.

"He is a good boy, this Mark Kenzie?" Mr. Fulton asked.

"Yes," Beulah answered him quietly, "I think so."

"How do you feel about him?"

"I—I don't quite know," she said honestly, but a clear, bright color flooded her face and in her dark eyes a sort of light glowed.

Her father looked at her searchingly and, although the girl did not drop her eyes, the flush deepened.

"Then go and find out," the man said gently. "Remember, Ruth went to Boaz. We cannot always sit waiting for things to come to us."

So Beulah wrote Julia, accepting the invitation. Mark met her, with assurance sitting like a banner on him. He knew that, once the family saw her, everything was as good as settled. Julia, trying hard to be fair and unbiased, stood off a little, in weak-willed aloofness. The whole family gathered in, and while she found them entrancing, like people in a storybook, it was Old Dade who fascinated her most of all.

About him there was a great sureness, a marvelous self-confidence, coming, she supposed, of having always lived well and without fear of what others might think of him. About the Kenzie way of life there was a great abundance of things—plenty of white meat at meals, great pitchers of thick cream, endless varieties of vegetables and fruits; good, substantial furniture in large, airy rooms; snug and well-painted barns filled with grain of all kinds; fields rich with lush crops or dotted with sleek grazing stock. The first Sunday of Beulah's visit had been the occasion for a big dinner—no one seemed to know, or care, how many had been invited. From a closet over the basement stairs, table leaves were taken, and, as the crowd increased, Ellie sent someone for extra leaves. No matter how large the table grew, there was still another cloth in reserve long enough to cover it.

The kitchen was an immense room, holding, in addition to all the necessary kitchen equipment, a rocking chair and a sewing basket. Ellie used the rocking chair to sit in and read, or sew a bit, while she was waiting for the men to come to meals. Any visitor, man or woman or child, might come in and sit in it, talking with Ellie as she prepared the meal. She had no dislike of being watched while she worked; some of the most satisfactory visiting she had ever done with family or friends was here in the kitchen while her hands were busy with cooking. In the center of the room was a table, long enough to be used for serving meals when the men were doing dirty work and did not want to clean up to go into the dining room. Usually, too, family breakfasts were eaten here. This Sunday, the table was being used for working space. Women, with aprons tied around their Sunday dresses, whipped cream, mashed potatoes, dished up preserves and pickles, cut cakes and pies.

Never before had Beulah seen so much food. At the parsonage, one was careful of every drop of milk or cream, every spoonful of fat. Potatoes were always boiled in their skins, to make them go farther. Bread was cut thin, and never eaten fresh, because that was wasteful. Cooking was something to be accomplished quietly and almost secretly, managing the best you could with what you had, making no apologies over the things you lacked, and talking not overmuch about the results. Here at the Kenzies', it was a public ritual, with everyone wandering in and out of the kitchen without seeming to disturb the workers in the least. Ben's three girls, at an age when they alternated between childhood and extreme adulthood, sneaked bites of pickles and cake frosting. Tom sat in the rocking chair, telling Mother how well his corn was doing. Mark took Beulah in, just to say hello to Gran'ma and, once there, the girl quietly offered to help.

"That's sweet of you," Ellie told her warmly, "but we're getting along all right in here. You and Mark can go out to the garden for some parsley, if you want. I need it for the plate of boiled ham."

Mark and Beulah went out the back door, past the smokehouse with its store of hams and sides and cured bacons, to the plot of ground that was the garden. At the extreme edge the orchard rose, dark and richly green, with early apples already turning red or gold. On both sides of the garden were oldfashioned flowers—hollyhocks, peonies, iris, snowballs. The outbuildings almost hid the plot from the house so that, with the orchard on one side and the flowers on the other, it seemed shut off from the world.

Mark bent down to gather the parsley and Beulah stood watching him. She had never noticed before that his hair had so much red in it—with the sun shining on it, it looked almost like his grandfather's. He rose quickly, caught her look on him. His eyes blazed, dark and arrogant. His eyes, too, were old Dade's eyes, as was the quick, unchecked urgency of his movements. But his mouth was soft and weak and slightly sensuous—the Callaway mouth. Or, it might well have come from the fact that never, in all his spoiled young life, had he been really crossed or denied anything he wanted.

Still holding the green stuff in one hand, he reached out and drew her roughly to him. Through the thinness of her muslin dress she could feel the strength and hardness of him. Because she had never felt a man's arms around her before, a great storm of emotions rose in her—panic and embarrassment and something else that made her relax, just a moment, against him. At this he brought his other arm across her shoulders, drawing her closer until there were only a few inches between her eyes and his. His lips came down on hers with a quick relentless pressure that brought her back to herself.

"No—" she said. "No—"

"Yes—" he urged. "Yes—"

She put her hands on his chest, pushing him back from her, her eyes clear and sure. Her very quietness convinced him as no coquetry could have done. He stood with his arms around her, but holding her loosely.

"I want to marry you, Beulah," he said. "You must have known that. Will you?"

"I—I can't be sure, yet," she answered.

She said it so simply that he knew she meant it.

"We must go back now," she told him, gently, as one would speak to a child.

They went back to the kitchen, scarcely speaking on the way. Ellie took the parsley from Mark, throwing it into a pan of water on the table. Beulah watched her with complete fascination. She was easily the queen of the kitchen. The oldest woman there, her movements were still the most deft and sure, her decisions the most final. Partly, of course, it was because she was in her own kitchen, but anywhere else she would have been confident and certain. She set her feet lightly but firmly on the floor when she walked, swaying her hips with an almost girlish grace. Her hair curled softly around her face; her skin was fresh and clear. There was about her an odor of soap and water and good powder, as well as the rose-scented cleanness of her Sunday clothes.

"Goodness, child," she said to Beulah, "you've got against some dirt. Brush it off her shoulder, Mark."

Mark reached to flick off the bit of earth, knowing he had put it there when he held her in his arms. At his touch, something flamed up again between them. Ellie watched with quick, bright knowledge in her eyes.

"U-m-m—" she said. "That's better, now. Take her out to talk with Gran'pa, Mark. He's scarcely seen her."

Old Dade, in his armchair, was in the yard with the men. In his hand he held a section of the Sunday *Star*, swatting flies with it. The other men were either in chairs or sitting on the grass near him. Children played behind the chairs—climbed trees, chased each other. Lanky boys lounged about, feeling grown-up and wholly masculine. More than likely as recently as a month ago they had been with the group of smaller children playing back of the chairs. Now they were with the men and were rudely unresponsive to the pleas of the children to come play with them.

Dade got up from his chair when Mark and Beulah came to him. To the day of his death he never lost his interest in and appreciation of a pretty woman.

He said, "Sit down, Miss Beulah. Has this young scamp been showing you a good time?"

Beulah took the chair he indicated and said yes, Mark had been doing his duty. Dade turned his own chair so that they were almost alone in the group, and Mark dropped easily at their feet. The other men went on talking their own particular affairs—weather and crops and the price of wheat and the prospects for corn.

Beulah did not have to be told that what was coming was probably the turning point of her whole life. There in the garden, with Mark's lips on hers, she knew that she loved him, that if she did not marry him she would never marry at all. As clear and sure as that, the knowledge came to her. Because she had never evaded an issue in her life, she could not do so now. She loved Mark Kenzie completely and unquestionably. Not for one moment did she see him for anything he was not, but she loved him because he was as he was. She knew, too, that what Dade Kenzie thought of her would determine whether or not they were to be married. There was only one way she could ever come into this family, and that would be with the good wishes and blessings of Old Dade himself. At that time, she did not know why it was so important to her, but it was.

From the very first she found him easy to talk to. That was why, later, when she tried to excuse herself for not telling him the thing she should have, she could find little justification for her failure to do so. Now she answered his questions honestly and without fear. She must have said the right things, for when one of Ben's girls came out to say that dinner was ready, the old man put his hand on Beulah's arm to hold her back just a moment after the others had started in.

"And when," he asked, his dark eyes searching her face, "are you going to tell that grandson of mine that you'll marry him?"

"The next time he asks me," she said.

And then they went laughingly into the dining room together.

There were twenty adults around the table in the dining room. The children ate from a table of their own on the side porch. Between Ellie's end of the table, where she served fried chicken, and Dade's, with the platter of ham before him, were scattered cousins, sons, in-laws, friends. Bowls of food were filled in the kitchen from what seemed an endless supply. Elaine kept the pitcher of iced tea going constantly. The ice was piled so high in the glasses that it rested, hard and cold, against their faces when they drank.

Beulah was conscious of Mark's nearness as he sat next to her. The magic of his presence was a part of the magic of the day—

close enough to touch, and yet, strangely remote and unreal. She and Mark were in a world of their own, their knees touching; even without turning her head, she was conscious of his eyes on her. She did not know what she ate. She picked up her fork and laid it down, automatically, as one in a dream. Old Dade, seeing how things were, said, as soon as dinner was over,

"There are some ripe apples on the tree over by the lane. Why don't you two go get us a basket full?"

The orchard was still and cool. There was a mingled smell of the freshness of ripe apples and a not unpleasant odor of rotting ones as well.

Mark set the basket down, and moved toward her.

"Beulah," he whispered. "Beulah, darling—"

All these things were moving through Beulah Kenzie's mind now, filling it with memories whose very beauty was pain. So, it was several minutes before she could get herself in hand and say, quietly and almost in her natural voice,

"I'm all right now, Mark. Let's go down."

~ V ~

DADE KENZIE often said laughingly that he had only one child. He meant his granddaughter Allison, Tom and Julia Kenzie's daughter.

She was the first grandchild, and before she was born Dade was confident that she was going to be a boy. Julia Kenzie devoutly hoped that he was right. She had never been wholly at ease around her father-in-law, although, goodness knows, the Callaways were every bit as good as the Kenzies. They might not have quite as much money, but they were good stock, and never did foolish, impetuous things and got themselves talked about, like certain people she knew.

THURSDAY

Julia was a great one for casting sly allusions. Her insults were the most subtle kind; one could take them or leave them. If people resented them, Julia denied any intent of evil at all, implying that it was a guilty conscience or an evil mind that made anyone take them home to himself. If they were ignored, she became more and more bold, going in for knowing looks and delicate emphasis on telling words. If her innuendoes drew a spark of anger, she retreated in hurt and frustrated confusion, saying she had always been misunderstood. Only Dade was able to handle her.

"Mean me, Julie?" he would ask, looking at her squarely from beneath shaggy brows.

Under his steady gaze she would become embarrassed, protesting that she had no notion of referring to him. Always she came out of these encounters breathless and incoherent. As the years went on, she profited little from her experience, never learning to refrain from veiled hints.

So the thought of a son was not unpleasant to Julia Kenzie. A grandson to carry on Old Dade's name would certainly make her supreme in the clan. Naturally he would be named for his grandfather—David Allison Kenzie. It sounded sweet upon her tongue, and she said it aloud several times, savoring it. Old Dade, learning of the plan, was mightily pleased. He said, however, it was confusing to have two people of the same name in the family, and maybe they better plan to call him Allison—that had been his mother's maiden name.

Julia was built small for childbearing, and besides that, had little courage. When she found her baby was not the son she had planned for, she burst into tears. Afterwards she defended herself by thinking that she was weak and had had a hard time, so that the tears were only a nervous reaction. But she never did get over feeling guilty about it, and remembering that her first emotion upon learning of her daughter's birth was one of disappointment. And because she felt guilty, she was often crisp and short-tempered with Allison, having little patience with the girl's independent ways.

Dade came riding over to see his new grandchild, and Ellie, who had been there helping with things, met him at the door.

"Now you go in and be sweet to her," Ellie bade Dade. "She's feeling pretty bad because it's a girl when she had hoped to have a boy to name for you. It's a fine baby—going to have red hair."

Dade went into the room where his daughter-in-law lay, very small and white in the great double bed. And defenseless. There would be no sly digs out of Julia today, nor for many days to come. He felt closer to her than he had ever been before.

"Hello," he said, taking her hand. "They tell me you've got a girl. We've been needing a girl around here for a long time."

Julia knew that he was pleased with her. She remembered, suddenly, the child Mary Ellen, and because she knew he was remembering, too, it was a bond between them. Purpose and courage flowed through her once more. She had got her baby into the world, and, even though it was a girl, Dade Kenzie was pleased with it, and with her. Besides, it had red hair.

"I'm going to name her like I planned," Julia said, a quick resolution flooding her soul and making her happy and confident. She had not thought of the matter until just this moment, but now it seemed a wonderful idea. "I'm naming her Mary Allison Kenzie. We'll call her Allison. How do you like it?"

Dade said he liked it fine. And now could he see his namesake?

Later, Julia Kenzie was to regret bitterly this impulsive act of hers. Maybe giving a girl a man's name wasn't a good idea to begin with. At any rate, because the child bore his name, Dade Kenzie seemed to feel that she was his to train, to rear.

It was not strange that Dade Kenzie should claim Allison for his own. In appearance she was certainly more nearly like him than were any of his own children. Hers was the only hair that might pass for red, although it was really more a mahogany color. She had, too, his red-brown eyes and quick flashing smile. But actually, the resemblance was more a thing of the spirit than of the flesh, although few were discerning enough to see that. They only said that Allison got more like the old man every day she lived, and Tom and Julia were going to have trouble with that one.

The child was very young when she began to realize how much she was like her grandfather. She was never to know whether he suggested it to her, or whether she came into the knowledge herself. Before she was ever able to put the thing into words, she recognized in herself his zest for life, his daring, his courage, and his fierce independence. She knew, too, she had his singleness of purpose and his ingenuity for achieving his own ends. Dimly at first, and later with more clarity, she knew what people meant when they said she was a chip off the old block.

When she was only five or six, he began to take her with him when he went about overseeing the place. He bought her a small pony and a saddle, and was inordinately proud of her complete lack of fear when she rode. The horse was more spirited than he had realized when he bought it, a fact which he and the child kept, with quiet understanding, from her mother. Together they would ride out to the fields where the hands were plowing the fat black land, to the pastures where the grazing stock was kept, across the creek to see the growing alfalfa. They had not been taking these rides long when she demanded overalls and a hat, "Like boys wear."

To Julia's disgust, Dade backed her in her demands.

"A dress isn't protection enough," he said. "We ride through weeds as high as a horse's back. Lots of times we climb barbed-wire fences. Get her some suitable clothes."

Julia, as much in awe of her father-in-law as ever, bought the overalls and hat, not without great sputterings.

They rode together over fields that sloped gently, dipping down from small swells to gracious valleys, then rising again to hills from which they might look across miles of farmlands to see homes and barns and tight outbuildings, standing secure and strong—the farms and homes of their friends and neighbors. The child Allison could even see very clearly several small towns—Belton, and the spire of the Baptist church at Midland, and even, when the air was right, smoke from Rockwell, twenty miles away. She felt that Grandfather rarely looked at these things, though. He was concerned chiefly with the fields that were his own.

These fields were laid off in checkerboard pattern, a design that was always planned and supervised by Old Dade himself with careful attention to what had been planted in them, not only the year before, but any number of years previous to that. Here would be forty acres of corn, tightly fenced, and green and tall and straight. Allison liked the corn. It was so fiercely independent, so arrogantly sure of itself. When drought came, as it sometimes did, and dried the corn up to but a sickly caricature of itself, she could not bear to look at it, refusing to accompany her grandfather on his rounds. She liked the wheat less, for it bowed so meekly to every breeze, rippling and waving in perfect harmony with each shifting current of air. But the greenness of alfalfa and the lushness of the bluegrass, with its grazing stock upon it, she loved, seeing in it a poetry of color and form.

A ride over the place with Grandfather was no small thing, for the old man had a farm larger than most—more than a section. He had bought, not only for himself, but for his sons as well. Now he and Tom farmed together the acres that had been meant for Ben to share also. But Ben had chosen to take a smaller place farther away—one with fewer conveniences, but his own to do with as he pleased. Julia said Opal's hand was in this, and she couldn't say she blamed her.

As the two rode together, old Dade Kenzie talked to his granddaughter as if he were talking to himself. He saw a certain kind of cloud that meant rain, and, out of more than fifty years of experience, said so. Or he discussed the cutworms in the corn and what their presence meant to the crop. Sometimes it was a more pungent, earthy wisdom that fell from his lips, and the child listened without shock or squeamishness. Later, when she discovered she did not have the false modesty and nasty-niceness of other girls about her, she laid the fact to this association with her grandfather. Privately, she scorned their attitudes, always feeling that the prunes-and-prisms people were the ones who had such a store of evil thoughts in their minds that they saw nastiness in the most simple and everyday phases of life. Having no lurking curiosities, no dark spots in her mind, she was never afraid to face things and talk them through. This she learned from her grandfather as she learned to ride—simply, naturally, and early in life.

Riding with him, she began to understand the feeling that a man has for his own land. She did not believe that anyone, even Grandmother, knew exactly how he felt about his farms. There was something in the love a man has for good, rich land that he feels for no other possession he may have, passing even the love he bears for a woman. She would watch him as he looked across fields laden with early morning mists, or bathed in the slanting rays of afternoon sun, seeing in his look tenderness and power and pride. As he bent to examine more closely a blade of corn just through the ground, she felt that here before her was the merging power of God and man—patience and wisdom fused together into a great partnership, each member depending on the other as on a worker intimately known and deeply respected. Old Dade knew, one and inseparably, the tremendous arrogance that comes of owning good land and the tremendous humility that comes of using it according to nature's plan. He knew, too, the exulting sense of freedom that came of looking at his own fields as they stretched out, a largeness that spread to meet the horizon, and beyond. So well did Allison understand this feeling of his that she could never interest herself in small things, or small souls. She did not play dolls as other girls did, and later she was not interested in fancywork, nor giggling conversations about nothing much, and new fads of dress nor manner.

It was not strange, then, that she grew up "not like other girls." Refusal to sew was only a part of the difference. She liked to climb trees, and was utterly fearless in doing so. Neither did she fear bugs and snakes and small creatures that usually sent little girls, with shrill feminine shrieks, to the nearest port of safety. She could throw a ball swift and true, and run like an antelope. It was no wonder that she would want to go for a ride in the first airplane she ever saw.

It was a small cheesebox thing that came to town in the wake of a circus. The pilot offered to take passengers up for ten dollars. The child, hearing this, raced straight as an arrow to her grandfather.

"I want to go up," she said. "Get him to take me."

Dade had been standing watching the machine—its smooth flow through the air like a bird flying, the glint of the wings against the blue, the look on the face of the pilot as he carried his passengers up, two by two. The man seemed to know his business, all right, and took no foolish chances. There was a boldness, a daring, about flying that caught at Dade's imagination. He turned with a start at his granddaughter's demand.

"Tell you what," he finally said, "if your mother will let you, and your grandmother will let me, we'll go up together."

Ellie was easy enough to manage. Julia, torn between her fear of the plane and her fear of her father-in-law, did not know what to say. While she hesitated, Allison danced off to tell her grandfather that it was all right—Mother hadn't said no.

Never in all her life would Allison forget that first wild, free gladness that came with flying. It was release from self, and from the world. It was a clean, bright loneliness that was not lonely at all; it was beauty of sense and motion blended into a surging burst of feeling that snatched at her heart until the hot tears came to her eyes. Always she remembered that Grandfather gave her that experience. Grandfather taught her what it meant to free the body as well as the soul.

Because everyone blamed Dade with her vagaries—her refusal to learn to cook or to sew or to keep house properly, her tomboy ways, her inattention in class—they likewise laid upon his shoulders the responsibility for her acting as she did about the speech for Children's Day. When the matter was brought to his attention by her mother, who did not fail to imply where the blame for the matter lay, he decided that perhaps he had better look into things. After all, every child took part in Children's Day programs. That was childhood's inalienable right.

"Why don't you want to say the speech they gave you?" he asked her, coming directly to the point as he would have done with an adult.

"It's silly," she said. "The whole program's silly. They get up there and mumble and nobody can hear what they are saying, and everyone says it's cute if they get up at all. I think a Children's Day program is about the dumbest thing there is."

"They've always had them," Dade said weakly, feeling a sneaking sympathy with Julia in her contention that the child was hard to handle.

"That's no reason they have to go on doing something silly, just because they've always done it," she said. "Besides, you ought to hear how Miss Laura told me to say my speech. She twittered just like a bird. No kid with any sense would talk like that. I told her I wouldn't twitter that way, and she got mad at me."

The child had a gift for mimicry, and she told him, word for word, how the spinster wanted her to talk. The exaggerated sweetness, the simpering coyness, were too much for the man. He knew Allison was telling the truth. Fifty years ago Laura had talked just like that when she herself said speeches. But, of course, he could not let the child know what he was thinking.

"You'll feel sort of funny Sunday morning, sitting back with the grown folks when all the other children are up doing things."

"I won't care," she said. "I can sit with you."

He looked at her sharply, into his mind creeping the suspicion that maybe folks were right when they said he was spoiling her, making her different from other children. Children's Day programs were silly. They were enjoyed only by the parents of the performers, having long since sunk down below the level where they had anything of entertainment, or even of interest, in them. But, even so, they were the big juvenile event of the year. Allison should be in this one, if only to refute the charges that she was different from other children. All the other little girls would be preening themselves in new dresses and ribbons. There would be a lot of silly gibberish about sweet and pretty things, said and sung in time with the waving of flower garlands and ropes of greenery. Allison was by far the smartest and prettiest of the lot. It was not proper for her to be denied the chance for showing off with the rest of them.

"How would you like to sing a song?" he asked. "Grandmother would teach you. She might play for you, too. She used to sing and play mighty well."

It ended with Allison's singing *Annie Laurie*, Ellie accompanying her. At first, the woman had protested that it wasn't quite the sort of thing for a child to sing on such a program, but Dade was adamant. It suited the child's voice. Besides, he had a memory of Ellie's singing it at a church social long ago, and he had a mind to hear it again.

Allison knew that she would always remember, too, the exulting gladness that came with singing. She was conscious of the people sitting out in the church, listening to her—Grandfather with a great look of triumph on his face; Miss Laura, horrified

THURSDAY

at hearing such a song in church; her mother, pride in the performance struggling with fear of what people would think of her for allowing it; Grandmother very erect at the piano, quite pleased at the way things were going, now that the break had been made. She saw them all, and others as well, and yet, she did not really see them at all. There was a detachment about singing that was like the detachment that came with flying. She was lifted out of herself so that it was not a girl who sang to them, but a spirit. The people listening must have felt the beauty, too, though at first they were mildly shocked at hearing such a song at Children's Day, for they wiped their eyes in tribute and afterwards told her how well she did.

As Allison grew older, she did not come into any greater likeness of girls around her. If anything, the gulf between them widened, so that she had even less patience than usual with their simpering, their self-conscious silliness, their small airs and graces. She got along better with boys, so long as they could climb trees together, or play games, or ride horses. But when they came to the age where they began to make shy advances at her, she would have no more to do with them. The mothers of these boys said sourly that the time would come when she'd be glad enough to get dates with their sons. Mothers with daughters had never liked her because her difference made their own girls feel uncomfortable. Now, they liked her still less because the boys she flouted came, smarting and humiliated, to the other girls as second choice, or not at all. Everyone asked who Allison Kenzie was to act so high and mighty.

The girl herself did not know who Allison Kenzie was. Others she could understand. She realized more clearly than anyone around her the magnificence of her grandfather—his power over each life he touched, his honesty and his courage, his great ease in life. She saw her mother with unchildlike clarity—the fussy busyness, the frustrations, the weak fear of her father-in-law. The girl knew that it was this feeling of inadequacy that made her mother take refuge in sharp, veiled insults. Allison saw, with calm objectivity, how weak and spoiled Mark was, and how lovable, knowing that he was this way partly from his inheritance and partly because Julia guarded him with a fierce, protective love that would have been funny had it not been, as well, a little pitiful. Mark was good-looking. Mark moved easily among people, charming them as his mother had never been able to do and as Allison refused to do. Mark turned to his mother with perfect faith whenever he wanted something. To him, she was wholly adequate, a thing she had never been to anyone else. Mark was her answer to the Kenzies. She, it was, who had produced the only grandson. Through him, and her, the family would be carried on.

These things about others she could understand. But Allison Kenzie—the hopes, the fears, the dissatisfactions, and the wild urges—she could not understand. All she knew was that she was not of this small isolated space that was the world to those she knew, and that she could never find happiness here. She began to dream of going away.

A few girls in the neighborhood who had felt like this met the urge by going off to school and studying to be teachers. Mostly, however, girls were satisfied to marry and settle down to raising families, the way a proper girl should do if she wasn't too ugly to catch a man. And, goodness knows, Allison Kenzie was pretty enough, if you liked girls that were sort of different looking. Allison Kenzie had no thought of marrying and settling down. Her dreams were of a different nature. As always, she took the problem to her grandfather.

"I want to go away," she said.

"You mean on a trip?" he asked.

"No—I want to go to school."

"What sort of a school?" he asked. "A teacher's college? That would be all right. Warrensburg is close to home, and good."

She said no, she didn't want to be a teacher; she'd like to study voice. There was a school in Kansas City—

Old Dade sat very still. From his chair on the side porch he could follow with his eye the gently rolling Missouri hills, covered with the shy and tender green of spring. Recently it had rained, so that the air was filled with the smell of it, and of fresh earth and sap, heady and thick in the trees. He could not understand why anyone would want to leave this. From where he sat he could see the part of the farm he had set aside secretly in his heart for Allison and her husband. The small knoll back from the road would make an ideal place for a house for the girl, who would like living on a hill so that she would never feel stifled. This he had planned for her as they rode together through the fields. And now he could see that he himself was to blame for the death of his dream. He it was who had encouraged her in her rebellions throughout all the years; and he it was who had set her to singing on that long ago Children's Day.

"Was it because you sang *Annie Laurie* that time?" he asked now.

"No," she said. "At least, that's not all of it. I would have found out I liked singing by myself, in time. That just made me know sooner."

"That wasn't a fair test," he said. "It won't be that easy, once you really get into it."

"I know it won't be easy," she said. "And I may find out I'm no good at it, or that it isn't really what I want to do. But I have to find out for myself."

That Dade could understand. A body had to know what he wanted in life, and, once he knew, he had to try to get it. That was the trouble with Elaine. Either she had not known what she wanted, or, knowing, she was too timid to go after it. He had never felt that marriage to Henry had been more than a compromise for her, a weak yielding to the pattern of life around her. Perhaps if Allison stayed here she, too, would fall into some grudging, reluctant acceptance of things as they were, trying to fit herself into a way of life hateful to her. This he could not bear, especially since he may have had some part in making her as she was. Music might not make her happy, but she must have the right to try it.

"What did you want me to do?" he asked. "Talk to your mother and father?"

"Not yet," Allison told him. "I'll tell them myself first. I just wanted to talk it over with you."

Allison went to Kansas City that fall. She stayed with a distant cousin-in-law on the Paseo, so that Julia was reconciled to the enterprise as being something almost respectable. She even began to speak a little complacently of the arrangement. After all, the cousin *was* named Callaway.

Kansas City was, at first, an answer to Allison's dreams. The streetcars and the bright lights, the people rushing purposefully about, gave a sort of circus atmosphere to her days. She walked down Petticoat Lane, looking into shop windows and hugging to herself a sense of freedom so real it was almost a thing to be touched. She was free—of her mother's querulous complaints, of all the small petty ways of the community that had been home to her. She went as she liked and came as she liked, and that alone made her days delightful.

Mrs. Benoni, the voice teacher, was a small, monkeylike woman. She had a monkey's sad, reproachful eyes, its wrinkled, clawlike hands which made quick, futile gestures, and when things went wrong, the same peevish spitefulness. From the first, she did not like Allison. The girl's quiet independence irked her, for she saw in it no virtue, but only insubordination.

The woman herself was full of affectations and mannerisms. Allison, always repelled by anything that smacked even slightly of artificiality, could make no pretense of covering her feelings. In her own mind she was scornful of the way the woman talked, of the very instructions she gave. And Mrs. Benoni, with an artist's sensitivity to moods, knew this. To her it was unthinkable that this young country girl, naïve as a roadside flower, should sit in judgment upon her. It was inevitable that things should go wrong between them.

"I will not say that you do not have the voice," the woman said to Allison. "I will only say that you do not have the wish to learn. You feel yourself—how shall I say it—you feel yourself better than you are. To sing takes much work. You are not willing to work. I think it best you stop."

Allison, too, knew it was best that she stop. Not because she did not want to work—never that. For something she wanted she could work constantly and painstakingly. But she did not want to sing, at least, not in the way she had thought she did. Even before going to Kansas City she had questioned that in her mind. But she had to know. Somewhere in the world there lay the thing she was striving for—something that she could pour her whole life into, gladly and fully, with no fear of losing her own identity or the integrity that was the innermost core of her being. Something that she could feel about as Grandfather felt about his land. Somewhere, somehow, she would find that thing. In her mind was growing another idea, and she wanted to talk it over with the old man.

Mother wanted her to come home anyway. Mark had gone off to Illinois and met a girl and now nothing would do but that he marry her, right off. Julia had written that the girl was coming for a visit, and Allison must come home and look her over. Allison felt nothing but pity for this strange girl, who must be looked over by not only the immediate family but cousins and in-laws as well—uncles, aunts, sisters, brothers, nieces, and nephews. There would be, as well, a battery of close friends and neighbors. Unless the girl was strong and healthy, with a will of her own as well, she would emerge from the ordeal completely worn out. Allison couldn't help wondering what sort of a girl Mark had fallen for with such speed and completeness. Probably some little featherbrain who would be a dead weight on his hands the rest of his life. At that, the responsibility would probably make a man of him, if anything could.

She had never been so surprised in all her life as she was at seeing Beulah Fulton. It was one of those things you could not believe, or, believing it, would dismiss as a phenomenon too good to last. Somewhere there must be a flaw in the girl, something she was hiding. No one could be that completely natural. But, as the visit continued, neither Allison nor anyone else could find the flaw. The girl went on talking quietly and candidly about herself and her family, making no effort whatsoever to impress anyone, yet utterly charming them all. But even that was not the remarkable thing about her. It was her relations with Mark.

Allison had not been long around them before she came to a strange conclusion concerning them. Mark and Beulah were each the separate half of a perfect whole. Complementing each other so completely, each took on new virtues in the other's presence. When they were together, Beulah's quiet sincerity glinted with charm and Mark's gay fecklessness became tinged with steadfast integrity. They openly adored each other—Mark with the bright impetuousness of a child, Beulah with an adoration that was a clear flame on the altar of her heart. Allison's one fear was that Beulah, trying so hard to be what the Kenzies wanted her to be, would give up all of her own personality in order to merge herself into the Kenzie way of life. That would be unfortunate. For Mark would love no one he did not respect, and he would respect no one who let him dominate her completely. She wondered if she should speak to the girl on the matter, and then concluded that it was, after all, none of her affair. Allison did, however, put the stamp of approval on the girl. It was only a form. Grandfather, as well as all the other Kenzies, had already expressed themselves in the matter, and things were settled between the two young people. So, Allison turned to her own affairs.

She managed to find Dade free and at peace, and so sat down to talk with him.

"How's singing going?" he asked.

"I've quit," she told him.

"Didn't like it?" he queried.

"It wasn't what I wanted to do," she said. "I had to find out, though."

"What do you have in mind now?" he asked. "Want to come back home and marry a good boy? There's a place over on the south eighty where a house would look mighty fine—"

"No," she said. "Not yet, Grandfather. I—I want to try something else."

"What's that?"

"Acting," she said quietly.

"You mean—on the stage?"

"Yes."

He sat quietly, saying nothing. Singing had been all right. Acting was another thing. He had seen a few plays—once he and Ellie had gone to one in Kansas City. Summer the stock companies made the little towns, playing "Tempest and Sunshine," "East Lynne," and others. He could not well imagine Allison in either of these. Mostly he associated actresses with the things he read in the papers—the tawdriness, the unrealness, the loose living. Again he wondered if he were to blame, as people said he was, for her ideas. In his heart he knew this was not true. Her very disposition made her be close to him, as young and old can occasionally become, ignoring all differences in age and sex, seeing only a oneness of hopes and dreams that transcends all other disparities.

Finally he spoke.

"Feel bound to be an actress, Allison?" he asked. "It's not just a notion you have to do something big and different, now that you fell down on the singing business?"

"No," she said. "That's not it. You know I've never worried about people thinking I'd failed. I just want to try acting. Or at least I think I do. If I don't have a try at it, I'd always be thinking there was something in it for me and I was afraid to try."

The man's eyes beetled sharply at her under brows that, once darkly auburn, were beginning to fade a little to a likeness of old weathered brick. As always, she had said what pleased him.

"I never did hold much with acting," he said. "Life is a pretty darned good thing, the way it is. We got no call to pretend things about it. Acting's like children playing house. Right pretty to watch, but no real substance to it."

"I want to go to New York," Allison told him. "I—I have a feeling that the way they do it there, it isn't pretending. I think they make it a sort of explanation of life that helps us understand the real thing."

"Could be," Old Dade agreed. "Only, I bet when you get there, you'll find the best actors are the ones who come nearest to giving a perfect imitation of the way real people do things. But New York—that's a different thing. I've always thought I'd like to go there myself just to see the sights, but I never could get your grandmother interested. What's your mother say about it?"

Allison told him the truth. Her mother was hurt and upset. She felt that life was dealing unfairly with her in bringing upon her at the same moment a son determined to marry and a daughter set upon a mad idea of going to New York to study acting. Julia had read, in the Sunday supplement, the story of how sin sat open and free on every corner of the town. Miss Laura Meeks had brought over a copy of the Sunday School *Herald*, in which appeared an illustrated story of what had befallen young girls who went there.

"Oh, so Laura got in on it," Dade said. "Well—you know a lot of that is true, Allison. I wouldn't want you to go off thinking it wasn't."

"It's true about Kansas City, too," the girl told him. "And right here at home, as far as that goes. People are going to find the wrong things to do anywhere they go. That doesn't mean I have to take up with them myself."

The old man chuckled. "You're awfully young and pretty to be out on your own," he said. "But you're smart, too. Do you think six months of that school would be long enough for you to find out if it was what you wanted?"

"Yes," Allison said slowly. "Yes—I think it would. By that time I'd at least know whether it was worth while for me to go on with it."

"Tell you what I'll do," he offered. "If you can get your mother's consent to go, I'll give you a check to cover the charges for six months."

The girl looked at him much the way she had, years ago, when he had paid for the plane ride. He must have thought of it, for in his eyes was the same look they had held then—pride at her daring struggling with doubts as to the wisdom of the enterprise.

"Don't feel bad, Allison," he felt constrained to add, "if you find it isn't the thing for you. Sometimes a body has to shop around quite a while before he finds his place in life."

In the end, then, it had been Dade's influence and Dade's money that had sent her off to New York to a life which, while it might have been turbulent and different from what she planned, was also satisfying and free. Eventually it had taken her to California, but still she would not have changed any minute of it for the safe, unchanging pattern that her life would have known, back in the circumscribed community that had been home to her when she was growing up.

This she knew, always giving her grandfather credit for whatever freedom, whatever happiness, she found in life. That was why, when the message came to her as she sat one morning at breakfast in a thick, golden California sunshine, she knew a shaking, surging sense of grief, as if the very foundations of her life were crumbling beneath her.

~ VI ~

VIRGIE MEADORS was awakened by the sound of muffled noises in the kitchen. Jim, bless his heart, was trying to cook breakfast by himself. For a moment she thought of pretending that she did not hear him and letting him go on without her. Then she pulled her unwieldy body up and sat on the side of the bed, panting from exertion. From a chair she took her cheap cotton kimono, slipped her swollen feet into house shoes, and went out into the kitchen.

"Hello," Jim said. "Why didn't you sleep?"

"I couldn't," she told him.

The water she sloshed over her face felt good. As she lifted her head from the granite pan on the table, she caught sight of herself in the wavery mirror.

"I look horrible," she said, lifting her hands to her hair.

"You look o.k.," Jim soothed her. "How'd you sleep?"

"Oh—all right—"

No need to tell him how many times she heard the clock strike during the night. That was why she looked so awful this morning—skin splotched and eyes like two burnt holes in a blanket.

"Here, give me that," she said, taking the coffee pot out of his hands.

Jim couldn't make coffee fit to drink. She couldn't tell him so, but it was a fact. This morning she must have good coffee—hot and black and clear. She must have it right away, too. After she got a little bit down she'd feel better, maybe, and not look so much like a worn-out dishrag.

"You can set out the butter and cream and things," she told him. "The oatmeal's ready to heat and the bacon's already in the skillet."

Jim began bumbling around, putting things on the table. She was not surprised, presently, to hear a crash.

"Gosh," Jim said ruefully, "I spilled the cream. Wait—I'll wipe it up."

He got a rag and began mopping.

"Look's like I'm more of a hindrance than a help," he admitted humbly.

"That's all right, don't worry about it. Where are you going to be working today?"

"Close to the house. I told Mr. Mark yesterday that I'd like to stick around close, and he said that was fine. This piece needs planting as bad as any."

"I wonder how Mr. Kenzie is?"

"He's a strong old man, and it wouldn't surprise me a bit if he pulled out of this. They said he was a little stronger yesterday."

"He must—" Virgie cried sharply. She felt Jim's eyes upon her. "I mean, he's been so good to us, and all—" her voice trailed off.

"Gosh, he has for a fact," Jim assented.

It was a matter on which they both agreed. Old Dade had been as much as life itself to them. He was the one who gave them each other. He, it was, who brought them up out of the Bottoms.

You had to live in the Bottoms, Virgie thought, to know what they were like, and what getting away from them meant. You had to be born there, and grow up there—dirt-poor, in houses that were not houses at all, but shacks, with big chinks around the windows and doors, letting in the dirt and wind. The doors hung crookedly on rusty hinges, and when something broke about the place it did not get fixed. Broken windowlights were replaced with pieces of cardboard, or even with bits of cast-off clothing. If a woman kept at her man to fix things up, she was a nagger.

"Herb," Virgie could hear her mother's shrill complaining voice, "there's a loose board in the porch floor. One of the young'ns is a-going to trip over it and break his neck. I've told you and told you."

"I'll get at it tomorrow," her father would promise. "I gotta piece of work to finish today."

The "piece of work" usually turned out to be fishing, or maybe hoeing a little in the melon patch, or maybe just visiting with the other men. There was no regular work, here in the Bottoms—that stretch of level land lying between the River and the bluffs. The lazy sluggish Missouri flowed, a tawny, sleepy cat, winding its way through fat black land. Harmless enough it might be at times, and then, suddenly, it was out with a roar and a swish, taking people and houses and even land itself before it, like nothing at all.

The people who lived on the narrow strip next to it were called "Bottomites," and, knowing its power, they accepted with a kind of pagan fatalism what it had to give. They knew it was no use to build fine houses, or plant rich fields, or make big plans. It was better to live each day at a time, taking what the River provided, asking no odds. Fish it gave freely, and those could be sold to the uplanders. Melons grew wondrously well, there in the damp sandy soil, and for them, too, there was a ready market. Slyly the Bottoms people laughed at the upland melons—the way the farmers tended them and hoped for them and then, like as not, had no crop at all and had to come to the Bottoms to buy, come August. Without comment they sold their own great melons to the upland farmer, thinking that at last these snooty people had come to the wise conclusion that it was no use to fight nature. The uplands were meant for big houses and fine crops of corn and wheat and sleek cattle; the Bottoms were meant for melons and fish and little shacks, and people who were wise enough to see the plan for things and not fight it.

There in the Bottoms, you grew up subject to the River. Because it was foolish to build a real house, since the River might go on a rampage any day and wash it away, you went on living in the same small huts—dingy and dirty and leaning crazily against the wind. Children came fast—maybe there were three or four by the time the oldest one started to school. They were never dressed right, and were always cruelly timid or loudly brash. They never had money for things like pencils and tablets and gifts to exchange at Christmastime. When other kids drew their names for partners in games and things like that there were smothered giggles, and like as not, when the time came for pairing off, there was no one who would acknowledge that the name had been drawn. Bottoms children did not get leading roles in plays or invitations to nice kids' parties. Nor did they learn well. Bottoms mothers knew these things and, knowing, ate their hearts out so that they got old and worn, and nagged. People thought these women were lazy and shrewish and didn't care. People were wrong. They cared so much they must mask their hurt in sharp words.

Virgie, growing up among these things, began early to wonder with an unchildlike wisdom why people in the Bottoms married and had children who would only repeat the pattern. You lived with your folks in a crowded and dirty house which smelled of cabbage and pork and wet clothes and old dirt. You did not think of things overmuch until you began to get bigger —maybe thirteen or so—and then, all of a sudden, you saw things as they really were. You saw them, as if you had come upon them unexpectedly, and for the first time. And you knew there was nothing you could do about it. Scrubbing, like they taught at school, might help a little, but really, there was nothing, *nothing*, you could do. And so you began hating it all, and wanting to go away; only there was no place to go except to the houses of the other people in the Bottoms and they were so exactly like yours that you might never have left home.

And then, one spring, when the dogwood was white on every bush and the wild crab apple a pink and white cascade of fragrance, you looked up and saw a boy you had known all your life. You saw him standing there, not saying much of anything, but suddenly he was strong and handsome and the answer to everything. Here was the thing that would take you away. Your heart was wild with the beauty of it, so that you could not separate the beauty of the dogwood and crab apples from the beauty that sang in your heart. You stopped trying, letting them all mingle together. The croaking of the frogs in the low places was a sound so beautiful it was a litany of love. It was all lovely, and life was lovely, and happiness caught at your heart until tears came into your eyes.

That was the way it was. And unless you were Jim and her, you got married and repeated the pattern.

Jim was four years older than she was. He was a quiet boy, and smart. He got along well at school, both teachers and kids liking him. He never came home with black eyes or clothes torn from fighting. Instead, he went quietly about his business in such a way that everyone, even the town kids, respected him. Even so, Virgie had never noticed him over much until the day he helped her plant the cosmos seed at the edge of the crooked little patch of ground that was called, more from courtesy than fact, the garden.

She had gone into the store for her mother and there among the coffee and sugar and flour were some packages of seeds. Something in the spring day had already sent the blood dancing through her veins—lilacs were a heady sweetness in the air and along the River's edge countless little wild flowers were blooming. She stood, immovable, before the seed rack, her eyes not on

THURSDAY

the bright-colored packages alone, but looking beyond them to dream of the sort of place they would grow around—a house, cool and white, with tight windows and doors and a straight white fence in front. She stood so long that the storekeeper said,

"Want to buy a package, Virgie? Only five cents." He had not had much hopes of selling them when the slick-tongued drummer put them off on him.

"Yes," Virgie said. "I'll take this one."

She handed him a nickel and took the package of cosmos seed, the bright picture on the envelope a medley of soft and delicate pastels. It was as if he handed her all she wanted in life—a symbol and a promise.

Once she got home she had to delay planting them until after she had prepared supper, for her mother had the misery in her back and had already gone, complainingly, to bed. It was twilight before Virgie finally got out to begin digging in the sandy soil.

She had only started when Jim came by. He stopped and began to talk with her. When he saw what she was doing, he came to her, taking the spade from her hand.

"I'll do that," he said. "It's too hard for a woman."

Virgie gave up the spade silently, but with surprise. Bottoms men did not think much of what was too hard for women. Or, thinking, they said nothing about it. If rarely there was a man who helped his wife with things, everyone felt sorry for him, saying he was henpecked, or worse.

In Jim's hands, the spade turned up the soil swiftly and with ease. Virgie watched it, and him. There was nothing you could say was different about Jim, and yet, as she watched him now, she saw that he was not like any other boy she knew. He was not so tall—maybe a little bit taller than she was. His eyes were blue, almost the same color as hers. There was nothing unusual about his straight brown hair. Yet he was different.

She was remembering many things about him—that he did

not go off Saturday nights, carousing and carrying on until all hours. He had never once got into trouble. He spoke differently —not loud and swaggering, but quietly and with a kind of modest assurance that made others listen to him. It was funny he should be like that, for he was an orphan, and, of course, the aunt and uncle he lived with had never bothered to teach him much of anything.

Finally, he said, "I have it all spaded now. Do you want to drop the seeds in? I'll come along behind you and cover them up."

She went down the row, dropping the seeds, wondering why Jim should take so much trouble for her. Although he was past nineteen, and could have gone with most any of the girls there in the Bottoms, he paid little attention to them. He came along just behind her now, drawing the earth carefully over the seeds she dropped. At the end of the row he put the little seed package on a stick.

"That's so we'll know what's planted here," he explained.

"I'll not forget," Virgie told him.

She knew that she would never forget. And while she was thinking that, Jim stood up and looked at her, and she knew that he would not forget, either. For while they had worked together planting the seeds, something had grown up between them. Perhaps it had always been there, and this had only brought it into flower. She knew, suddenly, that it *had* always been there. Always she had been conscious of Jim, quiet and aloof, going his own way, never mixing in all those things she hated about life in the Bottoms. Jim was different, even as she was different. They were not satisfied with the lives they had to lead. They both wanted better things. That bond had always been between them, and this evening the simple act of planting flower seeds together had made it tangible.

They stood still, just looking at each other. Off somewhere in the distance a whippoorwill trilled his plaintive melody.

THURSDAY

Around the bend of the River a hound-dog sent up his lonesome bay to meet the coming of evening. Voices of children, far off and unreal, sounded as they shouted at their games. There was a smell of spring in the air—things growing, and damp earth. Even the River was gentle with it.

Jim said softly, "Let's go for a walk."

They went around the bend of the River until the trees hid them from sight. Then he reached out and took her hand and they walked along together, not talking. He did not even try to kiss her.

Virgie was sixteen, an age at which many girls she knew were already married to brash-eyed youths, and living with their families. Violet Sawyer, who had "got into trouble" last winter, was just her age. It was not that she was too young for lovemaking; it was just a part of Jim's difference that he should see, even more clearly than she did, what lay ahead of them. In the Bottoms, one lived close to reality, so that you knew where "courtin' " led. Either it took you into a home, squalid and uncertain and precarious at best, or it led to "trouble." Either way was not for them. So they walked along, content just to touch hands, and it was as if the beauty and promise of the evening, and of the universe, flowed between them. Kissing they could save for another time. It was enough, now, that the two of them who were so different from all the others had found each other and that, together, they could walk along the path at the edge of the River.

The spring that was so bright and full of promise slid into a summer hot and sickly dry. When it was like this, people in the uplands did not buy many fish, which meant hard times for the people in the Bottoms. The meager gardens withered away, and food, always poor, was worse than ever. Flies swarmed into the houses which had few screens. Water got low in the wells.

And people got sick.

However, the sickness of Dulcie, Virgie's sister, was not the fever. When she got very green around the mouth one morning at breakfast, her mother looked at her with quick, sharp eyes.

"I guess you've gone and got yourself into trouble," the woman said flatly.

Dulcie made no denial.

"It's that Milt Phillips, I reckon."

Still Dulcie said nothing.

"I guess your Pa will be seeing Milt today," Mrs. Wrather went on, the voice that was usually so shrill and complaining now flat and cold. Listening to her, Virgie knew for sure that Bottoms women did care. They had their hearts torn out of them when things like this happened, just like—well, just like Mrs. Kenzie would if such things happened to her girls. Bottoms women could not let people know they cared though. If you ever admitted the weight of your burden, it would crush you.

Dulcie and Milt were married the next day. Dulcie was past seventeen, and Milt about her age. Of course, he had no job and no place to take her, so they moved in with the Wrathers, Dulcie's people. That made nine people living in four rooms. The heat beat down on the house, making an oven of it, and still there was no letup. Before long, Dulcie began "to show," causing a great nodding of heads and whisperings, and fast calculations on fingers. Soon, however, the fever struck, and people were so busy caring for their own that they had no time to think of Dulcie Wrather.

Doc Burgess came down to see the sick. Because there was no money to pay him, never would be any money to pay him, the people treated him with either jocular defiance or fawning gratitude. Flies buzzed about in the rooms where the sick people lay. A mingled stench of rotting vegetables, River smells, animals quartered too close to the house, filled the air. Sometimes the doctor was able to help. Sometimes he was not, and then one of the pitiful funeral processions of the poor wound up the bluffs to the town burial ground. There was no dignity in these deaths.

Virgie and Jim saw little of each other that summer. Virgie's mother was sick, and two of the younger children also. Dulcie was no help at all; the heat and the flies and the squalor were a battle Virgie had to fight alone. When things got too much for her she went for a walk, climbing to the top of the bluff that overlooked their house.

The bluff rose abruptly from the Bottoms, so she could see the whole pattern of her home and the homes of those who lived about them—the small crazy houses mended with bits of tin or tar paper, or, worst of all, not mended at all. She could see them, sitting crazily athwart the wind in the middle of small parched gardens. In one of these were her dead cosmos. For a while she had kept them alive by carrying water, and then when the water got low she stopped. However, it wasn't the water shortage, really, that stopped her. She could have gone down to the River and brought back buckets of the thick muddy water, had she really wanted to. The reason she stopped was that the flowers had been a symbol to her, a symbol of her difference, and Jim's. Now she knew there could never be anything between them that was any different from the pattern to which they were born and she was crazy for ever having thought so.

After they had planted those flowers in the spring she had planned brightly. She would finish high school—that would take two years. She would study hard, getting the help of the teachers in learning how to talk right, and dress right, and keep house nice and proper. Then, when she and Jim were married, she could do things the right way, not the poor squalid, inefficient way that was all the Bottoms women knew. Now she realized bleakly that she was not going back—high school was not for her. Nothing was for her. She had no clothes to wear, and there was no money with which to buy them. People had not bought fish, and there were no gardens from which to draw a store of food. Unless it rained soon there would be no melons. With Dulcie's husband, Milt, added to the family, there would be a struggle just to eat this winter. Coming from where she did, she couldn't expect anything. It was not worth while, struggling against fate.

Presently she went back down the path. Her mother's shrill complaint met her at the door.

"High time you got back. I've been a-slavin' all evenin', gettin' things red up. My back's a-killin' me."

Virgie knew that the only "slavin' " she had done was sitting in the rocker in the bare yard, complaining to the neighbors and dipping snuff. But she said nothing. It did not matter. Nothing mattered. She was free of ambition, of aching desires for the future. It gave a numbness that passed for peace. She could not be hurt any more.

That night it rained. The sound of it was brave and gay against the rooftops in the Bottoms. Its very sound was bright with promise—cooler weather, melons, late gardens for those ambitious enough to plant them, fish to sell to the uplanders. They rose next morning to feel new life running in their veins. Herb Wrather caught a string of fish and sold them, up at the store. A tourist who had slipped off the highway gave him three dollars for helping to get him back on the pavement. Herb was in an expansive mood. Seeing a pretty plaid gingham dress in the store window, he bought it for Virgie.

"You've been a good kid all summer," he said, handing it to her. "You can wear it to school this fall."

Virgie thanked him, without telling him that she was not going to school, this fall or ever. She had scarcely hung it away behind the limp calico curtain that served as a closet when Jim came by.

"Thought maybe you'd go to Camp Meeting with me to-night," he said.

People in the Bottoms did not go much to church. They did not feel at home there. Camp Meetings were different. Here they could slip quietly into the sides of the big tent and scarcely be noticed. The straw on the ground felt good to their feet, hiding their worn shoes. There was nothing high and mighty about Camp Meetings. They were likely to be right exciting, too, for people acted different here from what they did in church, even getting pretty happy sometimes when they got religion. Camp Meetings were almost as stimulating as weddings, or play parties, or fights.

Especially were the sermons to their liking. They were meant to stir people up, and had a lot of "Hell-fire-and-damnation" in them. The preachers didn't mince words, either, sparing no one who failed to mend his ways. Some way, you didn't feel that money cut much ice at Camp Meetings. Without being quite able to analyze it, the people in the Bottoms felt that hell wouldn't be so bad if it caught the snooty uplanders, too. They had visions of themselves looking down into hell with, say, Old Dade Kenzie on one side of them and George Marshall, the banker, on the other. It was a vision not displeasing.

Virgie said yes, she'd like to go with Jim. It was the first time he had ever really asked her for a date; always before it had been a sort of casual pairing off—a sliding up to her at parties, walking home from town together, dropping by for a talk or a walk along the River. Tonight was to be a real date. She took a bath and washed her hair and put on the new dress Herb had bought her.

She knew she looked nice and that Jim was proud of her. When they got to the Camp Meeting tent, they did not stop at the outer edge, where so many of the young people sat giggling and making passes at each other and holding hands in the shadows. Instead, they started down toward the front. An usher led them farther up than they meant to go, and when they sat down,

Virgie realized they were next to Dade Kenzie.

They sat together, she and Jim, quiet and proud. It was as if the usher had sensed that they belonged, not to the festering sore that was the Bottoms, but to the real substance of the Uplands. Old Dade smiled at them, and handed them a hymn book.

"Two-sixty-eight," he told them, just as he would have told George Marshall or Dr. Burgess.

He sat there, firm and solid, beside them. The cruel embarrassment Virgie had felt at being so far down in the tent dissolved into nothingness. By the old man's side she felt secure and assured. She belonged where she was. Jim felt it, too. When the music started, he began to sing—he had an awful good voice, better than anyone else around him. Old Dade looked at him approvingly under heavy brows. She and Jim stood when the old man stood and, with him, joined in the simple ritual of the service. It was as if he were their sponsor in this first public appearance of theirs.

This evening there was no hell-fire-and-damnation sermon. An earnest and sincere young man, still a student preacher, talked about the dignity of man and the preciousness of the human soul in the sight of God.

"What a wonderful thing man is," he chanted in a voice that was all beauty and poetry and music. "Thou hast made him a little lower than the angels—"

Virgie, listening to him, was no longer Virgie Wrather of the Bottoms. She was an individual, a human being, precious in the sight of the Lord, a person from whom great things might come. She thought, I'm going back to school. Some way I'll see it through.

The decision was of the spirit. She felt as if she were taking the vows of the church when she said it.

When the services were over, Dade Kenzie turned to them and told them his name. As if he would have to. All up and down the country he was a sort of legend. But he told his name simply, as if it were of no more importance than theirs. And when they told him their names, he listened carefully and said them over, so that they felt he knew them and would not forget them ever.

She and Jim walked home, their shoulders straight and square, their steps firm. Neither one said much. A moon so bright they could see each other plain as day by its light shone over them. Across the water sounded a hound-dog's mournful bay. Jim reached out and took her hand and they walked on together. Then he stopped, and she stopped, too, so that they stood in the narrow path, facing each other, close together. Jim put his arms around her. And then he kissed her.

Old Dade was always mixed up, after that, with their first kiss. Hope went into it, and beauty, so that it was a sort of sacrament. It was no greedy snatching at each other, or at any stolen happiness they might grab. It was promise of the future. It was love and great tenderness. It came of a self-respect that Old Dade Kenzie had given them.

That he had given them, and much more. He had, in time, brought them out of the Bottoms to work for him. He had provided this house, small and clean and tight against the weather. He was, in fact, their luck. So long as he lived, nothing really bad could happen to them. With him to bring her luck and courage, she could get her baby into the world. Without him, she was afraid, so afraid that she was sick and shaking all over. Jim, looking at her now, saw that fright in her face, so that, because of her fear, he was frightened, too, as one child catches another's fear without even knowing what caused it.

"Don't worry about Mr. Kenzie," Jim urged her, trying to soothe her. "He's strong. He'll pull through."

"He might," she agreed, trying to put courage back into herself, trying to ease Jim's mind.

Outside, the dog began a great barking.

"I'll see who it is," Jim said, going toward the door.

It was Ez Dowlin.

"Jim," he said, "Uncle Dade passed away this morning. We'd like for you to come up to the house. There are a lot of things to do—"

"Sure," Jim promised. And then he added awkwardly, "I'm awful sorry—"

Virgie standing behind Jim, heard Ez Dowlin's words. A great sickness swept over her, so that she knew she must sit down. She took a quick step toward a chair.

It was the cream on the floor. Jim, poor darling, hadn't scrubbed it up right. She caught at the back of the chair as she slipped, and missed it. As she fell, she cried, "Jim—"

That was all she remembered. That, and the pain.

~ VII ~

MISS LAURA MEEKS got up earlier than usual that Thursday morning. She couldn't tell why. There were times when a body just couldn't sleep, and that was all there was to it. She had no patience with folks who lay abed, once they were awake. It was just pure laziness on their part, and nobody could tell her any different. If Rose Marshall would get up earlier and find out a few things for herself, George might not be carrying on the way he was. It was usually the woman's fault when a man acted up. One way or another, it was.

She began dressing, getting into the things she had laid out the night before—the corset that laced up the back the way a proper corset should, the cotton-ribbed vest, the white muslin slip, the print house dress. She took the kid curlers out of her hair, putting them back into a little japanned box she had got for Christmas years ago. Dade Kenzie had given it to her when he got her name in the Sunday School class exchange. She combed her hair, parting it exactly in the middle and bringing

THURSDAY

the waves down in scallops on both sides of her forehead. Then she drew a net over it, pinning it carefully. She always dressed herself completely, and combed her hair, before ever she left her bedroom. She had no patience with people who went slopping around in those abominable things they called house coats. Like as not, these were the women who never combed their hair till after dinner. You'd think their husbands would get tired of such sloppiness and put their foot down on it. She had never let herself go sloppy around the house in all her seventy-eight years, and she did not intend to start now.

The kitchen was all in order, just as she had left it the night before. She couldn't abide people who left things every which way at night. If she got sick in the night, anybody in the world could come in and take over in her kitchen and find it in perfect order. They'd be sure to nose around, too, just to see how she kept things. Of course, they ought to come, in time of sickness. She herself always went—first thing—when someone was sick or in trouble. Not that people appreciated what she did.

She remembered what a fuss Thelma Kane made when she went up there the time that last baby was born. The house was all full of cockroaches, and that was one thing a Meeks never could abide. Of course, she went down to Butler's store and got some roach powder right off. In the first place, Thelma had no business leaving things in such a mess that they drew roaches. And she certainly couldn't expect Miss Laura to tell Cy Butler that she wanted the powder for roaches in her own house. He wouldn't have believed her, anyway. Everyone knew how clean she kept things. You'd have thought Thelma would have been grateful to be rid of the roaches, but she wasn't. And neither were her husband and those rascally young'uns of theirs.

One of those Kane boys delivered papers, and you couldn't tell Miss Laura in a hundred years that he didn't throw her paper off in the bushes on purpose. Every morning she had to go looking for it. She was a good mind to write the editor of the *Kansas City Star* and tell him about it. Even if it was a big paper, the editor would be interested in knowing how his readers were being treated. Come to think of it, she was going to write him. She bet that somebody—the circulation manager, or someone —would look into the matter. She was tired of having to go out looking for her paper like a child hunting for Easter eggs.

Sure enough, when she went out for the paper this morning, it was way off under the bridal wreath bushes. She got down stiffly to pick it up, muttering to herself. When she got up, she looked around her, sniffing the air for promise of what the day had to bring. This was going to be a warm one, like yesterday. That was good. She wanted to plant beans, and they needed warm, dry weather. The cutworms had taken the first planting because the soil was wet and cold. She wanted to be sure of this one because last night when she had checked her shelves she found she was short on beans. They were good in winter, cooked with onions and drippings and a touch of vinegar.

She lived well. She had no patience with women who cooked only because there were men in the house, lunching on cheese and crackers when they were alone. There were other things to live for besides men. She'd be ashamed—downright ashamed— to say that the only reason she ate was because some man wanted the things she cooked. She might as well plant some carrots, too. And some beets. Since it was so warm, it would be a good time, too, to wash the curtains in the front room. She could get this all done before dinner, and that would leave her the afternoon free to go see Rose Marshall.

She should have gone, long ago. When the first bit of gossip started, that was the time to go tell Rose Marshall, straight out, what was being said. In a way, she herself was to blame because she hadn't told Rose. It was her Christian duty to see that the woman found out.

At first, she had hesitated because she thought maybe it might

THURSDAY

not be true. Some way, a body just expected more of men like George Marshall. He had been off to school. His father had left him enough money so he didn't ever have to worry about having anything he wanted. He was president of the bank. And a steward in the church. Every Sunday morning he passed the collection plate, looking serious and sanctimonious. She, Laura Meeks, never intended to put another penny into the plate when he passed it; she'd sit somewhere else in church so that she could drop her envelope into another steward's plate. She'd do that, even though she had been sitting in this same pew for seventy-eight years. Right to that very pew Papa and Mama had brought her that first Sunday morning she ever went to church. But now, although it would break her heart and she wouldn't be able to hear a word of the sermon, she'd change pews rather than let George Marshall collect the money she gave to the Lord. Or, she'd mail in her contribution to Brother Kilgore with a note, telling him why she was doing it. The note might be the best way, after all. The preacher ought to know what was going on in his congregation. It was her duty to tell him. And if, as she suspected, he already knew, he should find out that the members of his congregation were talking about it. When a man had as much money as George Marshall had, a preacher was apt to get pretty broad-minded about his sins. Maybe if she wrote that note, it would stiffen up Brother Kilgore's spine to where he'd have the courage to tell the sinners a few things.

She went into the kitchen now to prepare her breakfast, measuring out the coffee, dropping the egg into the saucepan. She knelt to put the toast into the oven. She couldn't abide these toasters—crisped the bread outside and sogged it inside. Toast ought to be made in the oven, cooked until it was good and crisp and then buttered and put back under the flame to brown again.

Yes, she was going to see Rose Marshall. The affair had got past the rumor stage now, past the "I heard" and "Somebody told me" and "Do you suppose—?" Yesterday she herself had seen them together—George Marshall and Marta Sloan.

It would, be a good thing if women like Marta Sloan were made to leave town. They used to do it. She could remember when she was just a girl, there was a woman—a perfectly awful woman with bleached hair and a high shrill voice—who ran a millinery store. She lived in the back of it, going in and out through a door that opened on the alley. They said you'd be surprised any night after it got good and dark to see the men that went in that door on the alley—such good, respectable men you'd be shocked just to hear their names whispered in connection with such things. That woman never sold a hat—no decent woman would go into her place after they found out she was "that kind of a woman." But she kept on living there, and living well.

Finally, there was a red-headed Mrs. Raines who took matters into her own hands. She watched one night and, sure enough, she saw her husband sneaking in that alley door. She just took right after him, and went inside, too. She had a whip, most six feet long, with her. She stood there yelling at the top of her voice that she intended to use it on that yellow-haired milliner if she didn't get out of town. Anybody could see she meant to do it, too. The woman left without even packing her things. Of course, Mrs. Raines wasn't a lady herself, or she couldn't have done a thing like that. She didn't stay in town very long—it just wasn't the sort of place she felt at home in. But she did get rid of that milliner, and the women were grateful to her. That was the way somebody ought to do Marta Sloan. It was the only way to handle a "woman like that."

Miss Laura hadn't trusted Marta Sloan from the first day she saw her. She was one of those soft-spoken, smiling women. When she laughed, she threw back her head and a sort of soft, purring sound came from her throat. It wasn't honest, aboveboard laughing like a good woman did. It sounded more like she was saying to the men—she never paid much attention to women—"We know a secret, don't we? And isn't it funny!" When she laughed, every man in the room got restless, like he wanted to be closer to her. Her eyes got smaller and little wrinkles crinkled up all around them. On one cheek—the left one—a dimple popped out. It wasn't a natural dimple—Miss Laura had seen her pressing in on that spot with her finger, every time she had a chance. She had trained that dimple, and it was no more natural than her laugh was.

She said her hair was naturally curly, but Miss Laura didn't believe her. It didn't have any more natural curl than a stick. She went every week to a beauty shop clear over to Rockwell. It was scandalous to drive twenty miles just to get someone to curl your hair. A woman ought to wash her own hair and do it up on curlers herself. It was a waste of time and money to go off and have it done. It was a snare and a temptation, besides. When women went to beauty shops, they saw pictures showing the kind of hair styles young girls and fancy women were wearing. They got the idea that all they needed to do was to have their hair fixed like that and they could be young again, and get out and do all sorts of foolish things. Marta Sloan went to beauty parlors, and when she came out she forgot all about being a married woman. She got her complexion there, too, although a lot of people did think it was natural. But it wasn't—she put on all that stuff that made her look young and soft and pretty. And then men fell for her. That was all it took—a pretty face, and the men were off chasing the woman that owned it, forgetting all about their duties at home.

Even before Albert Sloan, Marta's poor, sick husband died, there had been "things going on." Miss Laura noticed it first, and then other people mentioned it as well. Marta had to go too often to the bank. It wasn't natural for a woman with a living husband to have that much business in the bank. And it wasn't natural that it should always be business that George Marshall had to see to himself, taking her back to his office and closing the door while they talked it over. Miss Laura was in there one morning, cashing a check, and she just stayed on talking with Rich Newton—she really wanted to ask him if this was a good time to have her house painted—and Marta Sloan stayed back in George's office, with the door closed, half an hour. She didn't know how much longer it was, for she left then.

Albert Sloan might have been sick, but he was plenty able to go to the bank and take care of his own checks, or do whatever it was Marta went to do. And why should his business take them out of town so much—to Belton, or Rockwell, or even to Kansas City? Once someone had seen the three of them—Marta and George and Albert—in Rockwell, taking in a show. Afterwards they went to the Elite Candy Shoppe, and Marta and George sat talking and laughing, eating banana splits (it was a crime to pay thirty-five cents for a lot of mess stirred up together when people in the world were going hungry). Albert was just sipping a cherry phosphate, looking sick and unhappy, the way he always looked. That was the way they "saw to business" in Rockwell. Heaven only knew what went on during those trips to Kansas City.

It wasn't long after that Rockwell trip that Albert Sloan died. It was awful, the way George Marshall acted then. He didn't wait for the man to get cold in his grave before he was up at Marta's "going over papers," and "getting Marta's signatures to things." At least, that was the story he told. But Miss Laura didn't believe them for a minute. One day she watched the clock and found out that he stayed a *solid hour*. Nobody could take that long to sign papers. Nobody, not even a dunce who had to draw his name like a baby would. After that, she timed him every time he came. It didn't always take an hour, but sometimes it did. It was easy for her to keep watch, for she lived just across from the Sloan house, and nobody could come or go without her seeing him. She didn't really neglect her work and set out to spy on them. She had a lot of mending to do, and she could get the best light at the front room window. Nobody could blame her for sitting where she could get good light on her work, and if it also happened to be the place from which she could watch the Sloan front door, that was just a coincidence.

Of course, at such times they always went inside the Sloan house, talking, so Miss Laura had never actually seen them together until yesterday. She had gone down to the grocery store, and since it was a little nearer that way, she had come out of Butler's store by the back door and cut across lots to go home. This way she had to go down the alley that ran back of the bank. The front door of the bank was closed and the shades drawn, for it was past four o'cock and all the help was supposed to be gone home. But George Marshall hadn't gone, for his window was up—his office looked out into the alley. As she walked by, she couldn't help looking in at the window.

George was not at his desk. Marta Sloan was sitting in his chair and George was bending over her. His face was flushed, like he might have been drinking. Only he hadn't—he was just so befuddled with that Sloan woman that he was worse than drunk. Her face was raised to his, the eyes almost closed, the lips slightly parted. Miss Laura knew, as well as she stood there, that he was about to kiss her. On both their faces was the look that people in movies got just before they kissed. Horrid things, movies. Watching them, folks got all sorts of loose ideas about making love. Used to be that all a boy and girl knew about lovemaking was holding hands. And now here were Marta and George, looking for the world and all like movie actors, ready to kiss each other. A married man, and a woman so recently widowed that she might as well be married, too. Miss Laura made a scandalized noise in her throat. She tried to stop it, but it just came out in spite of her. At the sound, the man and the woman looked up and saw her, standing there watching them. George jumped back like a shot. But Marta didn't jump. She just turned, slow and grave, and looked at Miss Laura. The way she looked, a body would have thought she was an honest woman, looking reproof at someone spying on her. Honest woman, indeed.

Rose Marshall ought to know. She, Laura Meeks, was going to tell her. It was her duty to do it. She wouldn't have a minute's peace in her own soul until she did what was right. As soon as she washed the breakfast dishes and got her chores out of the way, she was going. She must call and see how Dade Kenzie was, too. He had been sick almost a week now. Of course, Dade was still strong and able to shake off things, but she must call, anyway.

Dade Kenzie had been like all the rest of them—a pretty face and a bold manner, and he was caught. Men didn't want nice, modest girls. It didn't pay a girl to be sweet and good. That was always the trouble—a girl could be so good a man didn't want her.

She would never forget the night Dade met Ellie. He had taken her, Laura Meeks, to that party at Fullers'. He had been going with her pretty steady for almost a year. Papa didn't like him. He had heard things, down at the livery stable, and on the streets. Of course, he wouldn't tell his daughter what he heard, but he said that Dade Kenzie was a wild buck, and one that he didn't much want hanging around his child. Laura was sure that the things people said were exaggerated—men always talked a lot of things that weren't so. They were as bad as women about that, and maybe worse. She was sure Dade would be all right after—well, after— She never got any farther than that, even in her thoughts. Nice girls didn't.

The night Dade came to take her to the party he had a new buggy and a fast-stepping horse hitched to it. The buggy was so high it was all she could do to get into it without showing her ankles. Dade kept boosting her, and she kept getting redder and redder and more embarrassed by the minute. The horse was so restless that they really had an awful time getting off.

She could remember every detail of the ride, with Dade sitting there on the high buggy seat beside her. He was good-looking in a bold, reckless sort of way. His hair was a special kind of red—more dark auburn than red, really. It hadn't faded too much with the years. Even now when he sat in front of her at church, she could see a lock or two in the back that was almost the same color it had been that night so long ago. Red hair didn't fade like other kinds. He was a big man, too, and didn't shrink with age. His neck never got all webbed with wrinkles, and stringy. He didn't look his age by fifteen years.

You couldn't tell her, not if she lived to be a hundred years old, that Ellen Sparks didn't know that Dade was going to kiss her when she opened that door. No girl could be such a ninny as not to know that trick—it was as old as the hills. Ellie knew, and was ready for the kiss. She behaved like a—like a hussy. Her lips were all pursed up, ready to kiss. When Dade kissed her, she didn't even draw back, or scream, or slap his face.

Dade had tried to kiss Miss Laura once and she had told him—firmly and with no nonsense about it—that if he did, she'd scream. Papa and Mama were in the next room, and goodness only knows what Papa would have done. She wondered if she would have screamed, really. Dade was so close to her, grabbing at her hand and bending over her. There was a good smell about him—bay rum and tobacco and heavy woolen man-clothes. Maybe a little smell of horses, too, for he had ridden over to see her. He had a big, firm mouth. She looked at it, so close to hers, and began to wonder what it would be like, to have him kiss her. She got all panicky and flustered and tried hard to pull away, although, really, she didn't want to. But she had to pull away—he never would have respected her after that, if she hadn't. He was breathing fast and hard, and he said, under his breath, "Miss Prunes and Prisms, I'll kiss you yet—"

But he didn't. Because the next night was when he took her to the Fuller party and met Ellie. And after that, he never wanted to any more. He wanted Ellie, and he got her. He never even asked Miss Laura for another date. A man didn't want a decent girl.

Her father asked, "What's wrong with you and David Kenzie? I never see him here any more."

"I won't go with him," she said with elaborate carelessness. "He asks me, but I won't. I'm afraid the—the things you heard were so."

It was a lie, but it saved her face. Papa was glad Dade wasn't coming back any more. But night after night she herself lay awake, wondering what it would have been like, had she let him kiss her. If he had kissed her, like he did Ellen Sparks, would he have got engaged to her before Ellie came on the scene? Of course, if she had let him kiss her, he would have had to marry her. Papa would have seen to that. She lost him because she acted like a decent girl. Ellie got him, and all Miss Laura had to carry with her down the years was the maiden wonder of what his lips would have felt like against hers.

There was no accounting for men's tastes. Ellie was a good enough wife, she supposed. She cooked good enough, and kept house fairly clean, although she was usually a little late with spring cleaning and never did learn to can beans so that they were fit to eat. Such a pity, too—Dade had always been so fond of green beans. She settled down and had children and was several times President of Ladies' Aid. But she was big and ungainly looking—a cowish sort of woman.

Miss Laura often thought that Dade must look at his wife, with her big hips and bosom, and wish she were daintier. Miss Laura weighed the same now as she did when she was eighteen, when Dade had his last date with her. She had kept her figure, and had not let herself get big and fat and sloppy. Getting fat showed that a woman had no strength of character. Some women wouldn't deny themselves anything they wanted, even if they knew it was going to make them look like an old pudding bag. Once she went to Rockwell shopping with Ellie. When the saleswoman asked what sizes they took, Laura was proud to say she wore a fourteen. Ellie just laughed and said she guessed a forty would do for her—she had been putting on a little weight this summer because the fried chicken was so good she just couldn't turn it down. Dade was sitting there hearing it all. Laura wished she could have read his mind.

Well, she was through with breakfast now, and she must get at her chores. She rose from the table, taking her plate and cup with her. The telephone rang, and she hurried to answer it, wondering who could be calling her this early in the morning.

"Hello," she said, standing on tiptoe to reach the mouthpiece. The phone had been placed, years ago, at a height convenient for Papa, who was a tall man, and never in all the years since his death had it occurred to her to have it lowered.

"Hello," she said. "Yes—no—no, I hadn't heard. It's—well, it's too bad. Yes—I knew he was sick. When did you say the services will be held? Saturday? Yes—I'll look after the flowers. It's been a little cold, and things are late, but I'll do my best."

She replaced the receiver on the hook, looking smaller than ever. Then she crumpled up, so that she was no more than a bundle of laundry, there on the kitchen chair. She sat there a long time, and then she got up and began to wash the dishes. She guessed she wouldn't plant beans today, or wash curtains. Maybe even her visit to Rose Marshall would have to wait.

Dade Kenzie was dead, and they had asked her to see about flowers to decorate the church for the services. She reckoned she'd better get busy, getting the promise of them.

~ VIII ~

CHARLEY VANE took his bearings carefully. It should be about here. That spaced things right. "Ellen, beloved wife," and then, the exact same distance from the stone, "David Allison Kenzie." There were two mounds on the other side of Ellie. One was the child Mary Ellen, who, according to the stone, was "nine years, eleven months, and three days old" when she was called home. The other, and nearer one, was labeled only "Infant son." There were a lot of stones like that, scattered here and there in the cemetery, fragile little spirits who lived only long enough to die. When Charley first started helping out here, he used to wonder about them, and the reason for their brief span of life. He couldn't see why such things were allowed to be. He had long since ceased to wonder about the matter, taking it, as he did so many other things in life, the way it came.

Now that he was older, he was allowed helpers in the work out here, but this was a job he wanted to start by himself. That was why he sneaked off a day ahead of time, just so as he could be by himself to start things without anyone talking to him, or breaking in on his thoughts.

When they came to tell him about Dade, they tried to get him to turn over the actual digging to these helpers.

"It's pretty warm," they said. "You can supervise, but let the others do the work."

"I'll see to it myself," he said simply, and they quit trying to persuade him.

The earth was damp and cut easily, like cheese under a sharp knife. It wasn't going to be much of a job. He might just wind up doing it all himself. He was as good and strong as ever. Seventy-two is no age for a man that has lived right. Look at Dade—eighty, and sound as a nut till the very last. As much of this as he could, he'd do by himself. Dade was a friend of his.

THURSDAY

This was something he could do for him.

Charley could just hear everyone, all up and down the countryside, talking about Dade Kenzie, now that he was gone. The minute he died it had started. Over at Belton and at Handford, and even in Kansas City, for the *Star* carried a notice. Rockwell seethed with talk, for the old man had often gone there on business. He guessed they even talked it in Chicago and in that heathenish place in California where Allison Kenzie had gone. "Old Dade Kenzie," people would be saying. "I knew him well. Why I remember one time—" All the people whose lives he had touched would have something to tell about him, some memory to bring up concerning him.

Memories were strange things, queer as the keepsakes people put away in little boxes or in the family Bible. Little things, trifles, actually, with no real value of their own. They had no use at all, except to clutter up things. In themselves they were nothing; but, touched by the magic of memory, they were romance and tenderness, courage and hope, and sorrow which time had softened and blurred into a gentle semblance of beauty. They said if your house caught fire you went first to save those silly little keepsakes you had hidden away. Now, he knew, people were bringing out those things they had kept tucked away in their minds, maybe for fifty years or more, and were turning them over and over, like children looking at a beloved toy.

Mostly people would say the same thing—what a fine man he was, and how much good he had done, and how there wasn't anybody who could take his place in the community. Dade *was* a fine man. But mostly they said things like that about everybody who went, as if everyone was in a conspiracy to conceal all the bad things about a person, once he was dead. Some sort of a superstition, he supposed, that it wasn't right to say things about people who couldn't come to their own defense.

That wasn't the way Charley felt. He could turn up a shovel

of earth and remember the person, clear and true, the way he had really been. Maybe after people spent as much time out here as he had, they sort of lost their fear of death. He could remember just as well the first time he ever came out here to work, fifty-five years ago this summer. He was seventeen, and big for his age. Old man Ellsworth (dead these thirty years) had stopped him on the street to ask if he'd like to earn a few dollars. When Charley found out what he was to do, he hesitated.

"Don't be squeamish," the man said. "It's work that has to be done."

The first shock he had was not, as he had thought it would be, from the digging. It was hearing Mr. Ellsworth and the helpers talk. Then it was he began to see that the things the sextons said about the dead person weren't the same things his friends were saying, or what the minister said in church. Not a bit of it. Now he saw why. He thought things like that himself, and felt no disloyalty in doing it.

Take Old Dade, for instance. Most of the people who were talking about him today, or thinking about him, were the ones who had known him after he got to be a man—a good husband and a good provider, and a steward in the church. When Charley was a boy, there was a different side talked about him. He was a wild one, that Dade Kenzie. There were a lot of granny stories and legends about him, and whisperings. Good-looking young buck he was, with auburn hair and white teeth and a flashing smile. Women noticed him. That was the trouble —they all noticed him, and made a fuss over him so that it was a wonder he wasn't spoiled past all living with. There was that milliner, the one with the bleached hair. Goodness, he hadn't thought of her for years, and now he could see her, just as plain, and hear her laugh—that shrill, high-pitched laugh of hers. How the women all hated her, and snubbed her. They said one day Miss Laura Meeks met her on the street and drew her skirts close to her, just to keep from brushing the milliner's dress with her own. Maybe if the women hadn't been so catty toward her, she wouldn't have tolled off their husbands the way she did. Maybe she did it just to get even with them.

The men used to slip into the back of her shop at hours which the young ladies of the town didn't pick to receive callers. They said lots of men went. But the only one Charley ever saw going in was Dade Kenzie.

He was staying with Grandma Polk, who was town nurse, midwife, and comforter. One night she got a call to come to a sick baby on the other side of town. She roused the sleeping Charley.

"You'll have to go with me," she said, shaking him again and again, for sleep lies heavy on the eyes of a twelve-year-old. "It ain't that I'm afraid, but I got too many things to carry—"

Whatever the reason was, she kept at him till he was awake and dressed. Together, they went out into the windy, wet darkness. It was closer to cut through the alley, so that was the way they went. Just before they came to the milliner's shop, they saw an orange streak of light, saw the door open quickly, saw a man slip inside. The door closed in a flash again, leaving the night blacker than ever.

"I declare," Grandma said, "who was that—?"

Charley knew, but he didn't answer. It was Dade Kenzie. He never told Grandma, or anyone else, what he had seen. He hadn't thought of it himself, for years. Now that it came back to him today, it didn't make him think any the less of Dade. He turned out to be a fine man, one that shed all that boy stuff. You couldn't hold a boy's foolish ways against a man, for they were two people, really.

A body just naturally had to give Ellie a lot of credit for making a man out of Dade. She was the woman for him. She could keep up with him, for she had spirit and sweetness and dash. Dade couldn't fool with her, any more than he could fool with a spirited horse. She was all he needed, or wanted, in life. It was good for a man of spirit to marry a woman who was a match for him. It did not always work out so. Charley had only to raise his eyes now in order to see the graves of the women who had died with unhappiness and bitterness in their hearts. He could have written their epitaphs in fewer words than the stones took.

"She was a good woman," he would have said, "but not the one for him."

People talked about death with fear. They said it was a cruel thing which they could not understand. He could not see it this way. Death was not strange and perverse and unnatural. Life was the thing that was unexplainable. Death made sense, where life did not. A man and a woman could live together, fifty years maybe, the woman eating her heart out with loneliness and humiliation all the while. She'd be sitting in a crowd, but her mind wasn't there, or her eyes. They were both darting here and there, restless and wandering, seeing always the one who was separated from her. Maybe he was in the next room, or maybe downtown with the fellows. Or maybe he was at her side, but his spirit and his desires were far away. She knew no certainty, and no peace. And then death came and brought the two of them, no matter how unsuited they had been, together at last to lie decently and quietly together, as life should have done. Death brought peace and dignity, where life brought only despair and pain.

Well, life was like that, and the way he figured, you couldn't do much about it. You just had to take things the way they came, which, more often than not, wasn't the way you would have ordered them, if you had got the chance. He reckoned he wouldn't have stayed a bachelor all these years if things had come out the way he planned. There was a girl—a mighty sweet girl too. Sometimes, even now, he went over to that grave on the far side of the cemetery and placed some flowers on it.

Well, he guessed he had this thing pretty well started **now.**

He might turn it over to the workers tomorrow to finish, and he might not. If he felt all right, he might just finish up by himself. Now, he believed he'd go home.

Friday

~ I ~

FRIDAY was another hot day. Even while Elaine and Henry Waring were eating breakfast, she could feel the promise of its sticky warmth creeping into the kitchen where they ate. It had been cool for so long that these first warm days were hard to bear. They took her appetite, until she was able to drink scarcely any of her coffee, and could only peck at her egg and toast. Feeling Henry's anxious eyes on her, she tried to eat something.

"You might as well go to Rockwell with me," he said, breaking the silence that had lain between them during the meal. "Mark asked me to get some things, and there's no use of you staying here by yourself. I may be gone most all day."

Elaine said she didn't know about the trip. It was going to be hot, and the day would be long and tiresome. Besides, the Illinois kin would be in some time today, and she supposed she'd be expected to keep them. She ought to do something to get ready for them—change the sheets on the spare room bed, and maybe bake a cake, or something. If she had a little done beforehand, it wouldn't be so hard to take care of them.

Company always upset Elaine. When she was alone, her house looked all right to her—not like Beulah's, of course, but good enough. The minute company came in, she began to see things through their eyes—the dust on the window sills and the fuzz on the rugs. The curtains, which she had decided would do without washing until fall house cleaning, now looked limp and gray against finger-spotted woodwork. And no matter what luck she had with a recipe when she and Henry were alone, it always failed for company. Once every year she tried to have the entire Kenzie family, and always she knew that the next day she would be in bed with a sick headache. She had resigned herself to these headaches as the price she had to pay for discharging her obligations to the family.

Now Henry said to heck with the Illinois kin. He would help her get the room ready before they left, and they could buy a cake at the bakery. Nobody would ever know the difference. She needed the trip—she looked like a pound of soap after a hard week's washing.

Elaine ceased to argue. She said she guessed she might as well go, only he needn't help with the room. If he'd go on with his chores, she'd manage. As soon as he was out of the house, she did the dishes and went into the guest room to do some perfunctory straightening up. It wasn't as bad as she had feared—with all the damp weather they had been having, dust had scarcely come in at all. The room did have a damp and musty smell, but she wouldn't dare leave the windows open while they were gone. Never could tell when another rain would come up. But maybe she wouldn't have any of the kinfolks, anyway. The really important ones would go to the Ben or the Tom Kenzies', or stay on the old home place, with Beulah and Mark. More than likely the ones she drew, if any came at all, would be those who wouldn't mind unaired beds and bakery cakes. But whether they minded or not, she was going to Rockwell with Henry—not because she wanted the trip, but because she couldn't bear to stay by herself today.

Because of the recent rains, the country looked green and fresh. When Henry talked, it was of how well the corn looked, but how much it needed cultivating. Elaine said nothing beyond the briefest answers, nor did he seem to expect her to. As always, he seemed to sense her mood so that he knew she wanted to be left alone to think. What he could not sense was the agony of thought that swept her along until she felt an almost savage pleasure in her pain.

As if it were yesterday, she could remember how she felt when Barry left for school. There was an aching void of loneliness that nothing could fill—Aunt Ellie's kindness, or the new clothes Uncle Dade bought her in Rockwell, or the painting lessons she took from Miss Hallie Spangler. Perhaps the lessons came as near helping as anything could. She spent so much time with her brushes and paints that Aunt Ellie began to worry. She said it wasn't natural for a young girl to stay cooped up in the house all the time, daubing on china or canvas. She said she ought to get out and go places, and be with young people more. Elaine wanted none of this. The thing she lived for was Barry's letters.

They were, of course, written to all of the family, always beginning, "Dear Mother and Father and Elaine." At first, Uncle Dade had her read them aloud.

"Here, Elaine," he'd say, "I can't find my glasses. You read it to us."

And he and Ellie would sit listening while she read. Soon, however, she began to slip away when mail time drew near. She could not bear to think of reading aloud the words that Barry had written. Always, as soon as she was finished, Ellie took the letter so she might re-read it, reassuring herself that he was all right, that he had plenty to eat, that he was not studying too hard. In that way, Elaine was never alone with his letter, never felt it was really for her. If she could manage to be somewhere else when the mail came—cleaning her room, or painting—she would call down that she couldn't leave just at the moment and did they want to wait for her. Of course, Ellie could not, so she and Dade would go on and read it together. Later, after the woman had had time to read and re-read it, Elaine would come down and claim it. She had schooled herself to say casually, "If you are through with Barry's letter, I'll have a look at it now."

She liked to take the letter with her to her own room. Here she was safe from interruptions, and it was as if she and Barry were alone, talking. His writing was so individual that there was no mistaking it. He used a broad nib pen, and did not form his letters too carefully. In spite of his wide reading, he spelled poorly, always writing "truely" and "diden't." Later on, when he began to spell these words correctly, she noticed it and knew with a swift stab of hurt that he was slipping yet farther away from her.

At first, his letters were all Barry as she had known him. He was lonesome, and he talked about how he missed them all. He wanted to see them, and the farm, and the house, and all the people he knew. He missed his mother's cooking—nobody here knew how to fry chicken and you never saw real ham or biscuits. He reckoned it was Yankee cooking, and he didn't like it. He couldn't wait for Christmas, when he'd be coming home for vacation. Always there were special messages for Elaine, even though the letter was addressed to her, too. These she would read over until she knew them word for word, comma for comma. And, as his expectations for Christmas grew, hers stretched out to meet them.

She and Ellie worked hard to make things just as he liked them. There was mincemeat in stone jars down cellar, and fruit cakes ripening in tight metal containers in the pantry. They baked all kinds of cookies—the molasses ones he loved, the chocolate ones filled with nuts and raisins. As the time of his arrival drew nearer, the tempo of their preparations quickened. They boiled a ham, and had a turkey dressed. Dade, thinking the boy might like fresh sausage, had the hands butcher a hog, and containers of sausage and scrapple and headcheese were added to the rich store of provisions already in the smokehouse.

Barry came home for Christmas, but for Elaine it was almost as if he had not been there at all. She was foolish even to dream that his return would mean a reopening of the old intimacy between them. To begin with, he must visit all the members of the family, and they must come home to visit with him. The Ben Kenzies and their family, and the Tom Kenzies and theirs, came. All the cousins trooped in, and the neighbors and friends. Miss

Laura Meeks expected, and got, an invitation to Christmas dinner. She made the boiled custard for dessert, talking so much about its fine texture and good flavor that everyone was turned against it before they got to the table. She said, too, that she thought going off to school was a lot of stuff and nonsense. Just made a body think he was better than the folks he had grown up with. Barry was smart enough without going away to school, and all he'd get out of it was a lot of things he'd be better off without, and maybe the bighead besides.

Dade and Ellie did not answer her or argue with her, although privately they did agree that going off to school had changed the boy. Elaine knew better. Dimly she saw that he was as he had always been, and that going away to school had served only to intensify the differences between him and the others around him. All he had ever wanted was school, and books. They were enough for him, so that he never had felt alone in any situation in which he found himself. He was in the world of his family, but not of it. It never had mattered in the least to him that he did not excel in games, that he could not plow a straight furrow, that he had scarcely a girl's strength. These things were not important to him; they were, always, the lesser issues of life.

Going away to school had served to deepen in Barry the assurance of what he wanted in life. He told them all about his days in school—how he went each morning to class, and then to great rooms lined with books and newspapers and reading materials of all kinds. He told them that, if he read all the rest of his life, he would not be able to finish even a small portion of the contents of one side of one of these rooms. They listened, not really interested in what he was saying. Books were all right, but they were not the real things in life. Land was real, and the crops that grew on it, and stock that fed on the crops. Barns and silos and machinery were real. They knew that he was different, but then, he always had been a bookworm. If they felt anything positive toward him, it was a faint hostility that he should be so short of what they deemed right and correct for a man, and yet, remain so self-assured in his lack. If they could have picked flaws in him—seen that he was boastful, or arrogant, or stuck-up or even effeminate—they might have dismissed him with easy laughter. But because he talked quietly and well of the sort of life they held in scant repute, they were a little uneasy and resentful.

All this Elaine sensed, as none of the others were able to understand. As for herself, she had him for only one short evening. The family decided, rather suddenly, that it would be fun to rig up the old box sled and go to the Harmony Church for the Christmas program. The snow lay thick and white on the ground, but it was not bitterly cold, just the right sort of an evening for the enterprise. Everyone got busy making the plans—the men put straw in the sled and heated rocks to put in the bottom. Ellie busied herself looking for quilts and robes. They set out before it was quite dark, the sunset casting mauve and rose and violet shadows on the snow. There was a crisp, bracing bite to the air.

Barry sat next to Elaine. Under the robe his hand reached out and found hers. She slipped her mitten off and through their bare hands a current of warmth and light seemed to flow. They sat quietly, saying little, their hands loosely linked, scarcely conscious of the people around them or of the snow-clad hills through which they passed. Dade had found some bells for the horses, and their jingle was a gay chorus.

When they came to the door of the church, Elaine found that her mitten was gone, so she and Barry went back to look for it. In the shadow of the sled he drew her to him and their lips met, timidly, as if strangers were kissing. Three months' separation had spoiled for them the old childish intimacy that brought them together in the first place, and they had found no other basis on which they could meet. Elaine knew that it had been a mistake for them to kiss, for the intimacy of it had frightened them both. They were nearer to each other sitting quietly, touching hands. Once there had been something between them, elusive and beautiful as a gossamer, a thing of the spirit. It must grow of itself, and could not be forced or hurried. Stolen kisses, secret meetings, were not for them. Perhaps they could never go farther than they had been tonight. And, certainly, they could never go back as they had been when they were children.

Just then someone called that the mitten had been found at the church door, and to hurry back, for everyone was getting cold, standing there waiting for them. They went, and after that there was never another time during the visit when they were alone together. The next week Barry left.

As winter and spring passed, Barry wrote less often. He was no longer homesick. More and more he was finding the things he wanted in school. In late spring he wrote that he would like to stay on for summer school. Dade and Ellie talked it over and wrote him that if that was what he really wanted to do, it was all right. He came home only briefly for a vacation between the summer session and the fall semester. There was no time for anything then; Ellie complained that he might as well have stayed in Chicago, for all the good anyone got out of him.

The next summer he wrote that he had a chance to work on a magazine—just a temporary thing, but it might lead to something else. He had not been a month on this job before he knew that here lay the answer to all his dreams and ambitions. He did not go back to school again, staying on with the magazine, coming home only for the briefest vacations. It was a small publication, only getting started. But Barry said that it was going to grow beyond anybody's wildest dreams for it. Later, when it did become, if not so large as he had said it would, at least a magazine with a name well and favorably known all over the country, he never reminded his people of the way they had laughed at his early predictions. When he did come home for his short visits, Elaine was only a dear and beloved old playmate.

If he remembered how her lips had once been cool and trembling under his, he gave no sign. He had found the world in which he belonged, and was entirely happy in it.

Elaine did not know where the years went. They were made all of a piece, each day so filled with a familiar routine that there was no telling one from the other in any particular week. Monday was washday and Tuesday was set aside for ironing. All the other days, too, had their appointed tasks. Chickens came off in the spring just before gardening and house cleaning started. The summers were filled with canning and dozens of other seasonal jobs. There were strawberry socials when the berries were ripe, and oyster suppers when winter came. Church and Sunday School were as inevitable as the coming of the Sabbath Day itself. About a life which falls into such a pattern there is a lulling sense of security. If it gave little of change, it also offered less of hurt or pain. It was a vacuum in which nothing either of joy or of sorrow might grow.

The summer Elaine was twenty, Aunt Ellie became genuinely concerned because the girl did not go about enough with young people. Barry had been gone four years now, showing no intentions of ever wanting to come back for good. Ellie thought that the girl was too much alone with her and Dade, so she began asking young people home for Sunday dinners. Among this group was Henry Waring.

Henry was a good boy. He was short and heavy-set, with a thick, strong neck and a sunburned nose, which, in summertime, was always peeling off a little. When he took off his hat, his forehead showed very white and untanned above the rest of his face. His skin did not brown in the sun, but turned a dull mahogany. Against this rich background his eyes looked very pale, his brows and lashes a mere blond fuzz. In his Sunday clothes, which were always cheap and ill-fitting, he was awkward and uncomfortable. This he tried to cover up with a flip joviality, laughing too much and talking in a nervous voice, too high-pitched. He was far better-looking in work clothes—overalls and a shirt faded down by sun and many washings to a soft, muted blue, with a straw hat shading his pale eyes. During the week he sometimes came to see Dade on business, for he owned a small farm which he had set about in his determined way to make a paying proposition. In the work clothes he wore then there was always a certain quiet assurance about him; he talked less, and when he did speak, it was with greater ease and certainty. At these times Elaine scarcely noticed his crooked front tooth.

Dade and Ellie were both delighted with him. They talked often of his farm, his steadiness, his goodness. Almost every Sunday Ellie would ask him home to dinner with them, and usually he would accept, looking sidewise at Elaine to see what her reaction was. Often he came into the kitchen to help with the finishing up, his big hands strangely adept among the dishes and pans.

"Goodness," Ellie said one Sunday, "you're handy around the kitchen. My own boys are like bulls in a china shop, and Dade isn't much better."

Henry said he had got used to working around a kitchen since he began batching. And Ellie said he'd be a fine prize for some woman. Henry looked at her quietly, making no reply. That afternoon he asked Elaine to marry him.

The two of them were alone in the sitting room. Dade had taken Ellie off to look at a field of clover. It was early fall, and Henry had on a new suit, one he had bought when he took his cattle to Kansas City. It was the first time he had ever bought anything away from Rockwell, and his daring had given him new courage. The suit was a bright blue, with a stripe in it, which the salesman told him was the thing the young men were wearing, as it was. But no matter how many were doing it, the stripe was not for him. With it he had bought a tie—loud stripes of red and blue and purple. Above it, his face seemed even redder, his untanned forehead even whiter, than usual.

He was cruelly embarrassed at being left alone with Elaine. Although he sat on the sofa beside her, the girl was scarcely aware of his presence. Yesterday Barry had written that he might be home for a few days. He wanted so much to see them, for it had been a long time since he was home—he'd been so busy, and all. Now that watermelons were ripe and late fryers coming in, he couldn't think of a better time to come. Elaine was thinking of this letter—wondering if he, too, were remembering another fall when melons were ripe. Henry's voice, very hoarse and unnatural, broke in on her thoughts.

"Elaine," he said, "how about marrying me?"

She turned quickly, and as she did so, he reached for her hand. She watched his hand over hers with fascinated horror. It was thick and heavy, and short-fingered. Coarse reddish-brown hairs were matted so thick on the back that the skin scarcely showed through. His uneven, square-cut nails showed that he had never heard of manicuring tools, using, instead, his pocket-knife.

"Well," he went on, grinning foolishly, "how about it, kid?"

"No—" her voice was a horrified whisper. Seeing the stricken look on his face, she got herself under control. "Thanks, Henry," she added gently, "but I couldn't. I couldn't—"

"O.K.," he said, "I didn't much think you could, yet. But I thought I'd ask you. I'll sort of be sticking around, in case you ever change your mind."

He did stick around. Four more years. And then, Elaine married him.

Never for one moment did she deceive herself as to her reasons for doing so. She did not love him, made no pretense of it. Neither was she taking him because Barry was lost to her, although he was. His work was his life now, and when he came home it was all he knew, all he talked about. Already *The Criterion*, which was the name of the magazine, was beginning to be recognized. More and more Barry's bookish habits grew upon him. Where once he had recited "Horatius" and "Eve of Waterloo," now he read James Joyce and Virginia Woolf, discussing them so that his remarks were not pedantic, but lucid and right. Elaine, hearing him talk, picked up one of the books he left behind him, and tried to read it. And reading it, she knew that he was forever lost to her save in the dreams she had of him. There, he was hers, always. Certainly now, if she had ever known any hope of Barry's wanting to marry her, it was gone.

Nor did she marry because she felt herself a burden to Uncle Dade. He and Ellie were alone in the house, and the presence of Elaine was a comfort to them. She was as much a part of the family as if she had been born their own. They themselves would have been the first to admit that she gave them far bigger dividends in pleasure than they were able to repay her.

She married Henry Waring because one Sunday morning she looked around and saw Miss Laura Meeks sitting in her pew, alone, and she knew that she could not stand to live and die an old maid.

Here, as in all small places, people were strangely cruel to women who did not marry. It was, of course, although she was not able to analyze it at the time, a throwback to the primitive and superstitious age when all childless women were a reproach to a tribe, and to a clan. In a community such as this, there was no business, no philanthropy, into which these women could throw themselves, as they could in larger towns. Here there was only one pattern for a woman, and that was marriage. Her life was sewing and cooking and cleaning house, and with no man about, it was a lopsided design, not only crooked in itself, but one that threw the person who followed it out of focus as well. The uncultured feel a strange uneasiness in the sport or the specie that does not run true to form, voicing this unease in crude jibes. The men were bad enough about this, but the barbed remarks of the women were even worse. Later Elaine was to realize that usually the women who spoke thus were those who had so barely missed spinsterhood themselves that the narrowness of their escape still was a thing miraculous in their sight, blinding them to their own unsatisfactory marriages, making any kind of husband seem better than none at all.

Now she did not yet know these things, and when she looked at Miss Laura, a sort of horror came over her. Maybe Henry would not ask her again. Maybe she had waited too long, and, even now, he had found someone else. She stirred uneasily, and Ellie, sitting by her, was disturbed. The girl looked positively ill. Maybe she was coming down with something. Frail as she was, anything she got would go hard with her. She should stop fooling around and marry Henry. He was a good boy, and would take care of her, shielding her and never letting her do any heavy work. She and Dade weren't so young any more, and when they were gone, Elaine would be alone in the world. Maybe Henry wasn't quite a young girl's dream of romance, but he was solid and substantial, and loved Elaine devotedly. He would be good to her, never asking of her things that were impossible. Girls should think of things like that when boys came courting, instead of whether they were good-looking and had a way with them. Of course, if you can have all these good qualities, and love besides, it was better. Like Dade and her. Only, not all marriages could be like theirs. She remembered Dade as he had been when she first saw him, his darkly bright hair, his smile, his lips on hers. She flushed, suddenly and happily, right there in church. And Dade turned to her to ask anxiously if it was too warm for her, and would she like a fan. She said no, she was fine. She was. She was an old fool, but she was an immensely happy and an immensely content old fool. She mustn't forget to see about Elaine, the first thing when she got home from church.

The next day Henry again asked Elaine to marry him. He had come to see Dade about buying some pigs, and found that both he and Ellie were gone and Elaine was on the back porch, churning. He sat down beside her and took off his hat. As always, he was more at ease in his old clothes, more sure of himself.

"Here," he said, taking the churn dasher out of her hands, "let me do that. It's sort of tiresome, pushing that thing up and down when the cream gets heavy."

The churning gave him something to do with his hands, so he talked on with comparative ease. When he said the butter had come, Elaine went for a crock to put it in, and a stone jar for the buttermilk. She went back for two glasses and poured them each some buttermilk, and they sat there together, sipping it and talking more easily than they had ever talked together before. Suddenly Henry set the glass down and turned to face her.

"Elaine," he said, "I've been asking you for a long time. Four years, now. I don't want to make a nuisance of myself, and I'm not going to. But I'm going to try this last time. Do you think you can ever say yes to me?"

She scarcely hesitated at all. When she spoke, her voice was not loud, but it was sure enough, and clear. If he ever remembered afterwards that it was empty, like an echo coming from afar off, he did not mention it.

"Yes, Henry," she said.

He evidently had not expected her to answer so. "You mean—?" he asked uncertainly.

"I mean I'll marry you any time you want, Henry," she said, still in that quiet, dead voice.

He did not kiss her. Perhaps he sensed that this was no time for it. Perhaps he knew, even then, that he might never be able to kiss her, really, although she would marry him and come to live in his house and the two of them would become, as the wedding ceremony put it, "one flesh."

He sat there looking at her, on his plain face a beauty and a grandeur. He said, almost in a whisper, "I'll be good to you, Elaine. I promise."

They got engaged, and he didn't even kiss her. She thought of that now, as she and Henry rode along together across the rolling Missouri hills. But tomorrow, Barry would kiss her when he came home. He always did. All the Kenzies kissed each other, at meetings and partings. Riding along at Henry's side, she felt her heart reach out on tiptoe, straining toward Barry's kiss.

~ II ~

Beulah Kenzie was up very early Friday morning. Because this was the day that would bring many of the kinfolks, there was a great deal to do. With so many coming in, it was important that everything be in order, with plenty of food cooked ahead of time. Of course, friends and neighbors always brought in food at times like this, but more often than not, it ran to cakes and pies and salads. By evening, there would probably be fifteen or twenty relatives arriving. Some of these she would have to send to other people. Mother Kenzie, of course, would take some, and Aunt Opal others. If there was still an overflow, one or two could go to Elaine's, though she wouldn't send anyone there if she could help it. Company always upset Elaine.

Most of the Kenzies treated the girl with a magnificent, though kindly, disregard. Beulah always felt for her a yearning tenderness. She sensed that somewhere in her life was a great emptiness, neither presence of peace nor absence of joy. Elaine lived her pallid days through, each so like the other that there was no measuring the difference in any of them. She moved as one in a dream, a person oddly frightened of reality. Henry was good, and substantial, and real, but Beulah wondered if his wife was ever really conscious of him. Sometimes she felt that Elaine was, most of all, unconscious of herself. If only, Beulah thought, something—some great pain, or great joy, or great reality—could rouse her out of herself. Like a sleepwalker, she trod through the quiet routine of her days.

Beulah turned from thoughts of Elaine to consideration of her own affairs. Fortunately, she thought, the house was immaculate. In spite of bad weather, she had set about house cleaning early this spring. In March, she had seen that Grandfather was failing—nothing she could lay her finger on, but more of a general letting loose of life. He did not seem ill—rather there had been for some time a sort of fading out of energy and vitality, gradual as the fading of his magnificent hair. One did not see that it was taking place until one day you looked up and knew that it had happened. When she first noticed this fact, she began to watch him more closely, finally deciding that he might be sick later on, and it was well for her to get house cleaning, and other necessary chores, out of the way so she would be free to devote her entire time to him if he were ill.

She had taken the rooms one by one, washing curtains and hanging them back in place, taking out rugs and bric-a-brac, being careful to get everything back just as Grandmother had always kept it. It was with a great deal of reluctance that she had moved into this place after Grandmother's death, but once there, she had set herself with scrupulous care to keeping things just as they had always been. Elaine, coming over for the day, Allison, returning after months of absence, seemed each in her own way to be pleased to find things as they had used to be. It was a tie with the past that those two, so greatly different, seemed to have in common.

So curtains were clean all over the house, and woodwork shining. At first she had thought of painting, but because of the wet weather that seemed impractical. She was glad now that she had not undertaken it. Certainly it would have been a great mess in all the upstairs rooms, and, although she could have sent the in-coming relatives to other places to sleep, there were some who would have been disappointed at not getting to stay at the old place. Barry, of course, would have felt simply awful at having to stay elsewhere. Two of Grandfather's nieces who were coming from Tennessee certainly would not want to go off anywhere else. So she was glad she had the rooms in order for them.

Yesterday Ben and Tom and their families, as well as all the close kin on both sides of the house, had been here. Today they, and many other relatives, would be here. There would be many old friends, too. She must see that there were plenty of chairs about in the sitting room and parlor. People often just came and sat, not saying much, but seeming to want to be there. They would expect to see the members of the immediate family. The women all kissed, and the men shook hands in awkward quiet. The timid ones got out a single sentence, "You-certainly-have-my-sympathy," making it hurried and all of a piece, as something they must get over with because custom demanded that it be said. Beulah never ceased to be impressed with the kindness of people at the time of death in a family. There was no errand too difficult, no task too great, no offer too generous for neighbor or friend to bestow. People she thought Grandfather had scarcely known had come slipping in yesterday, bearing some gift which they offered with a simple dignity that made of the act almost a ritual.

She must get things cleared up as soon as possible, the dishes washed and the kitchen and porches scrubbed. Mother Kenzie would come early, but Beulah had to admit, privately, of course, that would not be much help. Julia had come as soon as she got the news yesterday. She was crying, and she was the sort of person who cried hard, screwing up her face and shaking until she could not say a word for sobbing. She often said she would give anything if she could cry easy like some women did, her daughter-in-law, for instance. Beulah could let the biggest tears fall, tears that looked like great crystal balls rolling down her cheeks to the front of her dress, and all the while her face would not show so much as a wrinkle. She could even carry on an intelligent conversation while she cried. Julia suspected such women, including Beulah, of not feeling very deeply in the matter.

Now Beulah tackled the dishes, left on the table from the midnight lunch she had prepared for the men who had sat up last night with the body. Because Ez Dowlin was to be one of the group, she had taken special care with everything. Ez was such a talker, that, if she failed in one detail, if the sandwiches were dry or the cake stale, or the pickles one degree less crisp than the standard set by Grandmother Kenzie, he would go out and spread details of the lack to all the Kenzie kin. She had been careful to get up, precisely on the stroke of twelve, to brew the coffee herself, and to see that there was real cream for it. And, with all this care, she must watch to see that there was no hint of waste or overindulgence about the meal she provided.

Allison, she knew, would have criticized her for catering thus slavishly to Ez Dowlin's tastes and opinions. But Allison had not yet come to understand that conforming was wise and often easier than was flying into the face of known opposition. To Beulah, there was a foolish and adolescent weakness about refusing to conform to patterns that were right and true, reminding her always of children seeing how close they could come to a bonfire without being singed. To her, there seemed nothing but childish bravado in deliberately setting one's self to do a thing that you knew would bring criticism upon you, especially when it was something that did not matter, one way or another. If there was a moral issue involved, she would, of course, defend her position to the end. But long ago her mother had taught her that often it is the little things over which people battle foolishly, losing friends, disturbing peace of mind, destroying serenity with no end in view save that they continue to defend the position which they have taken. It was far better, her mother pointed out, to give in gracefully, remembering that a fight in a lesser cause is never worth the struggle. She maintained that by doing so one gained everything really worth having, serenity, sweetness, and inner strength.

"Give in on the lesser, unimportant things," her mother would always say. "Then you will have established yourself as a person of judgment and when the time comes for standing firm, people will be inclined to respect your position."

Beulah wished, now, that she had someone here to answer the phone. It kept ringing, ringing, bringing messages from far away as well as calls from those nearer. Mr. Kuntz, the station agent, was keeping copies of all the telegrams, but he always telephoned them out ahead of time, so that if one needed answering it could be done at once. This latest one was from Allison, saying that she was leaving California by plane this morning. That meant she would be in Kansas City some time this afternoon.

She had felt all along that Allison would come, although Ez Dowlin had prophesied sourly that she would not.

"She won't make the trip," he said. "She's too high and mighty to come back at a time like this. You'll see—there'll be a wreath as big as the side of a house, and a message saying she can't get off from work."

Beulah was glad beyond all telling that Allison was coming. She loved her sister-in-law dearly and hated for people to misjudge her. It was true that Allison was different, leading the kind of life about which none of these people had even a glimmer of understanding. That did not mean it was a bad life. There was about the girl a kind of clear and shining honesty that refused to hide behind sham and pretenses. This quality people could not, or would not, see, feeling in her only something that made them uneasily aware of the fact that they might not be as good as they thought themselves to be. Because her own lack of pretense upset the sham in their lives, they could not forgive her. Of course, anyone could see that was the basis of Ez Dowlin's dislike for her.

But Beulah reminded herself that she must not criticize Ez Dowlin. One could never tell what made people act as they did, what strange motives, what unhappiness, what deep hurts lay back of their actions. Certainly she herself was open to criticism, every day she lived. The Kenzies had been kind to her; even when she came as a stranger, they had been kind and generous. They were a close-knit clan, proud of their family, anxious to carry on the Kenzie way of life unchanged. More than anything else in the world they would have liked one of the name to keep all the traditions going. And she, knowing that she could never give this to them, had still come into the family, not even feeling it was necessary to tell them of this before she married Mark. In her that was great weakness, and because they had never made her feel, by word, deed, or action, that she had done them a wrong, she must watch herself and never criticize anyone, regardless of the sin. She had wanted Mark Kenzie so much that she forgot herself and took him, giving no thought to what was right in the matter. Even now, she could remember every detail of that first visit to the Kenzies.

Julia Kenzie was the last one to give in to the marriage. At last she, too, yielded, although tearfully, making the stipulation that the marriage take place "right here." Mark had been born in this house and had grown up here. She could stand it better if the ceremony were said here among all the clan. It would be impossible for all of them to go to Illinois—she hinted that the state was foreign and alien, a place not entirely civilized and too far away to be of any real importance. Her most telling argument was that it would be hard for Dade and Ellie to travel so far in warm weather.

To everyone's surprise—no one had ever heard of a bride

consenting to be married in the groom's home—Beulah said if Julia considered it the wise thing, she'd write and ask her father what he thought about it. As far as she was concerned personally, it was quite all right.

His answer came almost immediately. He thought her idea a good one, especially since it was the wish of the Kenzie family. The congregation was most interested and desirous of her happiness. They had taken up a collection to buy him a ticket to come, if she wanted him or needed him.

Of course she wanted him. She told the Kenzies about it, showing great pleasure at the kindness of the congregation who had made the trip possible. She said she so much wanted her father and the Kenzies to know each other. She'd like for her father to perform the ceremony, if that was all right with Mark.

Mr. Fulton came to Missouri for the wedding. He was a tall man and spare, stooped from many hours of study. He had a gentle and easy humor, a great love of people, and the same complete unselfconsciousness that was his daughter's great charm. He did not tell many jokes nor try to demonstrate how folksy a minister could be. He fitted easily and naturally into the Kenzie family, making no less a success than his daughter had done. He and Dade liked each other on sight.

Through it all, Beulah managed to give a sense of rightness and naturalness to the situation. She went to Rockwell to buy a wedding dress, acceding to Julia's wish that it be white, but quietly carrying out her own point of buying something she could wear "afterwards for Sunday and for nice." So sweet and reasonable she was that Julia was reconciled to the lack of a veil and train, reflecting that the girl was going to be careful with Mark's money. How horrible it would have been for Mark to have married an extravagant woman who would have kept his nose to the grindstone all the time, making money for her to throw away.

Of course, there were those who were horrified at the arrangement. Miss Laura Meeks said it was the awfullest thing she ever heard of—a bride marrying outside her own home. Beulah Fulton's people were bound to be trash. There was something positively indecent about a girl who would chase a man all this distance, and then stay camped on the spot until she had him hooked and landed. She always did mistrust a woman who was too proud of her husband's family. The Kenzies were a good enough family, of course. The Meekses and the Marshalls had been around here longer than anyone else, but the Kenzies came early enough, and were good and substantial. Of course, when it came right down to family, the Meekses had them all bested. You had only to step into her house to see, right on the hall wall, the picture of Cousin Robert E. Lee. Miss Laura belonged to the U.D.C. She was probably the only person in the community who had papers for the D.A.R. She doubted if half of them even knew what the D.A.R. was.

Beulah Fulton was, in the first place, from Illinois. People from there were always different. They had too much of the Yankee stripe in them, so that they talked crisply and efficiently and in a way that seemed almost rude. They didn't think family mattered so much. Besides, Beulah simply had no spunk. She was so glad to marry a Kenzie that she was willing to give up everything she knew, just for the sake of getting him. She would pussyfoot through this marriage, catering to all the family, kowtowing, giving in. Mark would soon tire of that.

Allison, too, had her doubts. These she expressed one evening when the two girls were upstairs, getting ready for bed.

"Do you really *want* to marry here?" Allison asked. "You don't have to just because Mother wants it, you know."

"Yes," Beulah told her simply. "At first, I didn't know about it. And after I thought it over, I realized that the only thing against it was the fact that things weren't usually done that way. That wasn't a good enough reason for me to go back to Illinois when it suited everyone better for me to stay here."

"I wasn't thinking of that," Allison said. "I've never been the one to do the thing expected of me. It's just, well, Mother has always given up to Mark until he's sort of an absolute monarch around here. And now, if you start doing it, too—well, I don't think it's good for him to have his own way all the time. You may wish, later on, that you had started out differently."

Beulah sat for some time, saying nothing, her eyes quiet and thoughtful. When she finally spoke, her voice was low and sure.

"My mother used to say that having one's own way was the most lonesome business in the world. I'm not marrying Mark the way I'd go into a contest, determined that I'll come out winner. In a preacher's family we are always quoting scripture, and for weddings it's Ruth—you know, that part about my people being his people, and so on. I'm going to be a Kenzie, why shouldn't I do as they wish when doing so doesn't in the least bother me or my family?"

Allison, rarely given to demonstration, got up and kissed the girl.

"Why, indeed," she said. "You're too good for him by a mile, but I'm glad you're taking him."

And so they were married. The Kenzies' living room was banked high with fall flowers. For two days before, Julia had done nothing but cook and clean and make ready, so that by the time of the ceremony she was so nervous she would break into quick tears when anyone spoke to her. Opal came over to help and Allison proved remarkably efficient, a fact which, instead of pleasing her mother, only served to irritate her. If the girl, Julia reasoned, showed such aptitude in household tasks, why hadn't she been helping with them all these years instead of spending all her time outside with her grandfather? Miss Laura came to offer her services, and so got an invitation to the wedding, although she had not been on the original guest list. Nobody could make a white butter cake as well as Miss Laura, so she was set to making the wedding cake. Ellie personally took over the baking of the hams and the supervision of the chicken salad.

Through all the confusion Beulah moved, quiet and serene. She had long talks with Dade, and with her father. Whenever Mark was near her, there emanated from her face a sort of glow, like light showing through a transparent substance. Allison found it hard to reconcile the brightness of the girl's face with the life she would have to lead. The young couple would have no house of their own at first; until something could be arranged, they would move in with Tom and Julia. Allison knew, from a life-long subjection to them, the petty tyrannies that anyone living with her mother would have to endure.

Beulah seemed totally unaware of the difficulties that faced her. Of course, she would have preferred a home of her own. But since they were marrying so hastily, that was impossible. Therefore, she must make the best of things. Mother Kenzie was kind to take them in—it was not easy for a woman to share her household with another. Father Kenzie said that soon, maybe in a year or so, they probably would be able to build a place of their own. Building could not well be started now, in the fall.

Through it all, she gave no sense of compromise. Some instinct deeper than thought told the girl that this was the way to do things. This was Mark's family, and since she had cast her lot with them, their ways were hers. Beyond any doubt or shadow of reason, she knew Mark Kenzie was the man she wanted to marry. She was willing to take what came of marrying Mark, even though some of the conditions were not wholly to her liking. Allison, watching the course things were taking, felt that she was seeing a mother, wise and strong and sure, letting her fractious children have their own way in things that did not matter one way or another.

Only once did Beulah demur. That was when Dade came to her with plans for the honeymoon.

"I'd like to give it to you," he said. "A trip to Kansas City or to Excelsior Springs. Which would you like?"

Beulah hesitated. The only misgiving she had felt about letting the others make her plans for her was the fear that perhaps the old man would take these concessions on her part as confessions of weakness, even as Allison had intimated she did. But as time went on, she gained courage, feeling that Dade understood. He was never the one to let minor details stand in the way of reaching main objectives. Now she felt free to tell him her ideas concerning the proposed trip.

She said, unless Mark especially wanted to go, she'd rather stay here. As she spoke, she felt his shrewd kind eyes on her, knowing that he was seeing with certainty the thing she was not able to put into words.

She knew nothing of cities; she would feel only alien and strange in one. All her life she had lived in small towns, among simple, ordinary people. She knew nothing, either, of pleasure resorts such as Excelsior Springs. She had known Mark such a short time, really, that he was almost a stranger to her. She was not sure that she could grope her way toward him in a strange and different atmosphere. If they stayed here where she knew things better, she would feel more sure of herself, and of him.

In the end, Tom and Julia went to Kansas City for a few days with Allison, leaving the young people alone in the Tom Kenzie house for their honeymoon.

The wedding itself was exactly as the Kenzies would have had it. The closest relatives and friends were crowded into the room where the ceremony took place; the more distant ones, with friends and neighbors, filling the other rooms and even spilling over onto the porches. Beulah's father said the ceremony, simply and with a great deal of feeling. Afterwards there was a big supper, and the bride and groom cut the wedding cake. Miss Laura took a great deal of pains to tell everyone that she had made it, implying that no Kenzie woman had yet learned the secret of making a really good white butter cake, which was, in the last analysis, one of the attributes of a lady.

It was late before the last guest left, and Tom and Julia and Allison were off to Kansas City. Beulah and Mark walked upstairs together, through the wide, cool hall, to the room that was to be theirs. The August breeze had set the scrim curtains astir. There on the dresser was a vase of white asters Julia had gathered and arranged with her own hands, tearfully and with much self-pity. On the bed was a white candlewick spread. Already Beulah's things were in place—her brush and comb and other toilet articles on the dresser, her clothes hanging in the closet.

She said quietly to Mark, "Your things are already here. Your mother brought them in this morning."

She did not know what time she awakened. The moon was shining so brightly that it was almost like day. In a tree just outside the window a nightbird was stirring sleepily, making a soft, plaintive sound as it did so.

At her side, Mark was sleeping, sprawled across the bed, relaxed and quiet, like a child at rest after a full and happy day. Even his face was childlike, boyish, and unformed. The mouth was relaxed and soft. In the moonlight, his hair showed bright against the whiteness of the pillow.

Across the years a scene came back to haunt her. She could see the dust, smell the potted plants in the window, hear the slow drone of flies.

"You'll be all right," the old doctor was saying. "But it's extremely unlikely that you will ever have a child—"

It was a long time before she went back to sleep.

~ III ~

Allison unfastened her safety belt. The plane was in the air now, headed for Kansas City. Here in the clean blue of heaven space was infinite and time only relative. Perhaps, released thus from the ordinary pattern of living, she would be able to fix her mind on the letter she had in her purse—Harlan's letter, which had come to her only a few hours before she started.

Below her she could see Los Angeles and the surrounding territory—small dots that were houses, a glimmer that was water, and, in the distance, the blue haze of the mountains. It was like a block design that a child would make, without definite form or pattern. And suddenly there was wonder in her mind if she, too, had built the plan of her life as a child would—formlessly, and without pattern, putting strange and inappropriate blocks into place with no thought as to their suitability to the rest of the design.

Allison had come to California from New York. Julia Kenzie had been irreconcilable about the Dramatic School venture, hinting subtly that Dade was at the bottom of it, financing, as it were, the certain ruin of his granddaughter. But, when she saw how determined Allison was, she consented with a tight-lipped dignity, even agreeing to pay the girl's living expenses if she would agree to stay in the place her mother would designate. She had in mind a Girls' Hotel she had seen advertised in the Sunday School *Herald*, "A decent, safe place for girls alone in New York."

Allison did not care where she stayed, if only she could go. Accordingly, the necessary arrangements were made, and she was off.

Oddly enough, her first reaction to the city was one of disappointment. In some way she had expected the very bigness of it to reach out and knock her down. Kansas City was the only large place she had ever seen and, unconsciously, she had expected New York to dwarf Kansas City, as that place dwarfed Rockwell. It was faintly disappointing to her that she was able, almost from the first, to find her way about so easily in New York. The buses, with only minor differences, were not greatly different from those she used to ride down to Paseo to Mrs. Benoni's studio. After the first few bewildering encounters with the subway, she was able to manage with little difficulty. There was even a sense of flatness to find how exactly like her dreams were the places she saw—Times Square, and Rockefeller Center, and Fifth Avenue and Broadway.

Perhaps the ocean impressed her more than anything, for in her imagination she had no basis for comparison, having never seen a body of water larger than the muddy Missouri. The vastness of the water drew her with a strange and fascinated horror as the sight of depth will draw some people. Even as she shrank from it, she reached toward it, impelled by a force stronger than herself. Later on, the city was to become to her a magic fulfillment of her dreams, but just at first, it was a disappointment.

The place Julia had stipulated that she must stay was horrible, a hutch into which working girls crept at night after they could find nothing else to do. Her room was small, dank, and bleakly colorless. Its one window looked out on a small, bare court, reeking with smells of old cabbage and stale grease. The furniture consisted of a lumpy bed, a rickety chair, and a small dressing table. To take a bath she must go down the hall four doors to a bathroom shared by a dozen other girls. No light at all crept into this grubby hole save through a small, dirty skylight. The tub had been scoured so often that by now it was all of a grayness. She could not bring herself to sit down in it, choosing rather to stand up on newspapers which she carried with her for the purpose, and so bathed as best she could. She loathed the place with a fierce, shaking hatred, even as she loathed the twitchy-nosed woman who managed it. But it was respectable, and so long as she stayed there, her mother was reasonably reconciled to her being in New York. Besides, it was a price she did not so much mind having her parents pay for her. As soon as she could, she would get a job and support herself. Dependence, even on them, was a hard pill for Allison to swallow, but she was willing to endure it until she could do better.

Although she liked the Dramatic School, at first finding it stimulating and different, it was not at all as she had thought it would be. She had not been there more than a month of the six Old Dade had offered her before she began to feel a distaste for it. The whole program was slow and fussy and beside the point. They did not ever encourage her in thinking she had talent, a matter for which she did not criticize them. She had never felt sure that the stage had a place for her—she had only wanted to know for herself about it. She would have been quite satisfied with small parts, but they did not even think she could do those well. They tried her in maids' parts, not realizing that her acquaintance with maids had been so small that they might as well have asked her to play the part of the man from Mars. Her days at the Dramatic School held little of encouragement for her.

She thought on these things, deeply and gravely. Perhaps, as her mother said, the judgment of the school bearing her out, she lacked the spark. It was the same old urgent struggle for freedom that would never let her do things the accepted, the usual, way. Although she was too honest to offer this as an excuse, there would often come to her mind the picture of a little girl singing "Annie Laurie" at a Children's Day program when all the others were saying lyrics about flowers and sunshine and happy children. She was wise enough to see this as a symptom, not as an excuse, sensing dimly that the reason lay farther back than that—in rides with Old Dade across fields rich with clover or glutted with promise of wheat and corn growing, and with cattle grazing in the lush greenness of bluegrass pasture. Perhaps it was even deeper, rooted in the spirit of the first adventurous ancestors who had kept pushing on, always toward the free and open promise of new and untried country.

The stubborn, bright courage that had brought her to New York did not, however, fail her in the face of her disappointment with the school. She decided to go the rounds of the casting agents herself, trying for parts. With no outstanding talent, with no experience, she could certainly expect nothing but failure. And yet, there was about her a great lack of self-consciousness that struck people. They seemed to think that someone who was as completely natural and individual in the flesh might have some possibilities on the stage. Surprisingly, she got some small parts. It was while she was doing one of these bits that she met Olga.

Olga was not of the stage. She worked for an agency who handled the business details for the author of the play in which Allison was currently playing her small part. Her work with this agency was varied—she ran back and forth with manuscripts and messages, she did errands, she typed letters. That day she had come to rehearsal with a message, and stayed for a while. Sitting out in the bare and barnlike place, she was struck, first of all, with Allison. The girl was in street clothes which, though they were not the clothes of New York, were individual and different. Best of all, she wore them with a cool unawareness that captured Olga's imagination. She stayed on to see how this strange girl could act.

Watching, Olga put her finger upon the difficulty. The girl did not act. On the stage she was herself as completely as she was off it. That was fine in the flesh, but a maid in a sophisticated play could not be Allison Kenzie, and a charwoman in a psychological drama could not be Allison, and the girl who stands for one fleeting second starkly and blackly silhouetted against the background of a city skyline as she tells her lover good night cannot be, at the same time, Allison Kenzie. These people must be maids and charwomen and lovely girls. But she made of them all one person, and that was herself.

Olga waited for rehearsal to be over, and then she went straight to Allison.

"Hello," she said, "I am Olga Bischoff. I am with Tellers, who handle Ward Schmidt's things, the man who wrote the play. What do you say we have a cup of coffee?"

Olga was dark and petite. Her eyes slanted in her face. Her hair was smooth as satin, and all of a piece. She wore it parted in the middle and pulled back into a knot at the back of her neck. Her nose was small and straight and her skin had a smooth sallowness. She wore no rouge, but her lips were painted vividly. Looking at her, Allison felt that here, at last, was something she had come to New York to find. There was an easy sophistication, a smooth urbanity about the girl that appealed tremendously to Allison's country-bred nature.

Over the coffee cups there sprang up between the two girls one of those quick, easy friendships that come so easily to youth. Olga was Jewish, the first of that race Allison had ever known. In the circumscribed area of her childhood, God was an American, a Methodist, and, probably, harking back to the creation of man, a farmer. That there were other, lesser sons and daughters besides these favored ones was something Allison's family and friends were ready to admit in theory but were rarely called upon to recognize in practice. Now it was a strange and fascinating experience to find someone whose every tradition differed from hers, and who assumed naturally that her own way of life and thinking was the right and proper one.

"Do you have a good place to stay?" Olga asked Allison.

Allison told her about it, distaste shaking her as she spoke.

"That is bad," Olga said. "I know a better place than that. No, it is not much more expensive. And I think I know where

I can help you get a part-time job. You could do it, and still keep the parts you play, if you like."

Olga did not, that first morning, tell Allison how she felt about the girl's acting. Later she did, but by that time Allison was finished with it on her own accord. Now she asked where the job was.

"Donaldson's, literary agents," Olga said. "Tomorrow we shall go to see about it. Today, let us go to the place where I stay to see if you can get a room."

The room which, because of Olga, she got was a great, high-ceilinged one in an old-fashioned apartment overlooking the Hudson River in the University neighborhood. The room was small, but it was bright and clean. There were chintz curtains at the windows; she had only to push them aside to see far below her on the waters of the Hudson great ships, standing proud and free. The sight of them moved her with a force that was almost pain. She shared a bath with Olga; she shared, too, the kitchen with her and with half a dozen other women—two teachers working on their Masters' degrees at Columbia, a stenographer, and three older women who feuded among themselves with well-bred venom.

Allison got work at Donaldson's with little difficulty. Since she knew nothing of the work, at first hers were the humblest jobs. Later, she came to know it thoroughly, finding out all the intricate details of its services. The company acted as agent between authors and publishers. Their advertisements were in all the magazines, and they sent out, besides, circulars to any people they had reason to believe were interested in writing. "How would you like to sell what you write?" these brochures asked. "Send us a sample of your writing—and five dollars—and we will try to place your things for you. If they need revision, we will advise you as to the best way to go about it." Then they listed sales they had made for aspiring writers and letters of testimonials from them, sounding for the world and all like patent medicine advertisements.

Far out in distant reaches, people read these ads, and believed them. They sent in stories, women from lonely ranches and women in cities whose loneliness is often greater than that of people living in great spaces. College girls and boys who had been told, and often with good reason, that they could write, sent samples. Everywhere, people groping for that intangible thing which is called self-expression. Always, always feeling that, if only they could put their finger on the right word, there would come richness of understanding, wealth, and fame. There was about all of these offerings an incoherent urge that Allison, after she was allowed to read the manuscripts, understood. She could never laugh at them, as some of the other readers did, although in truth some of them were pitifully ludicrous.

It was her work at Donaldson's that made her know definitely that the stage was not for her. As usual, Grandfather had been right. The best the stage had to offer was only a pale shade of what real life was like. There was in no play she had seen an old man whose personality could in any way compare with that of Old Dade's; no grand dame who had the fire and sweetness of Ellie; no old maid as real as Miss Laura; and no weak character who approached the vagueness of Elaine. The stage, at best, was but a reflection of life. She wanted no reflection—she wanted the real thing in terms that she could accept and respect.

Dimly at first, and then with greater certainty, she came to know that her work at the agency was satisfying and, perhaps, even the thing she had been seeking. The things that books held, they were the good things, and the true. Books made no pretense of saying they were life. They only purported to tell about it. Theirs was a richness of understanding, a clear and honest beauty, a bright and urgent striving for truth. She could not write herself, but she could help others who did. So, she gave up all ideas of the stage and devoted herself entirely, with all the pushing drive of her nature, to the work with the literary agency. So great was her interest, so good her judgment, that before she had been there a year she was a trusted and valued reader.

That was the way she came to know Harlan Ranyak.

Miss Donaldson herself opened his manuscript when it came to the agency. She was a tall, raw-boned woman who dyed her hair and wore too much rouge. She had a nervous difficulty with one eye, so that it drooped a little, giving her a slightly lewd look. She was as hard as nails, but she knew ability when she saw it. If revision were needed, she could put her finger instantly on the trouble and tell the writer, clearly and concisely, what to do about it. She had no patience with writers unable, or unwilling, to follow her instructions. She seemed to feel no rancor over the fact that so many of her clients, ones whom she had started in pulps and little magazines, got another agent as soon as they graduated to better markets. She experienced little elation over a "literary find."

"Well, girls," she would say, "here's one that better go to the high-boys."

Thus did she designate, crisply and dryly, what others might term high-brows.

Now she flipped Harlan's story across to Allison.

"Read it," she said, "and tell me what you think of it."

It was a strange thing that Allison should have come to New York so that she might be helped to understand that crazy, perverse thing that was life, and here it was before her in a poorly typed manuscript by somebody from a Nebraska farm. It was all there—the eager searching, the deep, inner lonelinesses, the swift joys, and the sorrows that ever underlie happiness. The piece was naïve, as the country is naïve; crude, as hills are crude; natural, as woodlands are natural. Through it Allison could feel life pulsing—life here in New York, life as she had known it, life as it must be out there in that Nebraska farming community, different, as he pictured it, from any life she had ever seen.

She could feel Miss Donaldson's eyes searchingly upon her as she read.

"Well," the woman said at last, "I suppose there's no need to ask you what you think of it."

"It's—it's wonderful—" Allison said uncertainly.

"That's what I thought you'd say. You can take it over, if you like. I wouldn't be a bit surprised if we have a celebrity on our hands."

She said it with little elation. She did not care for celebrities. They had exaggerated ideas of their own importance, and went in for temperament. Give her a good, honest writer who became dewy-eyed and effusive over a sale.

She was right about the new writer. They sold three of Harlan Ranyak's stories in quick succession, and then a book. By that time, it seemed a good idea for him to come to New York to talk with publishers. Already they were saying about him much the same thing that Allison had sensed that afternoon she had read his first story. As she read each succeeding thing sent in, the spell of the powerfully crude material did not grow less for her. Not since she was a child, following her grandfather in his rounds, had she known such a sense of rightness as they gave her. Here were the wise solutions, the true. The restless mind of her and the rebellious heart came to rest under the spell of the new writer's words.

He came unannounced to the office one afternoon. Miss Donaldson was gone, so Allison had things almost to herself. She looked up to see a young man with blue-black hair and the high cheek bones of a peasant, standing before her desk. About his other features, however, there was no touch of peasant. The lines were long and scholarly, the mouth thin-lipped and sensitive. His eyes, deep-set and with lashes as long and thick as a woman's, were a dark, slate-gray. It was a shock to her, as it was to everyone seeing him, to note the contrast between those cool gray eyes and the dark olive tones of his skin, the blackness of his hair. He stood, tall and angular and uncertain, before her, and said diffidently,

"Hello—I am Harlan Ranyak."

She did not know why she should be trembling, or why she should be so moved by the sight of his hands, long and brown and big-knuckled, fingering his cheap straw hat. She did not know why she should feel that here, in this one person, lay all the answers to her dreams. But feel it she did—sudden and quick, like a summer rain coming up over the Missouri.

"Hello," she said, "I am Allison Kenzie. We have liked your stories here."

That was the way they met. Certainly he was not at all the sort of person she had thought he would be, and he grew less like it every time she saw him. There was, even as Miss Donaldson had foreseen, a growing arrogance that came with success, a series of small meannesses. There was a lack of self-control about him that, even while it infuriated the girl, had a strange and inexplicable interest for her. Here was no saint, passing out Jovelike judgment on others. Here was a man, weakest of the weak, who could rise at times to heights of insight that were almost godlike. Here was passion and power and frailty; courage, and deep sensitivity. Here, in all its contradictions, was a man.

She wanted to know more about his background, the things that had gone into the shaping of him.

"Your name," she said. "It's different. I never heard it before."

It was Czech, he told her. There was a bunch of his people settled in this particular spot in Nebraska. His father had been born in Czechoslovakia, but had come over when he was very small. His mother's people had been here longer. He had grown up there on the farm, and somehow managed to wrangle the right to go to high school out of his dad.

"He didn't believe in schooling," Harlan said. "But my mother helped me talk him into it. Later, I went to college."

He told her a little more about himself; not much, for at first he was strangely reticent. Piecing the bits together, she got a picture of a boy, different from his family and the other people around him, wanting different things, setting up different values. Naturally, he could not be happy among his own kind, even as she had not been. He had traveled a little, one summer on a tramp steamer. He had worked in harvest fields, too. His mother, only dimly understanding his desires, had tried to help him. But there was no one he could talk to, really.

"That's why I started writing," he said, simply.

Different as they were, Allison knew that she and Harlan had much in common. Basically, their roots were the same. They knew cornfields and pastures dotted with stock; they were familiar with small insular towns, units so complete in themselves that their abysmal ignorance of other ways and other places was, in itself, a wisdom profound and complete. Because these people knew nothing beyond their own locality and their own ways, they were content, their very contentment having an innocent quality like that of the first pair in Eden. They were happy because they did not even suspect the existence of the waiting serpent.

Like her, he had been fretted with the blindness of this content, the small-souled insularity. She had chosen to run from it, and he had chosen to write of it. For neither one had the way been easy. To fight content is a hard thing.

It was inevitable that they should be drawn together. From the first, Allison understood him as she felt no one else, not even his mother, ever had understood him. This was the bond between them. It was, as well, the source of conflict. He knew she saw all the meannesses in him, the small dishonesties. He knew it, and with the knowledge came resentment. And yet, it drew him to her as people, believing ever so little in mind readers and fortunetellers, will be drawn back to them again and again. And she was drawn as helplessly to him.

Theirs was a strange courtship. Harlan had come to New York on the heels of a quick and spectacular success. He had experienced no probationary period, no painful time of waiting, such as most writers must undergo. There is a discipline and stillness that comes of seeing hopes many times deferred, a strength that comes from waiting. These things he did not know. The book was coming into the promise his short stories had given. Success was new and swift, strong and heady. He did not know the town he had captured because of this success, or the people and their ways. The whole thing was a fantastic dream, with everything out of focus.

New as Allison was to this world, she already was wise in its ways. She knew this thing could not last, just the way it was, for Harlan. She saw, as he did not, the constant threat of transiency that lay over him. The public had a short memory, and shorter loyalties. Soon someone else would come along, someone whose success, perhaps, would be as swift and spectacular as Harlan's had been, and he would no longer be the most important person at any gathering he attended. She wanted him to see this beforehand, so that when it came, it would not bring with it hurt and disillusion. It was a hard thing to explain. She found that she could no more bring herself to tell him than she could have destroyed a child's belief in Santa Claus.

They went together one afternoon to a party given for Harlan by a woman whose name was known not only in New York, but by all the folks back in Missouri as well. Allison could have foretold many of the people who would be at the party—the large and gushy women, the thin and brittle ones, the flabby, weak-chinned men, the very young and arty ones. She knew exactly how these young ones would attach themselves to some older woman, lighting her cigarettes, running her errands, picking up her gloves, or handkerchiefs, or furs. Voices would be shrill and quick—there would be in the air the nervous tension of those who were trying desperately to attract the attention of someone who, they thought, could be of use to them in some way. And there would be the wary boredom of those in a position to confer these favors.

What she did not know was how Harlan would react to it. She made no effort to identify herself with him in any way, sitting apart, content to watch him, pleased to see how he stood out, in every way, from all the others who were there, with a sort of crude and vital reality that would make a real mountain cheapen a stage backdrop imitation of it.

She exulted in his embarrassment at the endearments the women heaped upon him; she was pleased that he made scant effort to disguise his scorn for those who suddenly professed great friendship with him. Afterwards, she remembered with pleasure that it was this party that really brought them together. Had he liked it, or been flattered by it, she could never have felt any real respect for him again. But because he saw it as she did, something full of sham and silliness, she knew with even greater certainty that the two of them had elements in common which drew them together.

Finally, he came to her. "What's the chance of getting out of this?" he asked her desperately.

It pleased her, too, that she was able to get him away, managing his departure with deft smoothness so that no one was angered at their going. Outside, they hailed a passing taxi which took them, magically, past Central Park, lying quiet and green in the middle of the city's fretful unrest. As if a single mind moved them, they gave the driver the signal to stop, and together they sought a bench. The traffic that slipped past them, continuously and relentlessly, was little more than a background for the quietness which they felt. People sitting on benches around them, or walking past them, did not bother them, either. Harlan looked at the trees, anchored as they were in solid rock.

"Gosh," he said, "you couldn't grow very good corn here, could you?"

They fell to talking about home, a thing they had scarcely mentioned before. They were a country boy and girl, who, in the great loneliness of New York, had found each other. The light fell away, and the traffic roared past as they sat talking. They went straight to the heart of each other so that they knew all the things that mattered in the lives of each—the fears, and dreams, and hopes.

It was strange that he, who could write so beautifully of love between man and woman, could find no words with which to tell her of his own. When he tried, he made a great bungling of it, such as the greenest country youth might well have been ashamed of. When he saw he was getting nothing said with words, he reached out awkwardly to draw her to him. None of the home boys, trying to kiss her on the way home from church or from parties, had ever been more awkward or inept. Even so, the world went singing around her ears at his touch, so that all of beauty and truth and love were distilled into that single instant when his lips touched her cheek. She clung to him and he kissed her again, this time with greater sureness. Afterwards, Allison knew for a certainty that this was, for him as well as for her, the first real kiss. Both of them had lived so much apart from their own age and their own kind that they had missed the love-making natural to the others. They, who thought themselves so wise, so vastly superior to those around them, were, in reality, tremendously ignorant.

They wanted to marry immediately. There was about both of them a bright tempestuous eagerness, an unwillingness to follow orderly processes of action, a complete and simple disregard for ordinary, practical considerations. They did not stop to analyze their chances for happiness. If Allison noticed that Harlan's weaknesses were such as she usually despised in other people instead of being the engaging ones which served to endear the possessor of them, she did not seem to think that was important. Nor did Harlan see in her a person fiercely independent, one who not only refused to yield one bit of her individuality, but who feared, with a fear almost an obsession, any threat to it.

They would not wait to go back to Missouri for the wedding. They would not even wait for Julia and Tom to come to New York for it. They slipped away quietly to the "Little Church Around the Corner" and were married like any little stenographer and her clerk lover.

The papers, of course, got the story, using both their pictures. The *Kansas City Star* picked it up, as did the Lincoln papers.

Harlan Ranyak made good copy. At first, the publishers had deliberately made him such. Later, he came into it in his own right. His sulky good looks, his naïve lack of social graces, even his not infrequent rudenesses, attracted people. New York, and later Hollywood, made much of him. Because Allison was his wife, she shared this publicity, a fact of which the Missouri papers, of course, made use. Allison felt no elation at this, anticipating the reaction of the home folks, especially of Miss Laura Meeks and Ez Dowlin. Certainly, they would not approve of most of the stories.

And now it was only a matter of minutes before the plane would land in Kansas City, and then only a few more hours before she would find herself back among her own people who had followed every detail of these newspaper stories about her and Harlan, including the most recent ones concerning their separation. It was not hard to imagine what their comments would be.

Looking down now, she saw the Missouri River, with the Kaw flowing into it, swollen from all the spring rains. The land looked surfeited with water as the great silvery plane slid easily over it. She gathered up her purse and gloves. The letter inside the purse gave a sharp little crackle, like a guilty conscience reminding her that she had not yet given the matter thought.

FRIDAY

~ IV ~

MOSTLY Virgie Meadors worried about making so much trouble. The pain was so bad she could not hide it, try as she would, which meant Jim insisted on having some neighbor women in to stay with her. It was such an inconvenient time for her to be sick, and most unfortunate that she had not gone to the hospital, as she and Jim had planned. When Old Dade had found out about her condition, he told Jim about a plan where they could pay out in advance, so that when the time came, she could be well cared for. But, because she had been careless, not looking where she was going, she had fallen and the doctor wouldn't let her go.

Yesterday, when Dr. Burgess came, after her fall, she had begged him to let her try to go anyway. But he said no—if she lay here still, *very* still—maybe things would be all right. He wouldn't promise, but they might. His eyes were red-weary, for he had been up most of the night with Mr. Kenzie. But he was still gentle and kind with her, even in her protests about going to the hospital.

"See here, Virgie," he said. "You want to get this baby here all right, don't you? Then you'll have to do as I say. I'll get some neighbor women in to stay with you. There's nothing I can do right now, so I'm going home and get some rest."

Virgie certainly had not wanted any of the neighbor women to come. They ought to be home cooking things to take up to the Kenzie place. A lot of kinfolks would be coming in, and Mrs. Beulah needed the neighbors to help her get ready for them. Virgie felt terribly guilty about keeping anyone away.

Anyway, she hated outsiders in her house, seeing her things. If she had done this properly, no one need ever have known that she had only six dish towels and two tablecloths. She washed out something every day, so there were always clean things. She told Jim she did this because she couldn't stand having dirty things lying around, and, really, that was as good a reason as any. Coming, as she had, from the squalor and filth of the Bottoms, cleanliness had become almost an obsession with her.

At first, schooled as she was to a great lack of everything, the few things she had been able to buy had seemed wholly adequate to her. Then one day she had gone to the Kenzies' to help with dinner for the hay balers and had gone, at Mrs. Beulah's request, to the kitchen linen closet for extra dish towels. Dish towels were there in abundance, and other kinds, too. There must have been fifty or more heavy Turkish bath towels, as well as little hand towels for guests and rough ones for the men to use when they washed up at the pump in the basement. She stood there gloating over them, feeling that great satisfaction that comes to a woman looking at a full linen closet. She almost forgot to go back with the dish towels. That evening she told Jim about it.

"Want some money for extra towels, honey?" he asked.

She said no—my goodness, and what did anybody want with so many towels, anyway? They couldn't use more than one apiece at a time, and it was best to wash them out right away, so as to keep them fresh. Jim worried about it anyway, and the next time he went to town he came home with two towels. He got them at the five-and-ten, and they were so sleazy that you could sift tumblebugs through them. But, of course, she didn't tell him so. She said they were wonderful, and just the right color, and it was sweet of him to get them.

She guessed all women were like that, maybe. She had spoken with awed respect about those towels she saw at Mrs. Beulah's, thinking it would make a good story to tell Jim. And he took it that she wanted more for herself. Towels didn't matter, not the least bit. There were other things that did matter, but those you mostly didn't mention, because down in your heart was a sick, scared feeling that kept you from saying what you really had on your mind. Maybe Mrs. Beulah hadn't really wanted all those towels, either. Maybe she wanted something else—although it was hard to imagine Mrs. Mark Kenzie wanting anything—but maybe she did, and talked about towels instead, so that Mr. Mark came home with them, thinking to give her what she desired. Men, bless their hearts, were big blundering babies at best.

Here was Jim now, underfoot and in the way of the women who had come to help. He shouldn't be here. Mr. Mark had asked him to come up to the house to see about things. Of course, that was before he knew she was sick, but anyway, he ought to go. With Old Dade gone, the young ones might decide they didn't need Jim. Maybe he wouldn't have a job left, after this was over.

"Pain bad, poor thing?" one of the neighbor women bent over her to ask.

Virgie shook her head. The pain was bad enough, but that wasn't what brought the exclamation to her lips. It was the quick, shuddering fear of what having no job meant. It wasn't right, the way things were.

Unless people had jobs, they didn't get the things that made living smooth and right. And jobs didn't come easy. Sometimes men had to fight for them, snarling at each other like hungry dogs. Then, like as not, they didn't get one, and came home with hurt shame in their hearts, and a great bitterness toward life and people. That was bad. They bowed and smiled to men who, sometimes, were not half so good nor honest as they were themselves, and then had to go and confess failure to their families. That was the hard thing. Outside, you could keep a brave face, and not show you cared. But at home, you were among people who knew your desperation so well that there was no pretending around them. Children were hungry, and needed things for school, like clothes and books. More often than not, there was another baby on the way, and heaven only knew what you'd do to feed it, once it got here. How many times she had watched her father come home from such an experience, until finally, he, too, became like the rest of the Bottoms men who stopped trying, and took what fate and the River had to offer.

Because Jim had seen it happen so many times, he was determined that, for them, things would be different. That was why he said they would not marry until he had a real job. He tried everything around home, but found nothing. People didn't have faith in the Bottoms men, anyway. How could they know Jim was different from most?

Jim went to Kansas City. He tried the automobile companies, and the farm machinery places, and the chemical plants. He went to the mail order houses. Most of the offices wouldn't let him past the waiting room. Down in the stockyards he did get to see one of the boss men. Jim told him he wanted a job.

"What kind of a job?" the man asked.

"Well—just a job."

"What sort of work do you do?" the man asked.

He was large and florid, and looked as if he did not eat the right things. His black felt hat was pushed back off his forehead, and an unlighted cigar hung from one side of his mouth.

"What do you know how to do?" he repeated, this time a little impatiently.

"I—I farm—" Jim told him.

Truthfully, that was all he knew of work. Hunting for coons he knew, and fishing in the muddy Missouri, and peddling watermelons, and doing odd jobs in the Uplands—those things he knew. But that was not what one could honestly call work.

"Listen, Bub," the man's tired, cynical eyes fixed him with a straight, level glance, "go home and learn how to do something. Don't go out looking for jobs until you know what you want. If you farm, get back to it. At least you have a place to eat and sleep."

Jim got out, mumbling something he meant for thanks. It was raining—fine mist between the drops so that the whole thing was a soggy downpour. His shabby suit was wet with it, his shoes a sodden pulp. He thought he'd better save streetcar fare to the station, so he started walking. The water slushed through his toes, ran down his hat in rivulets. He was still wet and soggy when he swung off the local at the station that evening and made his way to Virgie's house. The rain had stopped now, and the clouds were lifting a little. The moon was rising, lighting up the River, and the little islands in it were darkly etched against the water. Up the River a girl's laugh sounded, sudden and quick, and then there was silence again. Inside the house Virgie's mother was nagging at her father, and Dulcie's baby was crying fretfully.

"I—I didn't get anything," Jim said, the shamed hurt in his voice catching at Virgie's heart.

"It doesn't matter," she told him. "I don't know as I'd like living in Kansas City, anyway. Maybe you'll get something closer to home."

She knew he caught the sick futility of hope in her voice. He wouldn't get work closer to home, and they both might as well face it. People went right on living the pattern they were born to. All the families she knew did, and had, as far back as anyone could remember. The Kenzies in the Uplands were born to a pattern of plenty, and kept to it. And the Wrathers and the Meadors down in the Bottoms had their pattern as well, and it was foolish to think they could escape it. But these things she did not say to Jim.

"You'll get a place," she repeated valiantly.

But he didn't. The only thing that made him different from other Bottoms men was that he kept on trying. In the meanwhile, he worked his own melon patch and scrap of ground, putting away every extra penny he could get. He did odd jobs, but in the summer this was no good, for town boys got out and worked then.

Virgie tried hard not to worry. This was a little easier because she was almost too busy with Dulcie's baby to have time to think.

The baby was two years old now, and had never been strong. It was a thin and scrawny little thing, its hands mere claws, and in its sad eyes all the ageless sorrows of the world were reflected. There wasn't money to buy him all the milk he needed, but even what they were able to get did not agree with him. Virgie did the best she could for him, knowing an immense and pitying tenderness for the motherless little thing.

Dulcie had died when the baby came. Dr. Burgess came down and did the best he could, but he could not save her. He said he couldn't explain it, but she just sort of seemed to lose the wish to live. He said it to Virgie, who helped him.

Virgie didn't want to help, but Ma was down with the misery in her back, and there was no one else. Although she was only sixteen and too young for the responsibility, Dr. Burgess turned to Virgie as if she were a woman grown. The girl conquered her fear and horror enough to do the things he asked of her. But all they did was no use. Dulcie died.

"Of course," Dr. Burgess said wearily, "she wasn't built for childbearing, but that wasn't the main trouble. She just gave up—"

It was no wonder, Virgie thought, that she gave up. Nobody ought to have to suffer like that. God ought to think of some other way to get babies here. By this time, Dulcie had seen the pattern that life held for her and for her child. And when the pain came, she no longer wanted to live.

Virgie took over the care of the baby, and as she did so, a tremendous resolution grew within her. Until Jim had a job—a real one, outside the Bottoms—they would not marry. She would not bring into the world another life to suffer as Bottoms children suffered. If she lived and died an old maid—narrow and warped and the butt of all the community jokes—she still would not marry Jim unless they could offer something more to their children than they themselves had known.

It was in her eighteenth summer that she knew all the bitterness of frustration and dead hope. That was the summer she gave up.

It was August of that summer when Old Dade Kenzie came riding down to the Bottoms, looking for melons. Usually he had fairly good ones on his own place, but this year the bugs had got them. Jim waited on him, courteously and efficiently, and Old Dade eyed him sharply. Presently he asked,

"Haven't I met you somewhere before?"

Jim said yes, they had met. At Camp Meeting, a couple of years ago they had sat together. Dade said yes—of course, he remembered. The way he eyed Jim, a body could tell he had something on his mind, but he rode off without saying anything. It wasn't more than a day or two later until he came back. He said, looking at Jim shrewdly,

"Know a good man I can get to work for me?"

"I might," Jim replied, keeping his own voice level.

"I'd want a married man," Dade said. "They stay better. I'd furnish a house and a cow. You could raise chickens, and have a garden. I'd want someone I could depend on. Pretty good thing for the right man."

He named a salary.

"I think I know just the right man," Jim told him. "Me."

Old Dade chuckled. "I hoped you'd say that," he said. "I've been asking around about you, and you sound good. But where's the wife?"

"I'll have her," Jim grinned, "when I move in."

"That nice little girl that was with you at Camp Meeting that night?"

Jim said yes, thinking how wonderful it was that he should remember. People said he never forgot anything, and they were right.

The old man was scarcely out of sight, before Jim was over telling Virgie about it. She was alone when he came in, with an expression on his face as she had never seen there before. He tried to explain, but could not get the words out fast enough, telling the last part first, and then filling in the details. They talked about it almost in whispers, as if it were a dream to wake from.

"A house and a cow—"

"And we can raise chickens—"

"That's right—and flowers. I'll have some cosmos, and this time they'll grow—"

"How about it, honey—"

"Yes—oh, yes—Jim—"

He kissed her, and she kissed him. They were grown-up people planning a future so real and substantial they could almost reach out and touch it. This was the wedge into a new life for them—this was a marriage, and a home, and all the things that went with them. This was self-respect and dignity.

They were married the next day by a real minister. He was kind and pleasant, not indicating in any way that Virgie and Jim seemed any different from all the hopefully happy young people that came to him. The minister's wife had flowers in the room, and afterwards she had lemonade and cake. She said she had just baked a fresh one, so she put it in the middle of the table, with flowers all around it, and made Virgie and Jim cut it together. Then they drove over to Dade Kenzie's, proud and happy, and said there they were, and asked what he wanted them to do.

He looked at them shrewdly, taking in their bright happiness and their tremulous wonder at the good fortune that had come to them. He said they could go right over to the house and move in. Jim could take off a couple of days to help his wife get things in order. He wished them every happiness, and called out his granddaughter-in-law, Mrs. Mark Kenzie, to meet them. Mrs. Beulah came, her dark eyes glowing with kindness and good will. She leaned over to kiss the new bride, wishing her great happiness. Virgie would near-about die for Mrs. Beulah, she had been so good to them. She was the kindest woman in the world, and the best.

The four rooms of the tenant house into which Jim and Virgie moved were all clean and bright, with fresh paint and paper. Mrs. Beulah sent over some things for them to use—chairs and a table and a bed and dresser to supplement the few things already there. There was a magic wonder about fixing up the house. Such richness of spirit came to Virgie, just looking at the place. Four rooms, for the two of them! She used to waken in the night, gloating over all those rooms. She got bright-flowered stuff at the store and covered old boxes to make a nice settee kind of a thing in the living room and a dressing table in her bedroom. She found a picture in a magazine that showed how to make side drapes out of the flowered stuff, so she made them, too. Mrs. Beulah came over to see the house and said it was all lovely, and you could tell she meant it, too. She looked into the dining room where Virgie had the table all set for supper, napkins and silver and everything in place, the way she had learned how to do in cooking class at school.

"My goodness, Virgie," Mrs. Beulah said, "do you eat in the dining room all the time? That makes a lot more work for you, you know."

Virgie said they ate dinner and supper there. She didn't mind the work. It got pretty hot in the kitchen. She didn't tell Mrs. Beulah that never before in her life had she known what it meant to eat in a dining room. It was one of the chief symbols of the new life into which she and Jim had come.

Old Dade came often to see them. Once he happened by just at dinner time, so Jim asked him to stay and eat with them. Virgie's heart sang with pride that Jim could feel free to ask.

Jim would have died before he would have asked a Kenzie to eat with his folks in the Bottoms, but now he knew that while there might not be anything awfully fancy on the table, everything would be clean and neat and appetizing.

Virgie guessed that was one of the proudest moments of her life. When Old Dade came in, all she had to do by way of getting ready was to set another plate. There was even a small vase of bittersweet in the center of the table. She could see Old Dade's eyes taking it all in, knowing that the old man realized that this was the way she and Jim did *all* the time. People said you could drop into the Kenzies' any time, and find things nice and smooth, with everything in order and plenty of good food cooked up. They could say that about the Meadors, too. Her heart was like to burst with the happiness of it.

That next summer, she and Jim made a garden, and raised chickens. As things came on, she canned—fruits and vegetables of all kinds. They hardly needed to buy anything at the stores with her shelves so full. Old Dade had given them a hog, so they had hams and bacon and all their own lard.

They had been married a little over a year when she knew that she was going to have a baby.

At first it was wonderful. She and Jim would sit up late, planning the most marvelous things for the baby. That winter was a hard one; it snowed often and much, but the sound of the storm outside only served to give them a feeling of security. She began sewing. Mrs. Beulah said maybe there were some things around the big house, but Virgie said no, she had all she needed. This baby was to have no seconds, no clothes that had belonged to somebody else. That smacked too much of the Bottoms way of doing things. This was a Meadors baby, and she and Jim would provide all the things needful for it. It was March before she began to admit the dark specter of fear which, really, had been there all the time, crowded back into the far corners of her mind by the great happiness she and Jim knew. She was afraid she would die when the baby came. She brooded over it until, finally, Jim sensed her fear, and she had to tell him.

"Milly Fenner died," she pointed out.

"Milly didn't have the right kind of care," Jim reminded her. "There never was more than a shadow to her, and then she didn't take any care of herself."

"She was too poor," Virgie said. And then she added, "Dulcie died. She was big and strong."

Now that was the basis of her fear. Dulcie had been larger than Virgie, and stronger. Virgie wanted this baby more than anything else in the world, but, remembering Dulcie, she wondered if she were brave enough to get it here. Jim, in the depth of his awkward man-knowledge of the affair, tried to comfort her.

"You were just a kid when that happened to Dulcie. You hadn't ought to have been there, but you were. Try to forget it, now. It won't be that way for you."

It was soon after that that he made arrangements for her to stay in the hospital, thinking that would make her feel better. In a way, it did. She tried hard to hide from Jim the way she felt, for he was like a frightened child in the face of any fear of hers. It would have been better if she could have talked with Old Dade, even if he was a man. For Dade was their luck. Without him they were nothing. Whatever they had of peace or prosperity or dignity or worth was due to him. Without him they were sure of nothing, not even a job. Now he lay dead in the big house, and with him had fallen her last bulwark against fear.

She lay very still now, thinking that it didn't much matter what happened to her, or to her baby. It had been foolish of her to think that she could cheat the pattern of life and be different from her folks, anyway. You lived your life the way it came to you, not the way you wanted it to be. She and Jim were caught now, for sure. Old Dade was gone, and it was just as well if she gave up, too. Maybe it was better if her baby didn't get born. There wasn't anything ahead of him, with things the way they were. People were selfish to bring babies into a world where there was nothing but trouble—pain and worry and scramble for jobs as long as they lived. People lived, knowing nothing but trouble, and then they died. That was the pattern.

For a while she had thought that her baby was the thing she could shape into all her own dreams for a good life. The baby would be strong and wise and happy. Now, she realized that people seldom knew complete joy in their children. Even Old Dade—how did he feel about his? Not one of his boys was as smart as he had been; not one had his drive and force. Tom was a little fuss-budget, a small, opinionated man who, by himself, could never have made good. His father gave him a farm when he married—all stocked, and ready for use—and even now staked him to extra improvements like new barns or tight fences or some fancy and expensive implement. Without this, he would have been nothing. She'd have liked to have seen Tom Kenzie get out and scratch for a living, the way Jim had to.

Mr. Ben did manage a little more on his own hook, but he didn't have as much money, or as good a place, as Tom Kenzie did. They said Old Dade had always wanted a daughter, and then the only one he had, died when she was just a child. She knew he would have liked, although he never mentioned it, for the Mark Kenzies to have a boy so the name would go on. But, although they had been married eight years, now, there was still no child and no promise of one. The old man seemed to love Mrs. Beulah as if she were his very own, but people said he was fondest of all of the one in California, the one called Allison. Virgie wondered how he felt when the story about the trouble between her and her husband came out in the papers a month or so ago. Surely he hated knowing that she was having a bad time. Then there was the boy they called Barry, off in Chicago.

FRIDAY

They said he sat with his nose buried in a book all the time, and told the most miraculous stories when he came home.

No, Dade hadn't got a great deal of pleasure out of his children and grandchildren. Mostly, they were just ordinary people. Not so good-looking as their father had been, and no great shakes in the community, aside from what came of their father's influence. She wondered if the old man ever dreamed of the sort of children he might have had—boys who built bridges and made laws and ran banks. Men who had power and dreamed great dreams and had the will and force to push these dreams through to reality. And now he was dead, without ever having realized these dreams he might have had.

And she was dying.

She knew it, for true. And she didn't care a bit. She'd let go. It was easier than fighting, easier than facing things. It was very pleasant, now that she had made up her mind to go. Soft, like drifting on clouds. She could hear the stir and the confusion of the neighbor women, rushing about. Presently she was conscious, dimly, of someone else in the room. She couldn't tell for sure, but she thought it was Dr. Burgess. They were foolish to trouble him. He couldn't do anything for her now, and she knew it.

Someone kept calling her. It was a great nuisance. Why couldn't people let her alone. When people called you, you had to answer. Couldn't they see she didn't feel like answering anyone. Goodness, it was Jim calling. He sounded like a lost child, crying for his mother.

"Virgie—" he kept saying. "Virgie—" Over and over he said it.

Maybe she'd better come back, just for a moment, and let him know she heard him.

V

MISS LAURA MEEKS walked briskly down the street, a market basket over her arm. If she found any blooming flowers, she might as well take them now, for if she waited until morning it might rain and spoil them. She had no patience with people who dilly-dallied over their work. She always pitched in and did a thing as soon as it needed to be done. If she put things off, she would have no rest. That was why she felt bad about not getting to see Rose Marshall, even though the delay wasn't really her fault. She would go Saturday afternoon, as soon as the services were over. It was her duty to do it. If she put it off, no telling what would happen. Anything could come of that trip George Marshall was meaning to make Monday.

She wished she had a nickel for every time she had walked down this very street. She had been born in the same house she now lived in, seventy-eight years ago come August. Grandpa Meeks had lived there before her. She could remember him well —an old man with a great white beard sweeping down over his chest, and gnarled, blue-veined hands which he kept crossed over his cane. Everyone still called her house the old Meeks place, and, thank heaven, they weren't going to call it anything else as long as she lived. She had no patience with people who sold their homes and went traipsing off somewhere else to live. They didn't amount to very much in their own community, or they wouldn't be so willing to rush away from it.

Look at the old families. They didn't have any pride left. There was a time when they all hung together—the Meekses, and the Marshalls, and the Kenzies, and a few more families that really mattered. They visited among themselves and they married among themselves, and they kept trash outside, where they belonged. People had stopped doing that now. That was the reason such awful things happened. When she was a girl, a man in George Marshall's position wouldn't have looked in Rose Carney's direction, meaning to do right by her. And now here he was, married to her, and her belonging to the church and going to Kansas City to buy all her clothes, and having a maid in the kitchen. She'd even had a trip to California, and one to New York.

It made a person sick, remembering who Rose Marshall was, and where she came from. Her grandfather was old Tod Carney, and he had been a bushwhacker. It was common talk. Papa knew it. He had said,

"Well, I see George Marshall is after old Tod's granddaughter. He'd better not fool around there unless he means business. The old man will take a shotgun to him—he's had plenty of practice."

Maybe George had been born too late to know what being a bushwhacker meant. Trash of the earth, that was what they were. The veriest scum, who ravaged the country during *The War*. Papa knew all about them, and used to tell her stories of them. Papa kept his Confederate uniform until the day of his death, and after he was gone, she put it away in the attic in moth balls. On holidays he used to get that uniform out and walk downtown in it. Such times he'd remember things that happened during *The War*. One of these stories was about how he saw Tod Carney and a bunch of bushwhackers set fire to a barn, and make off with all the horses in it.

But George was bound to have Rose anyway, and when a man gets marrying in his head, there is no talking sense or reason to him.

Rose Carney had been one of those white, still kind. A man looking at her thinks she's an angel, and moves heaven and earth to get her, while all the time she just sits still, waiting for him to come and take her. Once a man gets a girl like that he's likely to find she's more dead than alive and that maybe it was just plain dumbness, and not some deep, tantalizing secret about her, that made her sit so quiet and ladylike, waiting for him. He'd get her, only to find that all she could do was to sit and look beautiful and remote—she couldn't cook or keep house or talk about a frazzling thing a man wanted to hear. Then he'd have her on his hands for the rest of his life—placid and quiet and about as interesting as a serving of cold bread pudding. Rose Marshall was like that. It was no wonder that George was out looking somewhere else. But that didn't excuse him. He had no business marrying her in the first place if he didn't mean to stick by her. Now that he had married her, he ought to make the best of things. A man ought to have to pay for his foolishness.

And George had paid. They bought just about everything in Kansas City. George had said his wife was too pretty to wear ordinary things. She was pretty enough, if a body liked someone with no expression or energy—just a doll-like look that never changed. Rose had even kept her good looks till this day, after a fashion. She still had a fairly nice complexion, but her eyes were sort of faded. Come to think of it, she had a faded-out appearance all over. That's what came of being trash. They didn't keep their looks. And if ever a woman had a chance to stay young, it was Rose Marshall. There hadn't been a day since her marriage that she was without help in the kitchen.

Goodness knows, it wasn't lack of time that kept Rose from keeping up with George. She just didn't know how to do a thing in the world but sit and look pretty. She probably wouldn't know the first thing to do, once she did find out about Marta Sloan. But whether she did anything or not, it was still Miss Laura's duty to tell her how things were. She'd do it, first thing after services tomorrow. She ought to go today, but she had a chance to go out to the Kenzie place, and she wasn't going to miss it. They said Allison would be there by noon, and she wanted to see the girl.

Miss Laura bet that Allison would come in just as brazen as if nothing in the world had happened. She'd never let on that her picture, and the picture of that writer husband of hers, had been plastered all over the brown section of the *Star*, saying how they were separated and were planning a divorce. Divorce, indeed! Divorce was the work of the devil. People got married now like they bought spring hats, thinking they could either make an exchange or buy a new one next season if this didn't suit. She had known that marriage of Allison's wouldn't last. The girl was too independent and self-willed to get along with anyone, let alone a husband. Besides he was just a foreigner—a Czech. Nobody had hardly heard of his country until Allison Kenzie popped up married to him. Probably carried a stiletto. No—she guessed it was Italians, and not Czechs, who did that. He had seemed right nice, that time they were home together. She couldn't ever be sure whether he was laughing at her or not, but he had been real polite and fitted in well, considering how different he was.

Maybe it was a lot Allison's fault that they were getting a divorce. The first time that girl was crossed, she'd surely fly her kite, never thinking what a horrible thing divorce was. Yes, it was probably a lot Allison's fault. Miss Laura never would forget the way the girl had acted that time about the speech for Children's Day. And Dade and Ellie had upheld her. It was their fault, really, that the girl grew up not getting along with anyone.

Flowers weren't so easy to get now—the spring had been too late and wet. There were some early roses out. And, of course, whatever she used, she'd mix honeysuckle in with it.

Dade had loved honeysuckle. It was sixty years ago this spring that Dade Kenzie had asked Laura Meeks for their first date. She had never gone anywhere with a boy before, so Papa and Mama had been in quite a twitter about it. They had bought her a new dress—a white China silk, made with a grown-up bustle and low neck and short sleeves. At first, Papa had thought the neck was a little too low, but when he saw how pretty she looked, he gave in.

She had been a pretty girl. She knew she had been. And that was the night she felt the loveliest of her whole life. Pretty inside, even, and soft and gentle, and sure of herself. She could shut her eyes, even now and remember that loveliness of hers—and of the spring evening, which was full of a sort of misty beauty, with flowers blooming, and just a hint of rain in the air. When Dade came for her, Papa met him at the door and the two men talked a minute, the way it was proper for the father and the escort of the girl to do. After a few minutes, she went into the room, and Dade stood up, and in his eyes she could see that he thought she was pretty, too. Her hair was soft and brown and curly then, and she had blue eyes—as blue as Rose Marshall's, but with more character in them—and her skin was good. She was so excited that her cheeks were all pink. Dade said he had the horse and buggy outside, but they decided to walk, since the party was only a few doors away.

Just at the Meekses' front gate was a honeysuckle bush. Dade looked at it and said it was his favorite flower, and she said that was funny, it was hers, too. They stood still by the bush, bound by the wonder that they both liked honeysuckle best of all.

"Want me to get you some?" he asked.

She said it was sort of high up, and hard to get. And he said that didn't matter a bit, if she wanted it. He got out his pocketknife and began cutting sprigs. The fragrance was simply wonderful. He handed her a spray and she reached up to tuck it into her hair. And then he put one in his buttonhole. They went on to the party, each wearing the same kind of flower. All evening it set them apart from the others, linking them together in a oneness both felt. Others felt it, too, nodding their heads wisely at the sight.

In a box at the bottom of her trunk, along with Papa's and Mama's pictures and copies of their obituaries, there was still a faded and brittle little flower, so brown and discolored that no one but her could ever know it was a piece of the honeysuckle Dade had picked for her sixty years ago.

The bush still grew at the front gate, and each year when it blossomed she remembered once more that long-distant evening when she was young and the world was young and Dade was so close to loving her that a push as slight as gossamer would have won him for her. She wondered if he had ever remembered it, too.

Tomorrow, when they buried Dade Kenzie, there would be the flower he had loved all around. She would see to that. She, Laura Meeks, who had shared its loveliness with him before Ellie knew he was in this world, would place it there with her own hands.

~ VI ~

CHARLEY VANE sat down on the grass to rest. Maybe he was a stubborn old fool for insisting on having his way about the matter, but he was glad now he had dug this grave mostly by himself. Let them think he was getting childish if they wanted to. Folks didn't look very close into other people's minds, anyway. Mostly they were too busy thinking about themselves. If they saw you at all, they thought there was no more to your thoughts than they could see on the surface. If you were old and bent and gnarled, like him, they dismissed you carelessly, thinking your mind was empty of all wishes, or dreams, or knowledge of beauty. Usually they were too occupied to think of you at all.

He could remember one time he was working out here at the cemetery when some of the Marshall kin from Kansas City drove up to bring some flowers. It was a rainy day—not a hard driving rain, but a soft summer one that looked like it was falling out of a gray chiffon sky. He had gone into the tool house to be out of it, although he really didn't mind getting wet. Rain in summer had a vital, growing touch to it that made people all the better for having it fall on them.

There he stood, looking out at the soft gray rain, slanting down over gray stones. Somewhere close a turtledove was calling, soft and mournful-like. There was about the whole thing a delicate gray beauty, of sense and of sound. And while he was feeling like maybe he and the Creator himself were sort of talking the thing over, up drove a bunch of women.

"Will you take these flowers and put them on the Marshall lot for us?" one of them asked, just like she was talking to a servant. "I hate to get out in the rain."

He stepped over to take them from her, and she handed him, not only the wreath, but a dollar bill as well. The money he handed back to her. He did not take tips. That was a city way of doing things. Out here, one man was as good as another, and all you paid folks for doing was a good, honest day's work. He and Old Man Marshall had been friends. They had gone to the same church and bought things at the same store. He knew his work out here in the cemetery as well, and did it as thoroughly, as ever Mr. Marshall did his at the bank.

The woman looked kind of funny at him, but she took the dollar, and then they drove off. They had no way of knowing that he was standing there thinking a poem when they came. If they thought of him at all, they saw only a small, bent man, silent and maybe a little surly, whose mind was as gray and empty as the day.

By and by, he took the flowers over to place them on the Marshall graves, thinking it a funny thing, the way the Marshalls did. They had their lot all walled off with an iron fence, painted white. There was a gate to it, and inside, there were iron benches for folks to sit on when they came out. Only, nobody ever stayed there long enough to use those seats. That was the older Marshalls—they thought they could shut out the rest of the world, even in death. But, only last week, at the meeting of the Cemetery Board, they had said the fence had to come down. Stuck up there in the middle the way it was, it made it too hard to cut the grass. So he guessed it wouldn't be long until that Marshall fence got hauled off for junk.

Death was a great leveler, all right. As far as that went, life was, too. Neither did it of themselves—it was time that did the business, and life and death both got their share. Here was a Marshall, married to a Carney. He wondered if the Marshalls, lying alone and proud in their walled-in section, ever knew that over in the far section of the cemetery, where the paupers' graves were, there was a sunken grave that held all the mortal remains of Hez Carney, Rose Marshall's great-grandfather. Charley doubted if anybody besides himself and the Carneys knew it was there. And he wasn't going to tell.

What was the use of telling? Mrs. George Marshall couldn't help what her folks were. She had always been nice to him, never giving herself airs just because she happened to have married George Marshall. Why should he set a pack of hounds on her trail by telling something that happened more'n sixty years ago, and wasn't anybody's discredit when it did. The Carneys were just dirt-poor then, and when the old man died they slipped out and buried him without even having a church service. He just happened to run across the grave himself, years ago, while the writing on the wooden marker was still legible. Now, nobody could tell who was buried there, and Charley just kept the information stored away in his mind, the way he did a lot of other things about the people around here.

Sometimes Charley thought he knew more about people than anybody else here did—even more than their own families, or Doc Burgess, or Brother Kilgore. They carried people just so far, and after that he took over. When you did his kind of work, you got over being squeamish. He saw the things most people didn't know about death, or, knowing them, tried to forget.

They didn't used to be so careful about marking off lots and sometimes now when he dug down—well, he knew more than most about death, and the things it did to the bodies people loved and cherished. In spite of that, maybe even because of it, he didn't have any fears about life—what it amounted to here on earth, and what came after it.

Life was good, just the living of it. Being born, and growing into a consciousness of the wheeling change of the seasons—spring marching into summer, summer into fall, fall into winter, and then back to spring again. Seeing that, you knew life had to be a circle—that death just sort of rounded out life. Knowing people was good, and eating and sleeping—and waking to dawns that sang like wine in your veins. Loving was good—yes, it was good even when it brought hurt and misunderstanding and tears. Work was good, and rest after work. Trouble and sorrow were good, for after them came resignation and peace.

Even death was good. It was good because it was the natural end of life, and part of the pattern. People were born, and they grew old, and then they died. It was their bodies that died, like the dried-up husks of corn when the kernel within had grown sweet and ripe for harvest. Better than most, he knew that bodies did not matter. They were nothing at all, save a house for the thing that man really was. A person got old and tired of his body, and he shucked it off because he no longer needed it to protect the inner heart of him.

Old folks died, and made way for future generations. Why shouldn't they? They had had their turn at a good thing, and now it was time to go on. Life was a privilege everyone had a right to—the ones that had gone on before and the ones that were here now and the teeming millions yet to come. He had noticed that usually when a person died in the community, a baby was born soon after to take the place of the one that had gone on. They said Jim Meadors' wife was mighty sick—might die, and the baby with her. But he bet she wouldn't. That

Meador baby would probably get into the world, all right. More than likely it would be a man-child, one to take Dade's place. The Lord sort of took care of things like that—keeping all the intricate parts of the universe spinning in their own places, and the people on the earth balanced and working things out according to his plan.

Lots of times people got excited and thought things were all going to wrack and ruin. They'd scream to high heaven that the world and the people in it were doomed. Charley never got excited at such talk. Things worked out. They always had, and they always would. Wars and plagues and panics and floods and droughts came. Bad men got into power, and everyone thought sure they'd ruin the country. But people lived through these things, and sort of scrapped a lot of bad things they maybe wouldn't even have noticed unless the hard things had come along to show them up. People made mistakes—awful ones—and then righted themselves and went on again, knowing they'd learned a lot from the mistakes they made.

It was like he heard a preacher say one time—one that was preaching from an awfully good text. Something about the Lord restoring the years that the locust had eaten. He said it meant that the Lord would give people a chance to straighten things out, even after they had made the worst kind of a mess. He said that, since the Lord had to work through people, he had to give them lots of chances to make good, just like a mother had to give her child more than one chance to learn a thing.

Charley liked to remember this, because it was what he believed. Things worked out. No mistake was final. Nobody's life was ever wasted. Lots of times people, in their blindness, thought somebody, or something, was utterly without use. But people didn't always know. Lots of them, even the smartest ones, couldn't see beyond their own noses, sometimes.

Saturday

~ I ~

EVEN before Elaine and Henry drove into the driveway at Uncle Dade's, she knew that Barry was already there. A dozen or more cars were parked—from Ez Dowlin's battered wreck to the shiny ones belonging to the more prosperous neighbors. The Kentucky license meant that some of Uncle Dade's nieces and their families had already got in. She did not have to see, however, the Illinois license to make her know that the gray convertible with the dark blue leather cushions was Barry's. No man here would have driven it, or trusted it had he done so. But Barry liked the car—the soft blending of blue and gray coloring, the slim, clean lines of the body, the feel of the wheel under his hands. Because he did like it, he drove it home, not even realizing that it was just another link in the long chain of events which marked him as one apart from the rest of the family.

Elaine smoothed the folds of her new dress nervously, knowing it was not right for the occasion, telling herself she didn't care if it wasn't. Yesterday, in Rockwell, she had seen it in the window and had stopped short, unable to pass it by. Henry, seeing her eyes upon it, said,

"Go in and buy it. Might as well—"

She did not mean to buy it at all, but she went in, as one in a dream, and asked the price. The woman said why didn't she just try it on, and, even before the dress slipped down over her thin body, she knew she would buy it.

It was a white background, with flowers deeply blue scattered about on it. That, in itself, was not remarkable. But the miracle was that it should be, in pattern and design, almost the exact duplicate of a dress she had had years ago. They said if you kept a thing seven years it came back into style. It had been more than twice seven years since Uncle Dade had brought that dress home from Kansas City to her. It was so very becoming that the old man was pleased with her, and with the gift, and with himself for thinking of it.

Uncle Dade's opinion did not matter so much. The important thing was that Barry liked it. Ellie found some blue velvet ribbon the color of the flowers in the dress, and she and Elaine had made bows for the girl's hair. When she came downstairs wearing the new dress, Old Dade got to his feet and eyed her appreciatively.

"Well, well," he said to Ellie, "just look at our girl. Looks like we have a beauty on our hands."

It was seldom he called her "our girl." Although he was never unkind to her, never even impatient, there was always in his relations with her the lack of warmth and that richly personal note he seemed to feel for Allison, and later, for Beulah.

Just then Barry came in, dressed for church. He had grown very fast that year, so Ellie had bought him a new suit. It fitted him well, molding his slender frame to show all its supple grace. Barry had never come to the awkward stage through which most boys had to go—his hands and feet did his bidding, and he made no fumbling motions that upset things. He carried himself with the light and easy grace of a young fawn, or of a reed swaying in the wind. He had not been strong enough to know the hard and grueling labor of the farm which sets its awkward seal upon the adolescent.

Seeing Elaine in her new dress, he stopped short,

" 'Oh, saw ye the lass with the bonnie blue een?' " he began, as always, to quote poetry.

Elaine stood there, dimpling, feeling very flustered and pretty, and happier than she had ever been before in her life. They were in the kitchen, and about the room there was a pleasant, Sunday sort of excitement—Dade in his best white

SATURDAY

shirt and Ellie rushing around, hat already on, seeing to the last minute things, so dinner would be easier to get once they were home from church.

"No—" Barry said, "that's not good enough. I'll write one of my own."

During the sermon, he paid scant heed to the preacher's words, but kept scribbling on a sheet of paper he had taken from his pocket. Elaine thought for sure Uncle Dade would call him down—the old man was pretty strict about behaving in church. When church was over, Barry handed her the piece of paper he had been writing on.

It was a poem. Even though she knew by heart every word of it, she still looked at it sometimes—if the day had been unusually hard, or she felt ill, or Henry was even duller than usual. The paper, broken and yellow from handling, had a musty smell about it. She did not need to look at it to remember what he had written—about how the skies were jealous of her eyes, and had stopped trying to be really blue any more, and the forget-me-nots turned pale with envy, seeing her. So many times had she read it that now the very feel of the paper was comforting and reassuring.

Yesterday, when she had seen this other dress, so like the one she wore years ago, it all came back to her. And, scarcely conscious of what she was doing, she had bought it. Henry, seeing it, said,

"Seems to me you had one like this a long time ago. I remember you looked awful pretty in it."

She did not want Henry to remember that other dress. Because it belonged to a time when she was not conscious of him at all, she did not like to think that even his memory of her could intrude upon that period.

She had on her new dress today, even though she knew Miss Laura Meeks would certainly talk about her for wearing anything so gay at a time like this. She wondered if everyone felt about Miss Laura as she did. Sometimes, as a little girl, she had a queer, mixed-up notion that God and Miss Laura were both watching her with an equally omnipresent eye, perhaps even with a slight advantage going to the woman who was, at least, visibly on the job.

So calm and impersonal had been Elaine's acceptance of Henry on the occasion of that long-ago proposal that she had been lulled into a sense of false security, thinking the rest of it would be equally easy. Over Aunt Ellie's protests that she would love nothing better than to give Elaine the sort of wedding she had always hoped she'd be able to give a daughter of her own, she insisted on having a very simple wedding, and Henry had upheld her. They were married one dull November afternoon, with only Tom and Ben and their families present. Elaine would not even allow Ellie to write Barry about it until it was all over. She said if he knew, he'd be sure to think he ought to come home for it, and there was no need, as simple as everything was going to be.

Through her own numbness, Elaine was conscious of the look on Henry's face—a strange mixture of simple dignity, incredulous happiness, and great tenderness. It helped her to go through with her part—through the ceremony and the good wishes that followed. It helped her to cut the cake that Ellie had insisted on, and to be casual about the parting that came when they were ready to leave. At last it was all over and she and Henry were driving to his home. No wedding trip, no pretenses that their marriage was like other people's. Henry understood the terms on which he was taking her, and he was content.

The house to which he took her was new and clean and bare. He had built it recently, buying only the barest necessities because he thought Elaine would want to fix it up to suit herself. There was food in the cupboard, and she set about preparing a meal—awkwardly, for she had never learned much of cooking.

Henry helped her, talking little. Together they sat down to eat, silent as strangers. His very quietness was, however, reassuring and soothing to Elaine. The day had been hard for her, and now to sit here in the cool stillness, making no effort to talk, needing to make no pretenses about the situation, was good. Henry said it was a beautiful night, scarcely cold at all, and maybe it wouldn't even frost. Elaine said, absently, that was fine. He said he was going to gather corn tomorrow in the east eighty, and she only nodded to that. By the time she began to wash dishes, the calmness had begun to do its work; she was relaxed and almost content. Henry wiped them for her, putting them back into the shelves the way he kept things when he was alone, and she made no attempt even to see what order he followed. Just as they got the last dish put away, the noise started.

At first, it was a great clatter of tin cans and then a ringing of bells. Someone fired a shotgun. Voices sounded then, as people began coming toward the house. Elaine turned stricken eyes toward Henry, and he said a single word, "Charivari—"

The charivari! She had forgotten this would be sure to happen. Into the midst of the quiet and calmness, the dignity which had marked the opening of their life together, this thing was intruding. Until it came, their marriage had been a private affair, something concerning only the two of them. Now it was a public exhibition, dragged out for all the community to see. She shrank, white-faced, against the wall.

Henry was looking at her strangely. Finally, he said, "We'll have to go to the door."

"Yes—" Elaine said. "Yes—"

She wiped her shaking hands on a dish towel, untied her apron, rolled down the sleeves of her wedding dress which she had not bothered to change before preparing supper. When she was finished, they walked together to the door, and Henry opened it.

"Hello," he said. "Come in—"

They came in. Mostly, it was the younger people of the community, with an occasional more mature person. There was a great deal of horseplay, many sly jests. If any of them noticed that Elaine had not yet even spoken to her visitors, they probably laid it to maidenly shyness. Henry was in complete charge, a great happiness upon his plain face. He had won the girl he loved and was the head of a household now. These people, his friends and neighbors, were here, carrying out the age-old custom of the community. Always, people went to charivari newly married couples. He had anticipated this very thing, and had provided for it.

"I got some pop and stuff to eat around here. Of course, I wasn't looking for you folks, or anything like that—"

A great laugh greeted his statement.

He got the soda pop and began opening the bottles, his strong hands flipping bottle caps as if they were made of paper. He got plates and stacked store cookies on them, Elaine still saying nothing, making no effort to help him. People ate and drank, went on with their loud talking and their jests.

With every passing moment, the horror of it engulfed Elaine more completely. These people came, assuming that this marriage was like any other, that she and Henry were lovers. For the first time since the ceremony, she realized that she was actually married. *Married*, to this stocky, clumsy boy whom she scarcely knew. It was as if she saw him for the first time now— the mahogany-brown face that, even in winter, did not fade out to a normal shade; the too-white forehead; the crooked front tooth; the thick stubby hands. The fact of her marriage came to her, with the sullen, final click of a jail door closing. She stood stiffly at Henry's side, bidding them all good-by. And when the last one had gone, she turned back into the room and sat down in a chair, dropping her head on the table. There, with the cookie plates and empty pop bottles around her, she broke into wild weeping.

SATURDAY

"Elaine," he said, touching her shoulder awkwardly. "Elaine—"

She drew back. No need for pretense now. She was his wife and she could not bear him to touch her, even in impersonal kindness. He drew back his hand, letting it fall lifelessly at his side. When she was finally quiet, he said,

"You're sick, Elaine. Go upstairs to bed. I'll stay down here and clean up the mess."

She went upstairs, so blinded with tears that she passed by the room Henry had got ready for her. Not until the next morning did she see the preparations he had made—a vase of fall flowers on the small table, a new footstool near an easy chair, magazines and books lying around. Tonight she passed this up, going on to the other bedroom which was small, and unaired. By and by, she heard Henry come upstairs and go quietly to his own room. And presently she fell into exhausted sleep.

When she came downstairs the next morning, he was already gone. Coffee was still warm in the pot, and on a plate lay a slice of ham, cut ready for frying. By the time he came in at noon she had herself under control, and had prepared a meal of sorts and had moved her things to his room. As if nothing out of the ordinary had happened, they took up the pattern of their life together. Henry took her as she was. If he had ever been sorry of his bargain, he had given no indication of it. Always, he sought to please her, to do things as she would have them, never questioning any of her wishes. Today he had driven her to the place where she would meet the person whose image had filled her life. He had done this as unquestioningly as he did everything else connected with their life together.

"Do you want to get out here at the front," Henry asked now, "or go 'round to the back gate?"

Elaine said to drive around to the back. She'd go to the kitchen first, for she had a bowl of Jello to take in. There was a subdued stir and bustle as she walked into the kitchen. Already women were there, working on the lunch. Beulah was in charge.

"Oh, come in, Elaine," Beulah said. "Put your bowl there on the table. Fruit Jello—that's good. There are always some people who don't feel like eating much, and this may tempt them."

Elaine stood looking uncertainly about her. Everything had about it a sense of arrested motion—as if, for a brief period, time itself was frozen into a pattern of solidity. Feelings, thoughts, emotions—even the ordinary humdrum acts of regular living, such as washing dishes and doing chores—all had the curious unreality of a dream. It was like a play she had once been in. The things she said and did in it had no relation to her life, really, yet they became so much a part of her that she felt that perhaps, for the first time in her life, she was really herself.

She could not move without feeling the presence of Uncle Dade. He was more vivid, more real, than the women who were present, helping in the kitchen. She could not understand how they could be so occupied with food at a time like this. Food, in this house, was always connected with Uncle Dade. Aunt Ellie might prepare it, or direct its preparation and serving, but it was always with her husband's tastes in mind. No meal could start without him. Either he asked the blessing, or directed who was to act in his place. Always, the main dish was set before him, and he served the plates. She wondered how anyone could begin the meal today without him.

"Let me help," she said to Beulah now.

"It's a pity to be working here in the kitchen in that pretty dress," Beulah said. "Why don't you go into the living room and meet the people who come? Somebody ought to do that."

Elaine said no, quickly. She knew she could not go into the living room, for Barry might be there and she did not feel equal to facing him just yet.

"I'll get you an apron if you are going to help in here," Beulah said, accepting, as she always did, anyone else's wishes.

SATURDAY

Elaine, knowing she should have brought her own apron, took the one Beulah handed her. Other women always brought their own, carrying them in newspapers, putting them in with their baskets of food, or in their purses. But Elaine could never remember to do it. She wasn't much help, anyway. She had no knack for household tasks.

She realized that, even with plenty of milk and butter and eggs, her cooking still bore the pallid look peculiar to her mother's. Even in the bright opulence of Missouri summers, her table never took on anything even approximately like the richness of those of the other Kenzie women. She could not bring herself to kill a chicken, so, unless she remembered to ask Henry to do it before he left for the field, she rarely had fried chicken—a dish which appeared, as a matter of course, on the tables of any Kenzie family from June until October. Even dressing one made her faintly ill—the smells, and the sight of the bloody water. After she had prepared a chicken for the table she could hardly make herself take a taste of it. Lots of times she purposely refrained from asking Henry to kill one for her. There were always hams in the smokehouse and, though she never could manage to cut through the thick skin and firm meat, usually Henry had more than enough cut for breakfast so that there was plenty left for dinner as well. That had come to be a symbol of their marriage—her coming into the kitchen to find slices of ham or bacon, neatly cut and with the skin trimmed off the outside and all the "sugar cure" scraped away, lying on the waxed paper bread had come wrapped in. Elaine did not "bake." She knew all the other Kenzies felt sorry for Henry because he had to eat bakery bread. She had honestly tried to learn to make bread. One of her happiest memories of living with Aunt Ellie was coming into the kitchen to find the freshly baked loaves, with butter still oozing out of the brown crust, sitting on the table to cool. She and Barry would beg for slices of it and Aunt Ellie would give it to them, spreading it with butter and brown sugar.

"Now, mind you," she would say, "when you eat it, get far enough away from the kitchen door so you won't draw flies."

More often than not, they would carry it to the crotch of the tree outside Elaine's window, and while the bread melted away in their eager, greedy mouths, Barry would spin tales of knights and great ladies.

Elaine followed every step Aunt Ellie tried to teach her about bread-making, but always the stuff was horrible. Finally, she stopped trying, and bought bread at the grocery store. At least they could eat it, for even though Henry tried hard to eat what she baked, most of it had to be fed to the dogs or chickens.

Now Elaine tied on the apron Beulah handed her, and set about buttering the bread. Beulah had Aunt Ellie's touch with bread. The feel of the loaves, their shape, the very brownness of the crust, were all as Aunt Ellie used to have them. Everything that Beulah did was patterned after Aunt Ellie's ways. Now that Elaine thought about the matter, things were all exactly as if the older woman had never left the house. The same kinds of meals came to the same table around whose sides the same people sat. The same ease and graciousness and great welcome met guests. Beulah, most alien of all of them, was the one who carried on the old ways, just as they had always been.

Mamie Bledsoe was cutting up potatoes for salad. It had been years since Elaine had seen the woman—so long that the girl was unable to remember whether the woman's distant cousinship was on Aunt Ellie's or Uncle Dade's side. The Bledsoes were very poor. About the only time they came to see their more affluent relatives was on the occasions of weddings or funerals.

About the woman there was a mixture of triumph and humility. She was secretly glad of an occasion which would bring her, legitimately, into the very core of the Kenzie home. She shared the knowledge common to every woman that until you get into the kitchen of a house you have no real intimacy with its owners. She was humble, too, always afraid of doing the wrong thing. Even Elaine would have known there was only one way to cut up potatoes for salad, and would have gone about the business with as much confidence as she would have summoned for any job. But for Mamie, each potato was an individual hurdle. She would cut an experimental slice or two and then ask Beulah uncertainly if she were doing it right. Beulah's responses were unfailingly kind and encouraging; she said it didn't matter at all, so long as the potatoes got cut. But Mamie kept asking.

Mamie's timidity was not shared by her sister Sophronia. Sophronia was everywhere, opening cupboards, looking into clothespresses, her sharp nose ferreting out everything. Once she got inside a house, her unlimited curiosity knew no bounds. Allison vowed that once at a family reunion she had occasion to open the icebox, and out popped Sophronia Bledsoe. Aunt Ellie rebuked the girl, but Dade roared with laughter and said he knew it was so. He said once he painted the back porch and then he and Ellie went off to town while it dried. When he came home, there were Sophronia's tracks all over the fresh paint. They knew the tracks were hers, because she was so darned pigeon-toed that the prints looked like rickrack on the floor.

Today Sophronia was carrying on her investigations unrebuked. She had run her fingers over the window sills to see if there was any dust; she had opened the door under the sink to discover whether by some chance the roaches might have got a start on Beulah. The younger woman was very likely not the housekeeper Aunt Ellie had been. Already Sophronia had been upstairs to see if the curtains there were freshly laundered. Let her upstairs for five minutes, and she could tell, right off, whether a woman was a good housekeeper or not. Lots of them kept downstairs, where they expected people to be, nice enough, but slighted upstairs rooms something awful because they didn't think anybody but the family would go up there.

Looking around her now, she saw that things were getting a little out of hand here in the kitchen. So many women working together were sure to make a mess. Making a hasty dive under the sink, she brought out the dishpan, soap, and draining rack.

"I'll just wash these dishes," she said.

She went about gathering up the dishes, setting her heels down so hard that the sturdy floor jarred under her feet. She picked up dishes roughly, as if she had a great quarrel with them for even getting dirty in the first place. All her movements were quick and resentful, but deft as well, with a kind of fierce, suppressed energy behind them. In their very forcefulness, they were a rebuke to laziness, to inefficiency, to weakness of all kinds. She banged the dishes into the pan, turned on the water with such force that it spattered the sink, her apron, and even the floor.

"I declare," she said, looking out the window over the sink, "if there ain't Barry Kenzie. I didn't know he had got home yet."

Elaine, cutting bread for sandwiches, felt a sharp pricking in the backs of her hands, as if a thousand small needles were passing through them. Blood surged up into her ears and her heart beat strongly and suffocatingly in her throat. She had only time to turn and face Sophronia when Barry walked in.

He came into the room easily, his slight figure moving as confidently among the pots and pans and be-aproned women as if he had never been away from this house and these people. His face had about it the aesthetic pallor of the student. What he knew of life came to him vicariously, through reading about the lives of others, by watching his friends and acquaintances. He could, and often did, read aloud beautifully to his friends' children about Peter Pan and Christopher Robin—characters more real to him than the child who sat in his lap. He had many friends into whose lives he fitted easily and graciously, so that he was always welcome in their homes. He made an attractive extra man at dinners, he played bridge well, his connection with the *Criterion* lent to him the somewhat pale hue of a celebrity. In a group, he would make humorous and pretty compliments to the ladies; alone with one, he was as impersonal as the morning newspaper. Even when he was fitting in best with a group, he seemed objective and aloof.

"Well, hello," he said now, the deep richness of his voice filling the room so that every woman stopped her work, smoothed her apron, and wished she knew how shiny her nose was. "Hello, girls. Goodness, Sophronia, I haven't seen you for years."

He bent to kiss the woman, and her sallow face, with its dark liver spots, turned a dull brick-red with pleasure.

"Up to your old tricks, Barry Kenzie," she said. And then, remembering the etiquette of the occasion, she continued formally and stiffly, "You certainly have my sympathy, Barry."

He said, "Thank you, Sophronia," simply and easily, so that you knew he felt the solemnity of the occasion, and was touched with the sorrow of it, and with the woman's sympathy.

Barry worked his way about the kitchen, shaking hands with neighbors, kissing all the kin, no matter how distant. Beulah he embraced warmly. She was delighted to see him. Always she had been fond of him, feeling that the others in his family did not understand him. Her own father had been a bookworm, so she knew that such people were not to be judged by the standards used for ordinary men. Although she loved Grandfather dearly, she had always felt a lack of understanding on his part for his youngest son.

As far as that went, none of the Kenzies understood Barry. It was no wonder that he got away from them. Neither he nor Allison fitted into the pattern. Thinking of them, Beulah sighed a little. Rebels were not happy. Barry's was no real life for a man; he should have something to turn to besides books. The very fact that he seemed content with them made her feel the situation was even more out of focus. While her father had turned to books, he had not made of them all his life. Allison, seemingly more foolish, was really possessed of the greater wisdom. She was not afraid of life, but was willing to risk hurt and disillusion. The girl was certainly not happy now, though. This divorce business was not good. But maybe she would work things out. She had the strength rebels must have, if they are not to be broken by the very force of their own rebellion. Beulah hoped she was wrong in suspecting that Barry had only a rebel's weakness.

Barry, in his greetings, had at last come to Elaine, who was standing by the cabinet, her eyes wide and blue above the flowered dress, looking like a young and timid girl arrested in flight by an artist's command.

"Stop," he might have said. "Stay as you are. Don't move—I want to paint you as you are."

She was, indeed, a study in arrested motion, and the poet that was ever a part of Barry felt it. The expression, the pose, the dress, were all the same as he had seen here in this very room, years ago. Nothing had changed. They were in the kitchen once more, and she was wearing a blue-flowered dress, and had known nothing, either of joy or sorrow or love or life, that had left its mark on her. Like one in a dream he moved slowly toward her and took her in his arms.

For Elaine, there was no reality aside from his lips on hers. The other women in the kitchen were only shadows. Henry did not even exist; the years that had passed since that long-ago Sunday morning melted into nothingness. All the long dreams she had known were crystallized into this single moment of fruition. Under its spell, she and Barry were at last a man and woman blending into a common destiny.

Beulah, knowing well that the watching women were anything save shadows, broke the silence. She did not quite sense the import of the thing, and yet she knew this was no ordinary kiss between cousins, even cousins who had been brought up as close together as Elaine and Barry had been. It would take very little, she knew, to start active tongues wagging.

"It's good to have you back, Barry," she said. "I hope you stay and make us a long visit."

Barry dropped his arms, turned slowly to face her. Elaine picked up the bread knife again, scarcely knowing what she did. The room surged and sang around her. For the first time, she had kissed a man adequately, and this man was Barry. Here, in the presence of all these women, she and Barry had kissed as men and women kiss, not as frightened children; not mechanically, as she kissed Henry.

"Can't you stay?" Beulah repeated. "Your old room is empty. I got it ready specially, so you could stay if you wanted."

"I'm afraid not," Barry said. He seemed now to be coming back, as from the far reaches of a dream. "I have some urgent business in Chicago next week, and then I'll be going to New York for a while."

"Bother business," Beulah said. "Can't it wait?"

"I'm afraid not," Barry told her. "It's rather special business. I'm going to be married."

A great clatter of congratulations followed, all of them urging him to tell them something about her. He said she was a teacher. He had known her for a long time—more than ten years. She wrote some—in fact, he had first met her and become interested in her through a little thing she sent to the *Criterion*. She was very nice. He knew they would all like her. Some day he meant to bring her back here for a visit.

It was Beulah's wisely kind eye that darted in Elaine's direction. What she saw made her cry out sharply.

"Elaine—you've cut your finger. I should have told you how

sharp that knife was—!"

Elaine did not answer. She did not, in fact, even seem to hear her. The girl stood, still and frozen, watching a pool of blood spread out on the cabinet. She did not know it was blood. She did not really see it at all.

~ II ~

Beulah Kenzie sat quietly at Mark's side, her hands linked loosely in her lap, her eyes intent upon the minister's face. She was conscious of a great many people about—in the pews, in folding chairs in the aisles, looking in at the open windows. She wondered if there was an able-bodied person in three counties who was not in the crowd.

It was a fine thing, she was thinking, to live one's life out in the same place, as Grandfather Kenzie had done. Things were all of a piece then, and you left your mark on the community. For fifty years to come—maybe even for longer than that—people would see the things you left and remember. It would be a long time before the Kenzie farm, even if it passed into other hands, would be known as anything save the old Kenzie place. And though someone else might take over Grandfather's pew at church, folks would still say, "That was old Dade Kenzie's pew. Man and boy, he sat there more than seventy years." The sight of his monument would call up old memories each year when services were held at the cemetery on Decoration Day. He was a good man, and had left his imprint on many places—in the community, in the church, in the lives of many people. His memory would live a long time, and even after it faded a little, he would live on in the lives of his children and grandchildren.

Beulah often had observed that the presence of death gave, in a queer intricate way, a better perspective on life. In its presence, people were stilled and quiet, so that the little, unimportant things faded out and one saw the big outlines of the whole plan. Then it was that you saw things the way they really were, with all the little pieces clicking into their proper places, until no longer were all your hurts and broken dreams without reason or justice, but rather were parts of a pattern that was, in itself, right and good.

Because of Grandfather's going, a great numbness had come over her. It was like an anesthesia which dulled her pain so she could conduct her own self-examination with certainty and clarity.

For a long time she had faced the fact that it was her fault there was no Kenzie boy to carry on the name. Knowing she could have no children, she had still gone on and married Mark Kenzie. Outside of Barry who was a bachelor and, as everyone said, not the marrying kind, Mark was the only Kenzie male who might have hopes of carrying on the line. After all these years, Barry said he was going to marry, but he was no longer young. He said his wife was about his own age, a woman he had gone with for a long time. Beulah had no great hopes for children from this match between two mature people so little in love that, with no apparent obstacle in the way of their marriage, they had waited ten years for it.

She found it hard to imagine Barry married. Beulah hoped his wife would be a wise and kindly woman who could bring Barry tactfully and gently into the ways of living with others. Sometimes his kind of people could not stand the shock of being brought from a life that was all books to a real one with real people. But, even if Barry Kenzie and his wife had a dozen sons to carry on the name, that did not alter the fact that Beulah had done the family a great wrong.

Even now, in this moment when she was trying to look honestly and courageously into her own heart, she could not think what she would have done had Mark, knowing she would be childless, refused to marry her. How fortunate she had been in having such a home and such a husband. To her, the life she led seemed the only one for a woman. Even so, she would not have gone into marriage as Elaine, who had apparently married Henry only because she had not the courage to remain single. Miss Laura's way, while a hard one, was really the more honest.

In a society that was built around a family unit, poor Miss Laura must have often felt out of place and alone. Here women met the rhythm of the season with an eye to family needs. They cooked and sewed and preserved and made soap; they planned homes and bought supplies and arranged church socials. And always, as they worked, they had in mind family needs. Even at those pleasant occasions, Sunday dinners, to which everyone was invited and with which everyone pitched in and helped, lone women were subtly out of things. Among married women there was a sort of freemasonry, making them talk with the greatest freedom and understanding of things that concerned them and their families. Even the youngest wife felt this, stepping into the circle with becoming assurance. But, even though these unmarried women were the best of cooks and housekeepers, their achievements were considered of little importance. It was as if these accomplishments had no real value in themselves, being important only when they were placed before the altar of some man's tastes. The unmarried women felt this. The timid ones shrank back at the knowledge, but Miss Laura and her kind became loud and aggressive, pushing themselves, by sheer force of will, into the inner circles of community life.

For Allison, life had not been like that, even though she had waited to marry until there was a great deal of talk that like as not she'd be an old maid, or go through the woods and pick up a crooked stick at last. Allison belonged to a world where women married or not, as they liked. If they chose not to marry they still found a full life and people did not make sport of them for living it that way. They found things that interested them and they were happy. Beulah could see why the people of the community looked critically at Allison when she came home. She violated their ideas of a woman's destiny. They felt she had no right to remain serene and unapologetic at staying single. Finally, when she did decide to marry, she did not act like a married woman at all, but kept on working instead of making a home.

Perhaps it would have been better had Allison decided to stay at home after her marriage. Perhaps it was not wise for two people, each equally independent and strong-willed, to marry in the first place. Marriage was made up of adjustments and self-forgetfulness. It was difficult to imagine either Harlan or Allison taking kindly to either of these virtues. Even Beulah, schooled as she had been in self-control and regard for others, found it difficult. Certainly, living with Mother Kenzie had not been easy. The fact that she had early realized that Ellie, not her mother-in-law, was the example to shape her own ways by, had not made the path any easier for her either.

She had learned to cook Ellie's way, distrusting with equal wisdom the bright pictures in the women's magazines which Julia followed and the pinched recipes handed down to her from her own mother, recipes for boiled dinners, one egg cakes, and foods "nutritious, yet inexpensive." Watching Ellie and asking questions, she had finally come to have at her finger tips the very essence of the older woman's art. It was not so much a matter of recipes as of instinct. No recipe could duplicate the butter beans floating in a cream sauce only slightly thickened with flour, cooked gently until every separate tender bean was encased in a delicate little coat of flavor; of chicken fried in plenty of homemade lard until it was brown outside and richly juicy within; of gravy made from the grease in which the chicken was fried—not doughy, but the consistency of thick cream, with small brown crusts left from the chicken frying floating about in it; of beans, glistening from small globules of fat that had come from the piece of side meat cooked with them. These things she learned to cook from trial and error, from practice, from a great wish in her heart to learn. She knew, too, Ellie's prize recipes—Jeff Davis pie and pound cake and sweet peach pickle and mincemeat, as well as dozens of others. She learned to fry ham the way Ellie did, too, and to make red gravy and light bread and apple pie.

It had not been easy, and she had made mistakes. One of the worst ones was the time she cooked beans, sliced very thin, and poured thick sweet cream over them. Her mother had cooked them so, only, of course, using milk instead of cream. Beulah prepared them for the Kenzies, thinking how wonderful it was to be using real cream. The family took one horrified look at the dish, and refused even to taste them. Green beans were not meant to be seasoned with cream, and that was all there was to it. She never made that mistake again.

All these things had been only a part of the big job of making herself into a Kenzie. She never felt anything but gladness that she should be able to take up their ways so easily. Of course, had things been as they should, she would have had sons and daughters to carry on the Kenzie way—girls to learn all Ellie's ways and boys with reddish hair and straight, strong backs, riding over the Kenzie fields. People looking at them could see Old Dade Kenzie in them, and Ellie, and their own father. And the Fultons, too. Then she herself could have kept a separate identity, and not worried so much about doing things the Kenzie way.

She had not been long at trying to master the job she had set herself before she began to see that this was not enough. Loving Mark as completely and unquestioningly as she did, it was hard for her to admit, even to herself, how spoiled and self-willed he was. His charm was something as effortless as light, blinding everyone around him to his weakness of will and selfishness of purpose. Unlike most masculine charm, it worked with equal success upon both men and women. Men liked him, and he could cajole women—from Miss Laura on down to Ben's little girls—into doing anything he wanted them to. His mother was completely under his spell, and Ellie, although she laughed and told him he was a spoiled baby, was scarcely better. Only Allison and Beulah saw through him—Allison with a clear objectivity that held no rancor and Beulah with a love deep enough to see beneath surface charm to deep and inner possibilities.

She was honest enough to wonder sometimes if, without Allison, she would ever have seen the dangers that lay ahead of such a man as Mark. Perhaps by herself she eventually would have come to see that, while it sat becomingly upon a boy, the irresponsible charm which Mark possessed did not always flower into a strong and substantial manhood. The fact remained, however, that Allison helped her to see this, and, seeing it, she knew her duty beyond that of making a Kenzie of herself.

If she could not give the Kenzie family a manchild, she could, at least, try to make a man out of Mark. To this she turned all her wisdom and her strength, working always quietly, without seeming to cast any reflections on Mark as he was, without becoming a bossing or managing woman.

Certainly it had not been easy, but she knew she had succeeded. Mark was a man now, solid and substantial. He it was that Dade had selected to run the home place. When, only this spring, the old man had decided that he no longer wanted to continue his duties as steward in the church, Mark, and not his father, had inherited the job. Men came often to consult with him on business. If he had lost any of his boyish charm, it was only a passing glitter that had gone, and nobody felt any real lack. Often now people said,

"Isn't Mark Kenzie a lot like Old Dade? Funny, I never used to notice it so much."

Beulah, hearing this, knew she had at last succeeded in the long job she had set for herself.

Now, sitting here at Mark's side, she knew she had still another task ahead of her, one which, so far as she could see, it would never be her privilege to lay down. Hers must be the work of holding the family together.

Dearly as she loved Grandfather, she had not really wanted to come live in his house after Grandmother's death. But when he asked them to come, she and Mark felt they could not refuse him. The decision was doubly hard because, after all these years, they were getting ready to build a house of their own. For one reason or another, building had never seemed possible, much as they wanted to do so. But, before they had time to make any real step toward building, Grandfather, who did not know of their plans, asked them to come live with him. It was a request that neither of them, regardless of their own wishes, felt justified in refusing. She pushed the dream of her own house into the back of her mind, thinking she could always pick it up again when the old man's need for them was finished.

Now, she knew they could never leave Grandfather's house. Very clearly she saw where her duty lay. She and Mark must remain where they were and, just as it had been her duty to learn the Kenzie ways, now it must be her part to keep them alive. Always, of course, she must work through Mark, but the real responsibility was hers—the Sunday dinners that had come to be a community institution, the keeping of the same church pew, the vital interest in all things touching community welfare. She must be the one to hold to family reunions, to succor those who were sick or in need. Cousins, no matter how distant or how disagreeable, must know that they were always welcome in the house.

She must keep the place exactly as it was, as it had been for more years than any of them could remember. All the relations would want it so. Even Sophronia, sniffing disdainfully at the waste and extravagance that went on, gloried in the prodigality, deriving from it a certain reflected glory. Elaine, pallid and passive as she might be, always brightened up at coming back. Barry exhibited a boyish joy that was both touching and satisfying. Allison shed a certain layer of sophistication and became relaxed and almost gentle. Usually so rebellious, so alien, the girl loved the place, seeming to gain strength and comfort from coming back. Because all the Kenzies gained something from re-visiting the old place, it was her job to keep it here for them to come back to.

The same ritual must go on—apple butter making in the fall, butchering in the winter, gardens and chickens in the spring. The same flowers must come up each year in the same places, and the same vegetables must always be found in the garden.

She realized clearly that in doing this she would not possess the place. It would possess her. Never would it be her privilege to move a chair, hang a picture, rearrange a room, without first recalling whether it had ever been so in the old days. More than that—inasmuch as she could bring herself to meddle with anyone else's life, she must do so now, learning to make wise decisions, learning to advise when called upon, learning to be a source of strength and comfort, even as Grandfather had been. Before Allison left, she must try to have a talk with her.

Allison was troubled. Ez Dowlin might say that divorce meant nothing at all to the girl, hardened as she was to the ways of the world. But Ez was wrong. Allison was deeply in love with Harlan, and the difficulty between them was causing her much unhappiness. Since they were both so rebellious, they could not work out their lives as easily as two people who followed more closely an ordinary pattern of life might have done.

Much as she liked Harlan, she had to admit that he was a strange person, fitful, erratic, unstable. She herself did not always understand what he wrote, or what he was talking about, even in conversation. Even so, she sensed beneath all this a clear and candid honesty, very appealing to her. If he wrote of great heights of generosity and nobility, letting himself fall into small-souled, petty ways, he did so openly and without subterfuges. He never pretended to be the people about whom he wrote. Little as Beulah knew about such things, she felt she must not stand him up beside the other men of her acquaintance for the purpose of judging him. For certainly, he seemed very different from them.

And that was well. Allison could never fall into a pattern of life with an ordinary man. She and Harlan were two separate individuals, each so independent and so different that it would be very difficult for them to be fused into one pattern. It was no wonder that they had experienced trouble. Marriage was easier, Beulah thought, when two people went into it without any false ideas about being able to maintain their own individuality. Oftentimes, the mating of such people as Allison and Harlan was like the mixing of two chemicals that, perfectly harmless in themselves, together produce a great explosion. The two atoms that were Harlan and Allison might never fuse into a perfect marriage, or a peaceful one—or even a very happy one. But, that did not alter the fact that they seemed to be made for each other. Perhaps a great many of the concessions necessary to their happiness would have to be made by Allison. Unless the girl would be willing to curb some of her independence of thought and action, this would be a difficult, perhaps even an impossible thing. At any rate, Beulah felt she must have a talk with her. Sometimes just talking things over helped. Maybe Allison would find it so.

Sitting here beside Mark, Beulah knew a great content. It was a good thing to hold the family together. A child of hers and Mark's might not have done this. A child does not necessarily guarantee perpetuation of the family way of life. Beulah Kenzie, herself, could do it, must do it.

So many times talking with Grandfather had helped her to

cut through to the solid core of thought in a matter. Almost she felt as if he had been helping her, even now. Almost, she felt him saying,

"It is a good thing you plan to do, Beulah."

~ III ~

ALLISON KENZIE RANYAK sat in the room just over the kitchen, the one that had been Elaine's. Against its windows the branches of the great elm scraped gently. All the children of the family—even the faint-hearted Elaine—had crawled out on the huge limbs to find a resting place there. Here, always, was a feeling of security. Here, at least, no grown-up ever came.

Within the room were the virginal pastels Elaine had helped to put there, years ago. Ruffled skirts on the dressing table, organdy curtains at the windows, and pale water-color pictures on the walls. Even though Elaine had been married to Henry for years now, the room remained more a part of her than of anyone else who had ever used it.

Allison never ceased to marvel at the impress some colorless people put on things and people about them. No real woman was Elaine—a lily maid, drifting wistfully toward Camelot, passive, inert, never really alive. Yet she dominated Henry so completely that he was but a shadow of her, fitting all his wishes into hers, having no way of life apart from her. She achieved this complete domination through weakness, not through strength.

Allison often wondered how Henry stood it. He was a real man, red-faced and on the clumsy side, but alive, who should have married some good, strong country woman to whom his every action would have seemed right and wonderful. Instead, there was Elaine beside him, cool and prim and aloof, bringing out with cruel clarity all the clumsy yokel in him. Among men he moved with a certain quiet sureness and power; only around his wife was he awkward and stiff, his hands inept and blundering, his feet and legs tangling with furniture and rugs. Yet, his complete adoration of Elaine was a touching and beautiful thing, like that of a mastiff guarding a child who remains utterly unaware of the magnificent protection which is his.

Perhaps in every relationship there must be one who takes and one who gives; as, in electricity, a positive and a negative current must exist before a perfect circuit can be formed. If this was true, it was a condition that should not be. Two people ought to be able to love each other with complete honesty and equal depth, never watching the quality of the other's love, gauging its strength, or wondering if it were time to draw back or advance, to wheedle or to pretend indifference. About love there should be a great honesty and beauty so that all which was best and finest in an individual would rise to meet it. It was a hard thing when it became, instead, suspicion and bitterness and hurt.

From the rooms below came the muted sounds of incoming relatives and friends, following the age-old custom that said they must arrive early on the day of the funeral services. She knew others would be coming, too—the curiosity seekers, the ones who never missed a funeral, those who came because being there made them seem important and necessary. Already the house was so well filled that the men had begun to spill out into the yard, talking in low tones as they stood around or sat on the grass or in yard chairs. A few children played soberly about them, reflecting the sadness of their elders as water reflects the image of the landscape around it—dimly, and with a certain distortion of values. Always, this place had been associated, for them, with great happiness and complete freedom. Now, over this accustomed joy of theirs was superimposed a layer of decorous quiet which, at times, broke away into spontaneous mirth, quickly hushed.

SATURDAY

The women, under Beulah's leadership, were busy in the kitchen preparing what was called simply "the lunch." Neighbors, following the established procedure for the occasion, had sent in food—cakes and pies and bowls of Jello, stiff with fruit and nuts; boiled ham and homemade bread and jars of thick, sweet cream; salads and pickles and jellies. The bowls were stacked so high in the kitchen now that it was hard to find a place to put the fresh offerings that came in. But Beulah's response to everyone was equally kind and appreciative. "A pie from Mrs. Cummings," she would say. "How good it looks." . . . "Mrs. Starke sent cookies. Hers are always so nice."

Beulah thought it was beautifully kind of these people to send things. Although she would have made no remark about their failure to do so, she would have thought it strange indeed if people did not bring food now. She herself always took angel food cake in times of trouble. They were so light that often people who had no appetite for heavier foods could nibble a bite with enjoyment. She always carried them in an enamel container which, between times, she kept on a certain shelf in the pantry. No matter how great the emergency, she never used it except to carry food to families who had suffered bereavements. Everyone knew it was hers, so after everything was over, it was not hard for those clearing up to get it back to her, or for her to find it herself if she came to call. Women, cleaning up, would say,

"This is Beulah Kenzie's cakebox. I'll see that she gets it and save some of the family a trip."

She never took it to basket dinners or aid meetings or such things, because sometimes people who had been in sorrow would be there and just the sight of the box would be enough to bring things back to them. It was just such little things, Beulah knew, that cut deep into the very core of the hurt, and could easily ruin the day for a woman who was just beginning to forget a little.

To Beulah, supervising the details of "the lunch," everything had a solemn rightness to it. To Allison, it was an orgy from which she had escaped early in the morning with the excuse that she would see to getting the upstairs rooms in order. Although she had long finished her self-imposed task, she had not gone back downstairs. It was as if she sat still while all the events of her past life went marching past her in solemn procession. She felt no guilt in staying away from the busy women in the kitchen; there were already so many there that they got into each other's way. Only the quiet, efficient presence of Beulah could have kept so many women working amiably together.

Within Beulah's own sphere, Allison reflected, there was no emergency with which the woman was not able to deal. She could take hold in all the great times of life—birth, and death, and marriage, knowing exactly what was the right thing to do, and doing it with confidence and self-effacing ease. She could go into a home bitterly poor and with her kind ministrations bring a semblance of peace and dignity to the occasion. Now she moved with the same instinctive rightness as, Allison felt, she would have displayed in any situation in which she found herself. She would even, Allison thought grimly, have known what to do at a tea for a celebrity, becoming, in her own right, one of the people sought after and looked up to. Beulah was at ease in life, an ease which she passed on to everyone else, no matter how fretful or unhappy the person might be.

The women working in the kitchen were like priestesses, performing the ritual of a tribe. For them, there was a kind of solemn pleasure in the work they did. Death was a moment of highest drama for the community. Births and marriages were secondary to it in that, by comparison, only a relatively few could take part in the proceedings. But there were none, from the largest to the smallest, whom death did not in some way touch. It was no wonder that people guarded jealously all the customs attendant on the occasion, seeing nothing incongruous in anything familiar or habitual, feeling rather a dignified and solemn satisfaction in having matters go forward in a way that was, in their opinion, the right and proper one.

This was only one of the ways in which these people preserved the pattern of their folkways. They went about their own business, oblivious of things which they felt did not concern their destinies, denying the very existence of these things. Theirs was, for the most part, a negative religion—a person was good not because of what he did, but because of what he did not do. They held in their hearts nothing but contempt and scorn for politicians, actors, writers, and people too highly educated, never seeing that these were the ones who shaped the very core of their existence—writing the books they read, shaping the laws that governed them, directing the radio programs which gave richness and color to their lives. They lived in their own tight little island of disregard for any way of life but their own.

There was no fathoming these people, she thought. Had they read about her in a magazine, or even heard about her in a radio serial, they would have lived vicariously in her struggles, wanting her to succeed, wishing her well, never judging adversely any of her actions, even her separation and impending divorce. But, knowing her, they were reserved and critical. It was only in stories that people would accept anyone who did not conform to the community pattern. Because she had never belonged here, they were aloof, feeling that her very nonconformity was implied reproach to their own set and circumscribed way of life. Grandfather had not really belonged here, either, and yet, by some great strength of his, he had made himself a part of it without ever surrendering his freedom or individuality.

She wished now, as always, that she could have come to

understand this pattern of freedom he possessed. Each time she came home she hoped she could get to the core of it, but always it eluded her. All her conscious life she had been groping toward freedom—something that would leave her soul and her mind in a still, bright integrity of will and action. No matter where she went she was always frightened of the pattern of things, drawing back from it instinctively.

At first, she had thought that California held what she sought. It was not long until she found she was mistaken. Here people were possessed by freedom, bound by it. In their fierce insistence on individualism, they were as provincial as ever Miss Laura could be. And yet, she liked California, and would have stayed there, even as an ant would like the freedom of a bowl better than that of the tea cup he had left. She would have stayed on without question, had Harlan liked it.

Allison often wondered why it was that she and Harlan should quarrel so. Certainly it was not lack of love for each other. In their love there was a magic and a wonder that two people, each one so different from those around him that he had never really expected to find anyone whose spirit would match his, should have found each other. It was a miracle to have someone who understood you—the little quirks of humor, the subtle ironies, the swift perceptions that cut straight through the outer layers of conventional thought to arrive, breathlessly and simultaneously, at the same conclusion.

From the very first she had found it difficult to reconcile the writer and the man. Harlan could describe, so movingly that one's heart cried out with the beauty of it, a woman, poor and alone, buying a cheap doll at a dime store counter at Christmas time. Allison would never forget the poignant beauty of that scene—the woman, turning from a doll with real hair, and eyes that opened and closed, to a small rubber one.

"Seems like I jest can't get away from this one," Harlan had the woman say. "I keep thinking how she'd love it."

At the end, he had her buy the cheaper one, and go out of the store. That was the sort of thing he did, with details that so narrowly missed mawkishness that the fact he did miss was the chief artistry of the piece. Then, having written a scene of that kind, he would go away from his desk to be impatient and even arrogant with a beggar on the streets or the scrubwoman who blocked his way.

They settled down to married life in the hotel room which Harlan already occupied. Harlan said he thought he could work better there, and since Allison was to be away at her own job much of each day, it seemed a most convenient arrangement. Evenings they were free to explore together the great wonder that was New York. Although Allison had been there long enough to feel that she was almost a native, she found that, with Harlan, she was seeing it through new eyes. Together they gulped it all down as children gulp candy—French bonbons and jawbreakers with equal appetite and lack of discrimination. It was no wonder, then, that before long the joy of it began to wear off, and about the city that had once been so magical to them there was little more glamour than could be found in Kansas City, or Omaha. And when this happened, they began to quarrel.

"There is no need for you to keep on working," Harlan protested sulkily, seizing upon the first thing that he could think of on which to pin his ill-humor.

Allison could not bring herself to tell him why she worked. Too often she had seen writers riding to a heady success, only to be forever unable to repeat their first achievements. She believed that deep within Harlan were untapped sources of many stories and books yet to come. But of this she could not be sure. Since their marriage he had done little real writing. Perhaps he was one of those people who write only to escape unhappiness or boredom. In their life together he had found so much of happiness and fulfillment that the urge to write was completely stifled in him. Lacking the bitter need to expose things which had hurt him, he found nothing else of which he could write. But, until she knew he would go on writing, she felt she must not give up working.

Besides, she liked her work. About it there was a deep and satisfying sense of self-expression which she had failed to find in music, or on the stage. It came to be a great satisfaction to her to be able to place a story where it might receive the understanding it merited. Scarcely ever was her judgment wrong on a piece, so that gradually all the promising material came eventually to her desk. Allison herself was not able to explain her success. Perhaps it was because she cut straight through to the heart of the thing, sensing exactly what the writer wanted to say, making him see how he failed in his purpose. No, she had no intentions of giving up her work, at least for the present.

"Maybe you would like it better if we had an apartment," she said, side-stepping the question with a certain diplomacy that made her remember, half-laughingly, her sister-in-law, Beulah. "This isn't such a good place to work, anyway. You should have more room to move around in, and a kitchen where you could get something to eat if you got hungry."

He was immediately diverted. Living in a hotel was like living in the Grand Central Station, he said. He got out the paper and together they began looking at ads, writing down addresses and telephone numbers that appeared at all promising. He volunteered to start looking the next morning.

For the next few days he went apartment hunting, coming home unsuccessful each night, but bearing with him all sorts of impossible and useless kitchen gadgets, bought at the five-and-ten, for Allison to see. He insisted upon having their dinner sent up, and could scarcely eat for trying to figure out whether this small affair that looked like a child's tinkertoy was a fruit knife or a dingus to get the cream off the top of the bottle of milk.

When he solved the riddle, as he usually did, he was absurdly happy, catching her in his arms and holding her high up, almost to the level of his shoulder, to kiss her. Swung thus off her feet, held away from any real foundation save the strength of his arms, Allison knew a strange feeling—as if they had a reality entirely apart from the place where they were now. She saw them, not as two lovers in a hotel room in New York, but together in a farm kitchen. Harlan had put down for the moment some useful farm object—a milk bucket, or a basket of eggs—and had caught her to him. The hardness of his lean body, pressed so closely to hers, was clothed in overalls and a blue shirt, and about him were the good farm smells—rich soil, the faint sweetness of hay, the musty opulence of corn.

Even after he had set her down, she clung to him, her shining dreams of independence submerged, for the moment, in a complete and elemental love for her man and the things that meant most to him.

It was Olga Bischoff who finally found the apartment for them. It overlooked the East River, and was all they had hoped for. At first, Harlan was entirely satisfied with it. They transferred their kitchen gadgets and the great dreams there. Allison found that she remembered enough of her mother's and Ellie's cooking lore to enable her to prepare their meals with efficiency and even pleasure. Harlan liked the simplest of food—steak fried country fashion and potatoes boiled in their jackets. She tried to prepare red cabbage the way he said his mother cooked it—"with a little bit of grease and some vinegar—yes, and some sugar, I know"—and made a great mess of it.

It was hard to see happiness so shining as this grow dull, but it did. Before long Harlan was complaining again. He could not write at all. The sight of the river distracted him. He was lonesome with Allison gone all day. He did not like the apartment. He did not, he said vehemently, like New York.

"Would you like to go home on a visit?" Allison said. "After all, you've never met my people. And I've never met yours."

"They—well, they won't be like people you've known," Harlan warned her.

"Don't forget, I grew up on the farm," Allison reminded him.

"It isn't just that," he told her. "My people are Czechs, you know."

He hesitated, groping, as always, for words with which to explain what he meant.

"Never till the day of my grandmother's death," he went on, "did she eat at the table with my grandfather. She served him, and then later she and the other women ate. My mother did that, too, when she was first married. But after we kids got bigger we were ashamed, and made her stop."

Allison understood many things now. The crudities, for example, which so many people had condemned in him. The timidity which cloaked itself in brusqueness. The age-old dislike for women who were anything but shadows of their husbands' lives. Fight as he might against the feeling, he was still outraged at the thought of a working wife.

So they went to Nebraska. Nothing Harlan had told her prepared her for what she found there, nor had any experience she had known in her own childhood on the farm given her an inkling of what Harlan's background might be like. His mother was a woman old beyond her time, with broken teeth over which she kept her lips self-consciously and tightly closed. His father was a huge, bearded man, taciturn and remote, in his eyes the stern gleam of a zealot. Beside him, Mrs. Ranyak was a small gray shadow whose comforting kindness and understanding was the only thing, Allison knew, that had ever come between Harlan and the wrath of his father. His sisters, married to coarse, peasantlike men, came in to see their brother. There was little satisfaction in the visit. Dressed as simply as Allison was, she still felt the women eyeing her clothes in self-conscious and disapproving silence. Always she felt that, if she could only be alone with Mrs. Ranyak for even a short time, she and the older woman would break through the barrier that was between them, coming to some understanding. But there never seemed to be an opportunity.

This was a life of which Allison knew nothing. Here was relentless toil, backbreaking effort, deifying work as the supreme end of all things. To Harlan's people, farming meant an eighteen-hour day, beginning with the milking long before daylight in the morning and ending with supper at ten o'clock at night. It was eating in the kitchen, by the light of coal-oil lamps, from greasy, oilcloth-covered tables. It meant a society in which women were little more than slaves.

The women worked all day, caring for gardens and chickens, between the regular housekeeping jobs. Theirs was more often than not, the responsibility of milking. Many of them worked in the fields beside the men. They knew nothing outside of the making, and saving, of money. And with the money that was made, the men bought more land, or machinery with which to farm the land they already had, or great barns in which to house the machinery and the stock and crops.

Allison had never felt so close to Harlan as she did there among his own people. Then it was that she understood the life that had been his, all the sensitive loneliness of the boy who had grown up, not fitting into it. Here was a group whose every ideal, every hope, every thought was different from his. None of the things dear to him, or easy for him, were standards which they felt very important. Of course, in such an atmosphere he had to develop defenses. He bragged, and he swaggered.

And he wrote.

And when he wrote, he took these people apart and showed them as they really were. Against this, they had no defenses.

Watching Harlan with his own people, she knew that he was never more alone than when he was with them. And when he came from being with them, she took him in her arms and comforted him, so that the things they had said and done were put into their proper focus, and did not matter so much. She knew, however, that Harlan shared the hurt common to all at misunderstandings coming from one's own people.

After this, the visit to Missouri was sheer joy. Grandmother was already gone, but Dade was still there and, under Beulah's reign, the old place had lost no whit of its air of gracious living—company dinners and Old Dade riding his horse over the farms to see how the crops were coming on. Harlan and Dade liked each other on sight, the old man feeling that here at last, with all his faults, was a man who could challenge the great promise that was in Allison. They might disagree, violently and even bitterly, but fundamentally they were meant for each other. It was a liking that was mutual.

"He's—he's magnificent," Harlan told Allison. "Like some great old king, with wisdom enough for himself and all his subjects. He's so sure of himself he's almost arrogant, and yet, he is as simple as—as earth—"

That was the key, Allison thought. Dade had about him the honesty and elemental fineness of good, rich soil. Because there was none who would question his greatness or his worth, he did not find it necessary to make pretenses about things. All his life had been builded on good things—wife and home and children and a place in the community. His very way of life was a justification so complete in itself that he was entirely free of the strain and fret of lesser men.

Beulah made a great fuss over Harlan, seeing that he had choice pieces of fried chicken and second helpings of ice cream. To him, she was a revelation. The farm women of his experience were little more than drudges—keepers of chickens, milkers of cows, bearers of children. With puzzled bewilderment he watched Beulah as she went about wearing pretty house dresses. She was poised, serene, quietly sure of herself. Goodness shone through her every act like a lighted candle in a piece of alabaster.

Here, peace came to Allison and Harlan. They slept late,

coming down to Beulah's breakfasts of ham and eggs and hot biscuits, jam and jellies and fresh fruits, coffee with cream so thick it had to be dipped from the pitcher. Afterwards, they went riding with Old Dade, or drove to town on small errands for Beulah, or took walks in fields sweet with alfalfa or clover. Now, at last, they could talk calmly of their future.

"Do you want to go back to New York?" Allison asked.

No—not that. Harlan did not like New York. He had done no writing there. Everything was crazy and out of perspective. Having in mind their new-found content, Allison asked,

"Would you like to stay here in Missouri?"

He said no to that, too. Here he was steeped in a rosy content that took from him all desire to write. Things were so right, so natural, that there was no need for him to get them, and himself, back into focus by writing about them.

"We aren't always like this," Allison warned him. "I have found almost as much here to dislike as ever you found in Nebraska. I ought to take you over to spend the day with Miss Laura. Or Ez Dowlin."

Oddly enough, when Harlan met Miss Laura, he liked her, seeing in her an acrid honesty which tickled his fancy. At first, she acted as if Allison had brought home a pet leopard to turn loose in their midst, but in the face of Harlan's genuine interest in her, she melted and asked them to dinner. They went, and over a table set with things that had belonged to "Mama and Grandmama," she told him stories of Missouri—of bushwhackers and old families and how to cook green beans and the way those Kane boys did about delivering the paper. Harlan listened intently, saying little himself, but drawing her out, so that, for the first time, Allison saw in the woman something that passed for charm.

"She has personality," Harlan explained later.

"She has a tongue a mile long," Allison amended idly.

"It is something beyond my comprehension," Harlan said,

"why we celebrate great tragedies in literature and persecute them in real life."

Even though Allison tried, she could not prevail upon him to explain, or expand, his statement.

And, while they waited idly, like a field lying fallow, destiny took over for them. Hollywood bid for the right to film Harlan's book. And would Mr. Ranyak like to come out to confer with the producers over details?

Allison and Harlan scarcely needed to discuss it all to know this was what they wanted to do. Old Dade, too, thought it was a good idea. California always sounded pretty good to him. The movies were mostly a lot of make-believe, but they were interesting, too. And so, with the feeling that a new life was opening for them, they left for California.

Hollywood fascinated Allison. It was not a town, but a state of mind. She went to movie sets with Harlan, and felt no annoyance, as he did, at the false fronts, the synthetic scenery, the simulated emotions. Behind these things she saw the true heart of the matter—a desire to make things authentic and real. Because it all interested her tremendously, she went every day to the lots to watch the filming of Harlan's book. She never blocked minor changes in the text of the story, but she did protest vigorously departures from the spirit of it, or from realistic approach to the nature of the country or the people whom it pictured.

"They would not do it that way," she would say. "A Nebraska housewife of that particular type would not act so. Here—let me show you—"

Recognizing the real knowledge she possessed in the matter, they listened to her, came to depend on her judgment. Without ever really knowing how it started, she had a job.

Mostly, she got her job by virtue of the fact that she knew, with unerring instinct, the things that would wow the natives in such box offices as Excelsior Springs and Sioux City and Lincoln. Because she knew the mind and the pulse and the heart of these people, she could speak with authority on the matter, and so, was often able to bring to the attention of the right people certain stories that might otherwise have escaped notice. Here it was that her experience in the agency proved of great value to her. And so she found work in California which, without having quite the responsibility that her place in New York had brought her, was still satisfying and absorbing.

At first, Harlan liked California, the freedom and unconventionality of it catching him up, as it did Allison. Together they went on picnics on the beach and swimming in the ocean. Harlan thought he'd like to stay out there permanently. The movie had gone well; the books were still selling. He thought they ought to take some of the money and build a house.

"What sort of a house do you want?" Allison asked him.

He didn't care. A house was a woman's business. She must go ahead and plan it any way she liked. He had an idea for a new book now, and couldn't be bothered. So, Allison took over the planning and supervision of the house.

What came of this planning was probably the strangest house in Beverly Hills. There the pattern was the unique, the bizarre, the magnificent, the unusual. Among those piles of white stone, colored stucco, the English, the Norman, the Italian, and heaven knows what other nations, she had built a Missouri farm house with square, uncompromising rooms and a hall running, dead center, through it. She had wanted, and got, porches front and back. She had it painted white with a green roof.

"Wouldn't you like green shutters?" the unhappy architect had asked.

She said no. She said no, as well, to the landscape gardener he wished to import to look after the grounds. Instead, she had personally supervised the planting of elm and maple and black walnut trees, of hollyhocks and lilacs and peonies, scattered about with unprofessional abandon. The house sat among its svelte neighbors with the slightly scandalized air of a maiden aunt who has come in from the country to visit her debutante nieces. Even so, it was the one house about which visitors invariably inquired. Something about it must have recalled for them past joys—roasting apples over an open fire, mincemeat in crocks down cellar, corn on the cob.

Harlan could have seen very easily what it was to be like, at those times when he and Allison came to look at it while it was under construction. But, either he was too preoccupied, or he had no vision in such matters, for it was not until they moved in that he said, violently, that he did not like it.

"My God!" he protested. "I'd think I was back in Nebraska."

They quarreled over it. They were quarreling more often now, anyway, and perhaps the house was only an excuse. Hollywood was not good for Harlan. It brought out all that was little and mean in him. It was too easy. And it was too hard. People fawned over him, telling him he was wonderful and sensational. And the next day they had forgotten what his name was. Here, as in New York, success had come so quickly that he was not prepared for it nor for the evils attendant upon it. The new book was at a standstill. Because he could not write, he blamed the country, the people, Allison—everyone but himself. He was bitter with Allison for working, not realizing that it was largely her contribution that was responsible for the splendid job that had been done on the filming of his book. Harlan wanted to leave Hollywood, going, of all places, to Nebraska.

"Not Nebraska!" Allison burst out. "To those—those people—"

"They are my own folks," he said stiffly. "What I am, they made me—"

She broke into hot, undisciplined protests. What he was he had made himself. He had nothing in common with his own people. She reminded him of the way they had treated him as a boy—the coarse lack of understanding they had shown when she and Harlan went there to visit.

"They would crush everything out of you," she said. "They belittle, humiliate, stifle you. They have no appreciation for you, or anything you do. If you want, we'll go back for a visit, and then you can see for yourself that what I have said is so."

He was not going back for a visit. There was a farm for sale, close to home. He was going to buy it, and go back there. He would farm, and he would write.

Allison listened to him with growing disgust and horror taking possession of her. Go back to Nebraska, to a farm close to that fanatical father, to that pitifully silent mother, to those brothers and sisters with their crude, peasant ways. That she would not do.

"If you want to be that blind and foolish," she burst out hotly, "go on. But you'll go by yourself. I have no idea of following you in a thing as mad as that."

That was three months ago. Harlan was now settled on his farm. Allison, living alone in the house in Beverly Hills, felt anew each day the bitterness of their parting. They cared too deeply for their separation to be an easy thing. To complicate matters still more, Harlan had become too much of a public figure to have a private misunderstanding with his wife. The papers made much of the situation. Miss Laura read the details in the brown section of the Sunday *Star,* as did the insufferable Ez Dowlin. Allison minded neither of these but she did hate her grandfather to be hurt or distressed over the matter. She might, however, have known what the old man's reaction would be. He said Allison and Harlan were both as stubborn and unruly as thoroughbred colts, and needed to have some sense knocked into them, a matter to which nature would attend. She liked to think of his words now as she sat here in this room where she had come so often as a girl. It comforted her to know that he had not been hurt by the story. Perhaps with his words in her mind she could at last come to a decision concerning the letter.

It bore a Nebraska postmark, and it was from Harlan. It said:

"You were right. It is all you said it would be, and worse. But the writing goes well. Will you come to me here?"

Nothing more. That was like Harlan. In his letters, even in his conversation with her, there was always a lack of eloquence. This she had never resented, feeling rather that it was a good thing. With her he was so completely himself, so honest and natural, that there was no need for fine speeches or careful cloaking of the things he said to her. Whatever had been the faults in their relationship, they always had gone, straight and clean and true, to the heart and mind of the other. Perhaps that was not well. Perhaps it is better to see one's beloved through a rosy haze that blinds one to all faults and weaknesses.

Now she sat, trying to face honestly what going back to Harlan meant. Not peace, certainly. Perhaps not even happiness. They were too much alike. Theirs was the same proud arrogance, the same wild love of freedom, the same strong will and utter lack of discipline. They had neither one ever bent their wills to fit with that of another. Marriage for such as they was never easy. Perhaps it was kinder and wiser to live apart

Since Harlan had left her, three months ago, this was the first word she had had from him. In fact, so stubborn had been his silence that she had thought first his letter was something concerning the divorce which rumor insisted was imminent, although neither of them had talked of the matter. When she saw that he had so far humbled himself as to ask her to come to him, she suddenly began trembling, as she had trembled that first day when she looked up and saw him standing before her desk in the agency in New York. Certainly it was not lack of love that kept her from him.

Nor did his letter present a problem to her which she had not already gone over many times, trying, even when hurt and anger were strongest in her heart, to see every side of the question. What did they have to give each other? Since their marriage Harlan had done scarcely any work of merit; and, though she still found pleasure in her own work, Harlan disliked the idea so much that certainly she must sacrifice any idea of continuing it, even before they could discuss reconciliation.

She was not meant to give in thus to another. That was for Beulah, and women like her. Always she had considered this quality a weakness in Beulah, a sort of spineless gentleness. Now she wondered.

Beulah was only a Kenzie by marriage, and yet she was more Kenzie than the family itself. She had preserved for this home the same smoothness and harmony that Ellie had made for it. Always, Mark had had his own way. Yet, in these very yieldings, Beulah had gained everything. She was the dominant figure in the home. With Old Dade gone, she it was who would hold the clan together. With unerring clearness she had long ago seen that few issues were worth fighting for—weren't those her very words, long ago? In her very yielding there was a great strength and a deep poise like that of a mother who says, wisely, "I will not struggle with this child. After all, it is such a little thing he wants."

In giving up, Beulah had remained the one true identity in the family. Others, with their small demands, their selfish seekings, were dwarfed beside her. Of all the Kenzies, she was the wisest, the one who had come nearest to freedom. For she was utterly and completely free of the domination of self. She was weak only as a fine steel blade is weak, bending easily to the slightest touch, and then flying back into place as clear and shining bright as if it had never bent at all.

What was this thing called freedom? Allison did not know. Was it the pattern of having one's way, eternally and completely? Certainly if one were to judge by Beulah, it was not. Was that what it had meant to Grandfather? She searched her memory, looking for clues, admitting finally that, not even for him, was it that. Grandfather had adapted himself majestically and completely to the pattern of life here, so that always he was oblivious to the fact that a pattern even existed. After all, was youth merely the time for rebellion, even as maturity was for adjustment, for working with the forces of life instead of fighting them, for a quiet yet purposeful acceptance of what life brought?

She had gone her own way, forever fearful of domination, forever wanting to be free. Always she had been afraid to give in to Harlan or make concessions. Had that fear of hers grown out of weakness?

Perhaps freedom came only with conformity to a pattern. In nature, this was true. One planted in season, and cultivated at the time for such things, and reaped at the period of reaping. The planets were free within the limits of their own orbits. The sun and moon and the seasons followed the great laws set for them. Must people, too, fall into a pattern, shaping their lives to meet its exigencies, bending wills and rebellious minds and hearts to fit in with the ideas of others?

She thought about the matter, deeply and gravely. It was not just the question of going to a Nebraska farm, hard as that experience would surely be. She felt that perhaps after a time, Harlan himself would grow tired of being there and so the matter would take care of itself. It was rather that her yielding would set the pattern for the rest of their life together. Even if he did decide to leave, would this be only the first of a series of many jumpings about from place to place, always hunting for something he could not find? Was she big enough for this? And, if she were, did she love him enough to do it?

She did not know. Always before, when she had a problem

too big for her, Grandfather was here to talk to her. Now Grandfather was gone, and she was alone.

She was alone, and she was a woman grown. She must think this through for herself.

— IV —

VIRGIE MEADORS lay, relaxed and quiet. She was not asleep nor was she really awake. Around her flowed the dear, familiar sounds of a new day beginning—Jim lifting the milk buckets from the place on the table on the back porch; the mother hens, full of soft cluckings and admonitions; the sharp click of a stove lid as a neighbor woman raised it to do something to the fire. These and a dozen more she heard, mingled yet muted, so that all her conscious world was one blend of them, familiar and dear, comforting and solid.

Fleetingly, she wondered if there was any action left in her at all; if, had she so desired, she might lift her hand off the bedspread. She dwelt on the matter with deep intentness, finally dismissing it as something that did not matter one way or another. The thing that mattered had no physical anchorage at all, no sense of motion or of sound. It was of the spirit, and the spirit was free, as she herself was free.

Free of pain, and free of fear.

She had been a foolish person, weak and silly. Because old Dade Kenzie had died, she had almost died herself and let her baby die with her. He was their luck, she thought, and without him she could not go on. She had given in weakly to all the great fears she had—fear of pain, fear of what people would think of her, fear of being poor. She had been afraid of everything.

Now she was no longer afraid. What happened to her did not matter only as it affected Jim and the baby. Out of weakness this strength had come to her, and it was not given her by old Dade Kenzie. She had got her baby into the world. She could still hear Dr. Burgess saying,

"It's a boy, Virgie. A mighty fine one."

She had not needed Dade Kenzie. He was a good man, and he had helped them, but he was not their luck. Nobody, anywhere, was anybody's luck. You were your own. You made your own life, for good or ill. She and Jim together could make this baby what he ought to be—brave and strong and kind and sure. He was rooted in the Bottoms, with its squalor and filth, but he must never be ashamed of this, or evade it, or pretend it wasn't so. He must not think that, because his folks came from there, that he had to take up the lazy, shiftless pattern those people knew. For he was of the Uplands, too—the pattern of good houses and well-worked fields and people proud and sure of their place in the world.

There was no reason the two patterns should not blend. The people of the Bottoms were proud, too. They were kind to anyone in trouble. They had hearts and souls and minds; they were men and women, just as the Uplanders were. There was no reason on earth that her and Jim's son could not grow up to be a fine man. Maybe, in eighty years or so, he could be a man as great as Dade Kenzie had been. Maybe people, coming to bury him, would say,

"He was a fine man—a power in the community."

Gradually, as she thought of these things, she could feel courage and strength flowing through her. Her hand was a part of her body now, and she could lift it if she wanted to. She was no longer weak and afraid and uncertain.

She could do anything in the world she wanted to do.

SATURDAY

~ V ~

MISS LAURA MEEKS settled stiffly into her seat. She had come early, on purpose, so as to get her own pew. Lots of people who never came to church ordinarily flocked to funerals, and when they did, they either didn't know or didn't care that they were taking other people's regular places in church. She supposed Lije Curran hadn't missed a funeral in thirty years, whether he knew the person or not. It had got to be a kind of joke, Lije showing up at funerals.

It was funny how a body got used to sitting in a certain place in church so that the services didn't sound right from any other spot. As she sat here, all sorts of things—little pieces from the patchwork quilt of her life—came back to her until she had the whole picture of it just by remembering what had happened to her here in this pew. From it, Papa and Mama had carried her to be baptized. Of course, she didn't remember that, but they had told her about it so many times that it seemed as if she did. She had been good, and didn't cry a speck, only just before the minister handed her back to Papa she had laughed out loud and grabbed at the older man's white beard. Mama had been terribly flustered, but Papa thought it was cute, and always laughed when he told the story.

She was sitting right in this pew the first time she ever saw Dade Kenzie. That had been—my goodness, it didn't seem possible that it had been seventy years ago this summer! It didn't seem a day hardly! She could remember it better than some things that had happened only last week. She was eight years old that summer. Mama had a party, and invited Dade. He behaved very badly. He climbed a tree in the yard, and soon had all the other little boys up there with him and it was only by being very firm that Mama was able to get them down to play the games she had planned. When refreshments came in, he ate more of the cake than anyone else did. But he smiled engagingly and said the cake was the best he ever ate, so that Mama quite forgave him. He remembered to tell her he had a good time, and Mama said he had been brought up right, and she must go call on Mrs. Kenzie and take Mrs. Marshall with her.

The Kenzies had the pew directly behind that of the Meekses. There were five of them—Mr. and Mrs. Kenzie and Dade and two little girls. The girls died later with membranous croup. Now they called it diphtheria. She didn't hold much with the fancy names doctors were giving diseases now; half the time they were just showing off, trying to make people think they knew more than they did. Anyway, the little girls died, and after that, Mrs. Kenzie was always too easy on Dade. When he was eighteen she died, too, leaving him without a mother to keep him in line. It was no wonder he grew wild and spoiled.

She could remember, just as well as anything, the Kenzie family filing into the pew that first Sunday morning. Hardly had they got settled when she felt a sly pull at her curls. She looked around, even though she knew without looking that the redheaded boy behind her had done it. Mama nudged her sharply. Of course, she wasn't supposed to turn around in church, but she did want to tell Mama she was doing it because the boy behind her had pulled her hair. But Mama wouldn't listen. She said, "Sh—" and looked straight ahead.

Out of the corner of her eye, she watched the boy. He was red-headed—well, maybe really just a dark auburn. He didn't have the freckles that usually went with a complexion like his. His eyes were dark, and had plenty of mischief in them. His mother must have taken him in hand, for he did not pull her hair again.

As soon as the sermon was over, the entire family went down to join the church. The preacher called all their names, and told where they came from. David Allison Kenzie, from Tennessee. How well she still remembered it. She supposed that was one of the few times anyone ever called him by his full name. And nobody ever thought of him in connection with any place but Missouri. He was as much a part of it as were its hills and trees and rivers.

Of all those who were present that day the Kenzies joined the church, only she was left. For a long time now, she and Dade had savored many memories together. He'd be telling a story and maybe forget a little something—not often, though, for his mind was as clear and bright as a young boy's, right up to the last—and he'd say:

"Now, let's see—how was that? Was it old Cale Marshall who was there, or was it Jeff Davis Curran?"

"It was old Cale Marshall," she would say.

Always he turned to her, not to Ellie, when there must be verification of a story long since forgotten by most. Ellie could not go with him, back across the long lane of the years, as Miss Laura could. There was a part of his life Ellie could not share. Miss Laura never gave a hoot if people laughed at her, all these years, for angling invitations to dinners and weddings and Christmas celebrations and things. Always these were good times to bring back old memories. And when they came, Dade would turn to her, as if Ellie had never existed.

Always, Miss Laura could meet that need of his. A body couldn't live all her life in a community, seeing people come and go—babies being born, and then growing up and getting married and having children of their own to repeat the pattern—without knowing the history of the community as well as you knew the palm of your own hand. There was no monument in the cemetery that didn't hold a story for her, of how those people had lived and died; no house that did not have its store of memories; no road or lane she did not know well. The very hills and fields had a fixed and immutable quality. She was here before any person now living had come, and now, she had even outlived Dade Kenzie whose span of memory was second only to hers. She shivered a little although really the church was quite warm.

She swept the church with her eyes, watching the people who came in. Now, almost half an hour before time for the services to begin, the church was already full, save for the seats reserved for the family. That was the way things should be. When a man had lived practically all his life in a community, he got to be part of it. People from all over three counties would be here, and a lot more from far off. It was bound to be a big funeral. That was good. Big funerals showed proper respect for the dead. A funeral was something that ought to be done right and proper.

She wondered how the Kenzies were going to take it. You couldn't tell her that people who didn't cry felt the death of a loved one as much as the ones who did. She remembered very well when Papa died. She went all to pieces, and afterwards had to be under a doctor's care for weeks. When a person really felt a death, it showed.

Look at the way Alvin Carter acted when his wife died. It took three men to hold him back to keep him from jumping right into the open grave with her. He cried and sobbed something awful. That was a real funeral. Alvin took it hard, like folks ought to. Of course, he up and married Hattie Kimbrough before the year was over, but that was a man for you. It didn't mean he didn't love his first wife, or grieve when she was taken.

Of course, there were no Kenzie daughters, and daughters-in-law couldn't be expected to be as cut up as a person's own folks would be. The grandchildren would feel bad, for they loved Dade a lot. He always had a way with children, not joking and teasing them, but listening to them as if they were real people. They'd feel bad for sure. Allison wasn't the kind to believe in crying, though. Even when she was a child, Dade and Ellie encouraged her in her strange ways. She'd never forget the spectacle Allison made of herself, singing that outlandish song for Children's Day, with Ellie playing for her, like all possessed. It was a scandal. She was surprised Brother Hickman didn't stop them, right in the middle of it. But he was sort of light-minded himself. Come to think of it, he was the one who said he didn't believe in hell. They got rid of him next year. She told the stewards she didn't ever intend to pay a red cent on the salary of a man that preached doctrines like that. It was putting sin right in the way of the young people. She'd like to know where the world would be if people didn't have the fear of hell to hold them in line.

Maybe Beulah Kenzie would take it hard. She cried so easy, though, you'd never know she was shedding a tear. Privately, Miss Laura was never able to understand why everyone raved so about Beulah Kenzie. She wasn't specially pretty. Always reminded a body of a cow—big and placid, with soft, swimming brown eyes. You couldn't fool her—she knew Beulah Kenzie's folks had been poor and tacky. The very idea of a bride coming to the groom's house to be married. Anybody could tell what sort of a family would allow a thing like that. But to hear the Kenzies talk, you'd have thought she did a wonderful thing. That was like the Kenzies—when they made a mistake they went right ahead pretending it was what they meant to do all along. She wouldn't wonder a bit if that was why Dade always acted so crazy over Ellie. He didn't want anyone to know he had made a mistake in picking her.

My goodness, there were a lot of flowers already in place in the church. That meant they probably weren't going to have flower girls to carry them. More than likely, that was Allison's doings. Having flower girls was a nice thing to do. It gave friends of the family a chance to have a part in the services. Of course, they weren't always what you could really call girls. Lots of times Miss Laura herself acted. But that was natural, because she knew so many people here in the community that they just called on her lots of times to show respect. Having the flowers placed in the church ahead of time was kind of uppity, like you meant to put folks into their places. When she got home this afternoon she was going to make out a list of the flower girls she wanted at her funeral.

Come to think of it, she'd have to change her pallbearer list, too. Twenty years ago, when she first made it out, Dade Kenzie was at the head of the list. It made her feel queer, thinking how often she had since revised that list. At first she had George Marshall on it. That was right, for the Marshalls and Meekses had been friends for more than seventy years. She had felt a little uncertain about leaving him on after he married Rose Carney. After he got to carrying on the way he did, she crossed him off.

Now that Dade was gone, she'd substitute Tom Kenzie's name. No, she wouldn't, either. She'd put Mark on the list. He had grown more like Dade than any of the rest of them had. He had some fire and spunk in him. Every once in a while he said something—just a phrase or two—or turned his head quick and impetuouslike, and for a second it was almost as if she were seeing the young Dade Kenzie again, the way he looked that night he drove her to the Fuller party. She'd ask Mark. He was a Kenzie, and so long as the family was represented, no one would think it amiss that she had the son instead of the father.

She didn't know who Dade's pallbearers were to be, although she had gone to the house twice, thinking to find out. They were waiting for Barry before making the final decision, and he was late getting there. Any way they tried to do it would be hard. He has so many friends that a lot of people could rightfully expect to be asked. She had known many hard feelings to come of picking the wrong ones. It was easiest to have something definite to go by—pick all nephews, or cousins, or something like that. It was a delicate business, and people ought to be very careful about doing it. They ought to have a list prepared ahead of time, the way she did. She must remember to go home and put Mark

Kenzie's name on it.

She couldn't make up her mind whether to go around the casket when the invitation was given to the congregation, or to wait until after the family had left. Of course, they would open the casket. They'd remember what a scandal it caused when the Marshalls didn't. She had gone around the casket twice at Katie Grigg's funeral—once with the friends, and again after the family left. She and Katie had been good friends.

The honeysuckle certainly looked awfully pretty. She had mixed it in with the vases of roses on the piano, and with the blue flags on the table in the entry. At the last minute she had even twined some around the stairway posts. It looked pretty and it smelled sweet.

Maybe it was the smell that was making her feel a little faint. It was surely a funny feeling she had, like once when she was a little girl and got lost from Mama and Papa at a picnic. She didn't know why she should think of that now, when she was here among people she knew and there wasn't a thing in the world to frighten her.

There was nothing to frighten her, but a mounting sickness crept up and engulfed her so that she thought for a while she might have to leave, even before the services started. And then she got herself in hand. She would not leave; she would stay right here.

She had loved Dade Kenzie better than anything else in all this world. She loved him before Ellie ever saw him, and kept on loving him long after she was gone. Nobody had loved him as long as she had—neither mother nor wife nor children. Today, in the very spot where she had first met him, she would see him for the last time.

Certainly she would go by the casket twice.

Saturday Evening

~ 1 ~

ELAINE had not even bothered to take off the blue dress, but lay crumpled up on the bed. Her hair clung dankly close to her small head and her eyes, always the one feature that gave life and animation to her face, were closed so that she looked like something carved out of stone. About her face there was neither warmth nor color.

Henry was moving about the room, clumsily quiet, putting things to rights. She could hear him opening drawers and closet doors, knew he was putting away gloves and purse and hat in their accustomed places. He adjusted the shades to keep the light out of her eyes. And presently he came to sit by her bed, quietly, not touching her, not speaking. She did not have to open her eyes to see him sitting there, his face concerned, his hands awkward and stiff upon his knees. She did not need to, yet she must see for herself if it were true, as a child must make sure in the night that someone is near.

When she did look, sure enough, there was Henry, with no line of face or form different from the way she knew it would be. Seeing him, she felt a child's relief. When her eyes opened, Henry spoke.

"Feel better?" he asked.

She nodded, without speaking.

"Want an aspirin?"

She shook her head again. She did not want an aspirin, or anything else. She wanted only to lie here, free of all need to talk, or move, or even think. Her world closed around her like a great empty bowl. Every way she could look, emptiness spread out before her. Uncle Dade was gone, and some great source of strength, some permanent anchor, had gone with him. She was like a person who, having lived all his life in the shadow of a great mountain, suddenly finds the mountain gone, with only flat, blank plains stretching endlessly out before him. She lay contemplating this emptiness, washed around by it, engulfed with it.

Barry, too, was gone. All day she had kept this thought in the back of her mind, as a person crossing a narrow gorge will push from him all thoughts of the great depth lying below him. Later, she would tell herself—later, when I am home—I will let myself think of this. Now she was home, and she could face it.

Barry would marry. Because he was married, she could have no more dreams of him. This was the death of beauty, and the loss of hope, like shutting a heavy door against the one source of warmth and light in her life. A great, shuddering breath shook her, as if she had been running far, and in great fright. At the sound of it, Henry said,

"Why don't you cry? It would do you good."

She did not answer, but a few tears slipped slowly down her cheeks and she made no move to check them. She could not really cry. She was empty, too, of tears.

"Elaine," Henry said, "maybe it's no time to tell you this, but I've known all along how you felt—well, how you felt about Barry. Even before we married, I knew—"

Elaine jerked her head quickly on the pillow, fixing her wide eyes on his face. She could feel a great surging beat of her heart; the blood was rushing into her ears, beating in the pulse of her throat. She opened her lips to speak, but no words came.

"I just wanted you to know I'd clear out, if you want me to," he went on.

His words were as matter-of-fact as if he were offering to do an errand for her. But they crashed around the room like cymbals, their echo hitting the walls, shattering into minute pieces, dashing back to her as she lay motionless upon the bed. She began to cry, her slight body shaking convulsively, sobs tearing her throat.

At first, Henry made no effort to stop her. Finally, he reached over and patted her shoulder with a gentle, impersonal touch. She grew more quiet and presently she lay spent and exhausted, but calmer. Then he got up and left the room, coming back with a pan of cool water and a cloth. He bathed her face gently, pushing the soft hair back out of the way of the cloth. When he finished he put the pan aside and once more came to sit beside her.

Elaine lay very still, her body drained of all strength. But her mind was working more clearly than it had ever done before. Henry had known, from the very first. And knowing, he was still willing to take a shell of a woman who lived only to nourish a dream in her heart. Never had he been blind to the fact that he was little more than a shadow in his own home. Even now he would release her, not because he was tired of his bargain, but because he thought it might be best for her to go. This Henry was willing to do for her who had never done anything for him.

Uncle Dade was dead now, and with his going, her childhood, too, had gone. And Barry was gone, taking with him the whole frail structure of a dream. Only Henry was left. And this thing he offered her was reality; it was strength and certainty to fill a great emptiness of mind and heart.

"I didn't want you to feel bad," Henry said uncertainly. "But I thought I ought to tell you—"

She put out her hand, reaching gropingly toward him. He took it, and when she tried to rise, he put his arm under her shoulders, raising her until she lay against him. She felt the great gentleness and strength of him, knowing it was of the spirit, as well as of the flesh.

"No—oh, no—Henry—" her voice tore from her in a great

sob, and she turned toward him, clinging to him with desperate strength, pressing her face against him so that under her cheek she could feel the great thundering of his heart.

His arms tightened, ever so little, about her.

"I want to stay with you—" she whispered.

"Elaine—" he said thickly, not quite believing, not quite sure.

"I do, oh, I do—" she cried.

The great wonder of it swept over her, like a light shining in darkness. She did, indeed, want to stay with him. In spite of her weakness, a sort of exultation came to her, and a great sureness. She lifted her face to look at him.

She did not know whether it was her own tears, or his, that were on her lips. She did not care. In spite of them, her lips were warm against his. And his arms were strong and confident about her.

"Elaine, darling—" he whispered.

She clung to him like a child, lost and frightened, who has, at last, come home.

～ II ～

BEULAH KENZIE, back home in her own room, was slipping out of the dark sheer she had worn, into a house dress. She moved swiftly and deftly, without sudden or undirected motions. And as she dressed, her mind ran on ahead to the things she must do.

Long ago she had heard her father speak of the Greek tombs which told of no great grief but rested rather on some remembered scene from the life of him who had gone on. He said the best monument to a man was to continue some good act that had been habitual with him. Grandfather had been the lodestone around which the family always gathered. He was the force that held them together. She could best associate him with the big dinners given at the Kenzie place with neighbors and friends and relatives of varying degree gathered around him. From these occasions people went away refreshed and inspired, happy and strengthened.

It was this thing she had in mind when she had asked all the family to come to supper this evening, stilling their protests that it was too much trouble for her. It was no trouble at all. She wanted to do it this way. How happy Grandfather would be to know that life was going on at the Kenzie place much in the way he liked to have it go, without break in the habits of the clan.

Most of them were coming. Elaine said she had a headache. Beulah hoped she was wrong in suspecting it had been brought on by the knowledge of Barry's approaching marriage. Perhaps the girl's memory of Barry was what had kept her all these years from being a good wife to Henry. Beulah had often noticed that people did not appreciate the good things life offered them, being often most happy when they were least aware of it. To her it seemed a great tragedy for a woman to go on blindly, never seeing within her own life the materials from which joy is made. Beulah tried to savor every moment of her own life, holding fast to the thought of its manifold joys.

Of course, she had missed having children. But she had often noticed that people, for some reason known only to God, failed to have the thing they wanted most in life. She had long since discovered that one must not dwell upon this lack but must think of all the things possessed in great abundance. It was not well for one to think overmuch of himself, anyway. Part of the happiness in marriage came from the necessity, and the privilege, of thinking first of the needs and wishes of someone else.

She would have a good supper tonight. There were plenty of things left, and besides, she had a cellar full of pickles and jellies and fruits of all kinds to supplement what was on hand. She would make an omelette. There would be coffee for the grown-ups and plenty of milk for the children. They would all gather around the table, remembering with a solemn happiness all the greatness of Grandfather and his life here in the community.

Her father had said that no small particle of matter could be moved without touching others, influencing them to movement of their own. He said it was just like throwing a pebble into a pond; things would not stop at the place the pebble struck. So it had been with Grandfather's life. Everywhere he went, people felt the force of his personality. There was no telling how many lives he had helped to shape, lives that maybe got his influence only indirectly, themselves scarcely knowing of his existence. So goodness and strength and force are spread as ripples spread when the stone is thrown into the water. His destiny, enlarged and multiplied, was passed on and on. Death did not finish such an influence as that. It was a lovely thing to remember. It was a great privilege to try to carry on, as she had set herself to do, the work that had been his.

When the clan gathered around the table this evening she would put Mark at the head, in Grandfather's place. In that way, everyone would know that she and Mark had decided to stay on in the old place, as Grandfather had wanted them to do. As heads of the house, hers was the right to arrange the seating, Mark's to ask the blessing, or to designate who would do so in his place. She would make no suggestions to him in this matter. A man rose in stature, both in his own eyes and in the eyes of those around him, in direct proportion to the way his wife looked up to him. She thought happily of how Mark had grown until he was perfectly capable of taking over the responsibility she would place on him, not only in the matter of the blessing but in countless other things that would come up as she tried to carry out the work to which she had set herself. She let her mind run ahead of her down the long lane of the years, seeing with bright happiness a Mark, wise, kindly, strong, and just, holding together a family and a community.

She went downstairs swiftly, tying an apron around her waist as she went. Soon the others would be coming home. Just now, she was glad to have things to herself. About the house there was a sort of benign stillness, as if every room, every piece of furniture, was resting in quiet approval of the things she had done. The setting sun slanted across the yard, on flower beds and clipped grass and great trees. Down at the barn the hands were milking—she could hear the clink of buckets and the occasional soft lowing of the cows. A great peace and certainty came over her.

Of course, whatever Mark decided to do was all right. But she hoped he decided to ask the blessing himself at supper this evening.

~ III ~

ALLISON asked her father to wait a moment while she went into the station. She got out of the car and started up the cinder path to the greenish-gray building, with its two waiting rooms, its stale, unaired smell, its clicking telegraph instrument. Negroes sat on the platform edge, not speaking, relaxed and quiet, looking as if they were a part of the landscape. She never remembered coming to the station when there were not Negroes sitting here, just as they sat now. About them was an age-old patience. What they waited for she did not know; nor, probably, did they.

"—evening, Miss Allison," one said, and she spoke to him, not remembering his name, seeing in him only someone who used to help Grandfather. He was just another part of the fixed unchangeableness of this place.

She was glad, really, that she stood where she did—not quite of this place, certainly not exactly of the world in which she lived. Like Janus, looking both ways, she could see this community with its small, provincial people, understanding both it and them; and she could understand, as well, the rich stream of life, the shifting values, the great strength and the great weakness of the broader world in which she had come to live. She was of both. Always, because of this, she could never be sure to which she really belonged, and was fated forever to be a little lonely, a little sad. The world of her grandfather feared her and her way a little, holding aloof in disapproval even when they made her most welcome home; that other world of her choice did not accept her entirely, either, feeling always within her a withdrawing which was, to them, an implied criticism and dislike. Because she was of neither one, really, she could see with great objectivity the shams and hypocrisies and evasions of both. To neither one had she ever surrendered, even as she had never really bent her will to Harlan, greatly as she loved him.

She remembered a game they used to play as children. One of the rules said that they must touch "home base" at intervals, failure to do so disqualifying the players. She was like that. Coming back here, to the very roots of her existence, always helped her. Perhaps Harlan was like that too, but with a difference. There was stored up in him a great lot of hurt and bitterness; perhaps, when he had written out the last drop of that, he could leave Nebraska. Maybe then he could even write a different, and a better type of thing. Great love and happiness and adjustment in life should make as good material for writing as did great hurt and humiliation. Now there were only two facts she knew for sure. One was that he was writing, and the other, that he wanted her. These things she knew, and she had another great knowledge that had come to her as she sat, quiet and listening, at the services today.

Life was not just for the little time you were here. This was only a small piece, a perishable part. You could not do things just for the moment. You could not always do what you thought was safe, or what would give you greatest happiness. You did what needed to be done, and took what came of it. You could not run away from life any more than you could run from death.

They said that just at the last Grandfather had called to her—to Grandmother. That was the tie that held, past life, into death. It was the tie that would hold Harlan and her, different as they were, impetuous and weak and self-willed as they were. Together, life would never be entirely happy for them. Perhaps, in the end, it would be up to her to make most of the concessions, most of the adjustments. Perhaps she did not have the wisdom and strength and courage to do this, but she could try. The last three months had taught her one thing, at least: life with him might not be easy, but without him it was a great and aching void.

She had come now through the station door and stood at the ticket window.

"I want to send a telegram," she told the man behind the wire grill.

She took the yellow slip he handed her, wrote briefly upon it. When she handed it back to him, he looked at it uncertainly.

"You gotta right to send ten words for the same money," he told her.

"No—it's all right as it is," she assured him.

She walked back down the cinder platform where the Negroes still sat, each exactly as she had left him. She was not thinking of them, but of the telegram, already on its way to the small, bleak farmhouse in Nebraska. She wished she might see Harlan's face as he read its single word.

The word was "Yes."

~ IV ~

Jim was very firm about sending the neighbor women home.

"I can do all that's needful myself," he said. "We're much obliged to you for coming, but I know now you have things at home you need to do."

After they left, he came into Virgie's room, sitting on a low chair by her bed. The room was very full of their joy. It was good to know the three of them were alone. Neighbor women, no matter how kindly, made a body feel as if the house did not belong to the family.

Jim smelled faintly of the tar soap he had used to wash up with; of milk, for he had only recently finished with milking the two cows; of hay, which he had thrown down to the cows before leaving them. More than likely he had also come back by the chicken yard to care for the fowls there. Cows, grain, chickens—that was the pattern of their lives, and it was a good pattern. It was good for them, and it was a secure and steady way of life for the baby to come into.

Jim took her hand and they sat together, not saying anything, linked together by a great happiness and a great content.

Finally, he spoke. "It was a big funeral," he said. "Like we knew it would be. You never saw such a crowd. Nobody would have known if I had stayed away. I kept thinking about you, and wondering if you were all right."

"We would have known if you had stayed away," Virgie said. "Good as he was to us, one of us had to go. You know that, Jim. Besides, I am doing fine. The doctor came back a while this afternoon, and he said I was. He said he never saw anybody snap out any quicker than I did."

Jim said she looked grand, and he guessed one of them did have to go to the funeral, all right.

"He was a good man," Virgie said. "You live your life right

and people take notice when you die."

"Yes," Jim agreed. And then he went on. "I told Mr. Mark I'd be over, first thing in the morning, if he needed me. He said for me just to stick around here with you for a few days."

"Do you suppose—" Virgie began uncertainly.

"Yep," Jim did not wait for her to finish her question. "He said he hoped he could be counting on me to stay on with him, now that his Grandfather was gone."

"And you said yes," Virgie said, her voice richly happy.

"You bet. And he said Mrs. Beulah wanted to come over and see you and the baby tomorrow. She was sorry to be late, but there've been so many people there, and everything—say, do you want me to bring him over here to you?"

He laid the baby on the bed beside her and together they regarded the wonder of him.

"Look at them little fingers," Jim said, in awed tones.

They were, indeed, a miracle. Ten fingers, all perfect. Two little hands. Feet exactly as they should be. A heart that beat strong and sure. Everything about him was perfect.

"Doc Burgess said he didn't know as he'd ever seen a stronger baby," Jim said, finally, calling down expert witnessing to bear out the miracle they felt in their own hearts. "What are you thinking about naming him?"

Virgie said, "Jim, of course."

Jim sat quietly thinking.

"Had you thought of one to go with it? Kids always have two names, don't they?"

"Well, no," she admitted. And then she added, "Had you?"

"Sort of. David, maybe."

"You mean—?"

Jim nodded.

"Of course, we wouldn't call him that," he went on. "There might be a Kenzie boy they'd want to name that. But we could use it for a second name, and we'd always know it was there.

Afterwards, we could tell him why. He'd be proud, I think."

David, of course. Old Dade Kenzie was gone. His shadow was long on the community, and he would not be soon forgotten. As yet there was no little David Kenzie to bring to mind the great kindnesses, the wisdom, the infinite goodness of the man who had dominated the community for sixty years or more. Had it not been for him, the baby would never have had a chance at life in the first place. What better memorial could be raised to Dade Kenzie than a man-child, strong and wise and good, bearing his name?

"That's grand," she said. "We'll name him James David."

Little James David Meadors stirred in his sleep. It was as if he saw, through the great arches of the years, the promise of the life that was to be his—love and sorrow and happiness and the wonderful joy of life itself.

He saw it, and was not afraid.

~ V ~

AT FIRST, Miss Laura thought she would not eat any supper at all. A sick feeling caught at her throat and her hands trembled so she could scarcely remove her hat and gloves. Her knees seemed ready to fold up under her. Always, as soon as she came into the house, she went to put her things away exactly where they belonged in shelf or drawer. Now she threw them heedlessly on a chair and sank down on the old couch in the living room.

The air was full of the scent of honeysuckle from the bush at the gate. At the smell of it, she trembled still more, and would have gone to shut the front door, only she felt giddy and unable to move just then. Tomorrow she would have a man come and grub it up. It got in the way of the gate so she could hardly get the thing open and shut.

She lay still for awhile, and presently the trembling stopped a little. Maybe she would feel better if she ate something. After all, it was well past her suppertime. Usually she ate at five-thirty, sharp, but today she had been delayed at the cemetery because, since she had driven out with Tom and Julia Kenzie, she had to wait until they were ready to come back. Lots of times people who came from a distance didn't get to see the family until out at the cemetery, so there were a lot of people wanting to speak to Tom and Julia.

She got up and went into the kitchen. There was plenty of food in the icebox, but there was no use getting it out. Always she prided herself on eating nicely, with napkins and a tablecloth and flowers on the table. She had no patience with women who snacked out of paper bags just because they happened to be living by themselves. Now she had no desire to take pains. She set a box of breakfast food on the kitchen table, and a bottle of milk. Then she got a dish and a spoon, and sat down.

Her hands were shaking so that she spilled milk at every bite she took. Presently she gave up trying to eat and went back to the living room couch without even bothering to put up the remains of the supper or to wash her bowl and spoon.

She got up to go to bed. It was scarcely seven o'clock, and not yet dark, but she was going anyway. This morning she had planned for sure to see Rose Marshall and tell her what was going on, but now she wasn't going. Not this evening, or ever. She didn't care what George Marshall did. That was for him and Rose to settle. Let him carry on any way he wanted to. It didn't matter. Nothing mattered, really.

For more than seventy years this community had been her life. The things that happened to the people here had been, in a sense, the things that had happened to her. All that she knew of love, or sorrow, or excitement, or change, had come to her through their doings. She had lived their lives as they lived them, seeing people born and growing old and dying, knowing of a truth that all men were mortal. But in her own heart she had felt that she herself escaped mortality. Because she identified herself with each new generation, she did not grow old. Nor did Dade Kenzie grow old. His strength and wisdom and his personality grew stronger with his increasing years, and, watching him, she felt strong and wise and a part of things. He was her interest, her hold on life, her reason for being.

And now, Dade Kenzie was gone.

Without even turning on a light, she threw her clothes—her Sunday dress and the fine white underwear with its handknitted lace trimming—across the back of a chair. She buttoned on a high-necked, long-sleeved nightgown and, not even bothering to put her hair on curlers, got into bed.

She was conscious of the lack, knowing that by morning her dress would be so wrinkled it would never look like anything and that, without the curlers, her hair would be a stringy mess. But she didn't care. It didn't matter now what she wore, or how she looked.

She was just a trembling old woman, and nothing mattered. Nothing, in all the world.

~ VI ~

CHARLEY VANE took a satisfied look around. Now that everything was just as it should be, he could go home. But it was so quiet and peaceful out here, he really wasn't in any hurry to leave. The flowers were simply wonderful; he didn't know as he'd ever seen any more of them in all the years he'd been working here. That was because a lot of people were touched about Dade's going, and flowers were their way of saying so. Folks liked him fine. He was a good man. They said that now, with him gone, there was no man of his measure to take his place in the community. They said you just didn't find men like him any more.

Shucks, they forgot that Old Dade himself wasn't so much as a young man—just a gay young buck that the grannies whispered about. But he outgrew his mistakes, and became a fine man. It ought to be a lesson to folks not to criticize young people. Never could tell from looking at a tadpole what kind of a frog he'd turn out to be.

Besides, nobody jumps into goodness or greatness all of a sudden. They work at it for a long spell of time, never once thinking they're busy making a fine person out of themselves. Fact of the matter was that the less they thought about what they were doing, the nearer they'd come to doing a good job of it. They just kept on minding their own particular trade— the Kenzies looking after their farms and Doc Burgess getting babies into the world and keeping them reasonably healthy, once they got here. George Marshall staying in his bank, watching folks' money, and Old Man Butler selling goods across his counter and getting some of the money back. Miss Laura sticking her nose into everybody's business, and likely keeping a lot of people straight that might have got out of line if she hadn't been on the job. Allison Kenzie's husband writing his books, and somebody must be reading them, or he wouldn't keep turning them out the way he did.

When these people stopped, there'd be others to take their jobs over. That was the Lord's plan. He was getting the world's work done through people, and He would see to it that He had enough to keep things going. There was that baby born up at the Meadors place yesterday. A boy, like he thought it would be. Jim Meadors was just a hired man, but that baby could be anything he wanted—president, or anything else. If he just made an honest, upright man out of himself, though, that would be good enough. Maybe a president was getting born somewhere else. One thing you could be dead sure of, and that was that one was going to be born somewhere. Always did find that when we needed a big man, he turned up somewhere. The Lord took care of things like that, well in advance.

The funeral was over now, and people would go back to take up their own lives, just where they'd left off three days ago—Barry and Allison off on their separate ways, and the other relatives and friends to their fields and homes and jobs. For a while Old Dade's going had been a ripple that had disturbed the even flow of things, but now it was over and everything had smoothed out again. That was the way it should be. Life had to go on, and nobody, least of all Old Dade, would want the world to stand still forever just because he happened to leave it.

Well, he believed he'd go home. Didn't think, long as he'd worked out here, he'd ever seen a prettier sunset. Red sunsets meant good weather. That was fine; the corn sure needed a warm dry spell.

Yessir, it looked like tomorrow was going to be a mighty pretty day.

The End